The Bachelor Duke

The Bachelor
Series

D1713592

CECILIA RENE

For more information about the author: www.ceciliareneauthor.com

Twitter: @cecilia_rene
Facebook: @authorceciliarene
Instagram: authorceciliarene

Edited by Misti Moyer
Cover Design by Holly Perret, The Swoonies Book Covers
Formatting by Champagne Book Design

To Papa, I love you always.

The Bachelor Duke

Chapter One

*The Bachelor Duke has arrived in town for the Season. I am
sure there will be broken hearts from here to Bath. It is an
unfortunate truth that he shall never marry.*

London 1821

HENRY LIVINGSTONE, THE MARQUESS OF Heartford, read the scandal sheet out loud as if he were an eager debutante.

Remington Warren, the seventh Duke of Karrington, bristled at the description of himself. He greatly disliked that infernal title. The idea of breaking the hearts of eager misses gave him a very sour disposition. He'd have to engage them to break their hearts, and he had no plans of engaging them—at all.

He sighed out of frustration, sitting straighter on the Queen Anne settee. All he wanted to do was sit in his parlor and enjoy his brandy. He did not want to discuss the possibility of marriage or the cursed title.

The title was a bitter reminder of the fact that he would never marry; what he did not understand was why was it anyone's damn business. It was true he had lived unmarried the past ten years. He'd never met a lady he desired enough to want to be in her presence for the rest of his life, let alone a fortnight. At the age of eight and twenty, he was not in any rush to marry and, frankly, did not care if a distant relative on his father's side inherited the cursed dukedom.

"Please stop reading that filth in my home." Remington used his most annoyed voice.

"You have to admit it's very entertaining!" Heartford said excitedly.

"Entertaining for you perhaps, but for me, it's loathsome." Remington stood and walked over to the sideboard to pour himself another glass of brandy.

The large, lavish room was a prime example of his vast wealth. While he poured his drink, his gaze landed on the imperfection on the edge of the sideboard. A shiver ran through him as he looked at the old nick. The memory of his father beating him in this very room was fresh in his mind as if it was happening. The silver-plated cane with a curved hook was his sire's favorite. His father had cornered him beside the sideboard and swung violently causing a young Remington to fall against the furniture. The last swing was aimed for his head but missed when he dashed out of the way, officially damaging the dark wood.

For years Mother Di begged him to replace it, but he kept it as a remembrance of what a cruel bastard his father was. A reminder that he never would be like him.

Mother Di had made it her mission to redecorate every room in both their London townhome and the ancestral home in Norwich. She was determined to rid their lives of the man she had married, three months after her friend's death. She only married him for the sake of Remington, the child she had loved as her very own.

Remington's gaze darted across the fine furnishings as he turned to listen to his friend continue reading.

"As you all know the Bachelor Duke is in position of one of the most powerful dukedoms in England. There is no end to his family's wealth, another attribute that any lady would find appealing in a husband. Not to mention his dashing good looks." Heartford continued reading, ignoring his friend's mood.

The blasted title, *The Bachelor Duke*, was a constant reminder of his failures to fulfill the Warren family legacy. One he would rather forget. He'd seen firsthand the effects the Karrington dukedom had on the Warren men. They were cruel and violent to their families, each son worse than the father.

Remington Warren was a man who would never inflict harm on an innocent wife and child.

"It seems as if you will be the talk of the Season … again." Heartford looked up from his reading, a mischievous look on his boyish face. The jovial man of seven and twenty had bright green eyes and white-blond ringlets that bounced freely as if he were still a boy in nursery strings.

"How fortunate I am," Remington growled, not looking forward to the beginning of the London Season at all.

It always began the same way, countless balls and functions where one met overeager mothers and daughters—and even fathers—desperate to unleash their unmarried debutantes on any willing gentleman.

Silly girls with air in their heads and no concept of the cruelty of marriage or the hunger of men. He would protect them from himself, even if their parents did not have the decency to do so.

It was bound to be a long Season if he was the topic of the gossip sheets so early on. And to think, it had only begun.

"Please do not read that rubbish in my home," Remington stated in annoyance, walking back to take his seat. His long limbs stretched out in front of him as he relaxed, not caring for propriety in front of one of his closest friends since childhood.

Heartford laughed, knowing how much Remington loathed the title. "Come now, man, you knew you would be the talk of the town."

Yes, Remington was aware that he usually was the talk of the town before, during, and after the Season. He'd also hoped that a new subject would entertain them. Obviously, his hope was for naught.

"I had rather dreamed that a new gentleman would grace the pages of the gossip sheets, but I see the obsession is still so very strong," Remington said.

Years of being at the forefront of the gossips had not dwelled well with him. The entire ordeal, for lack of a better word, was exhausting.

"Every eligible lady dreams of becoming a duchess. Surely, even you can forgive the paper for appealing to their audience." Heartford raised an eyebrow in challenge.

"I will do no such thing. See how forgiving you would be if it were you with such a reputation." Remington tilted his head at Heartford.

"I shall welcome it, Karrington. After all, I'm only a lowly marquess. It would be a pleasant change to have to fight off the ladies," Heartford teased with a roguish grin.

Glaring, Remington adjusted his waistcoat before lying back to ease his stiff muscles. The aches and pains were a familiar reminder of the strenuous activities he partook in daily. This morning's boxing match had done nothing to calm his nerves, after listening to the gossip rag.

To avoid any manner of deprivation, Remington took great joy in several activities that would not bring scandal to his name as he had once done. Daily trots on his steed in Hyde Park, fencing every morning at his club, and boxing, all contributed to keeping both his mind and body occupied from the lack of feminine company.

"A marquess is as good as a duke in any eager mama's opinion." Remington tipped his glass toward his friend and grinned.

The scowl on Heartford's usually buoyant countenance caused a bit of joy to fill Remington, especially after his friend was so pleased with reading that damned article.

"I am well aware of how my title ranks in society. I do not need a lesson in the peerage. It is not my title that makes me less appealing than you … it is the fact that you have one of the wealthiest and most powerful dukedoms. You cannot deny that makes you far more exciting than I with my boyish charm," Heartford replied too cheerily to fight.

Remington groaned, knowing Heartford never would willingly spar with him on superficial subject matters. That was the difference between them. Where Remington was usually in a foul temper and ready for a verbal assault, Heartford had always been a happy sort of fellow.

"Do not underestimate yourself; you are also an eligible bachelor with sizable coffers. Trust me, any number of gentle ladies would find you appealing. Besides, you are more suitable for a wife than I." Taking a sip of his brandy, he let the smooth taste soothe his rattled nerves.

"Perhaps I am a catch, but you forget my family's greatest scandal." Heartford's body tensed, and he bowed his head slightly.

"Yes, your illegitimate sister, Lady Amelia Evers." Remington shrugged his shoulders. "That particular scandal will always follow you, especially as Lady Evers is an extremely active widow."

Heartford's sister, the widow of the late Viscount Evers,

bore a remarkable resemblance to her brother, bringing truth to the rumors that the Duke of St. Clara was not her father. The truth came to light when she was only a girl. The duke never disputed her legitimacy, keeping his wife's affair a secret. But there was no denying her true paternity, especially since she shared the same vibrant white-blonde hair, green eyes, and long elegant Livingstone nose, as well as their tall, slender stature.

"I've grown to care for her, but the constant reminder of my father's affair with her mother, and her affairs since her husband's death, is all very unsettling." Heartford ran his hand through his hair.

"Well, I believe she hasn't been seen in town, so perhaps she has settled for one of her many suitors." Remington took a sip of the dark liquor.

"I have not heard from her in some time. We did exchange missives during the winter months. It drives my mother mad that we've formed a friendship, but she is my only sibling, and I found I wanted to get to know her despite the scandals. I'm sure she will show for the Season. Amelia lives for it." Heartford stretched his thin frame.

"I should've remained at Hemsworth Place. I do not know why I even partake in the Season, too much bloody drama." Remington swirled the liquid in his glass, wishing he stayed at his ancestral home.

He found refuge and peace in the old home and the grounds that surrounded it. After his brief but disastrous youth, he took joy in the land and his tenants. It was one of the only things the Warren line had done correctly since King Edward VI granted them the estate for showing loyalty to the crown.

Heartford stood, chuckling as he walked to the sideboard. "If you did not attend, Mother Di would have your head."

Bloody hell, Remington would rather had faced Napoleon at the battle of Waterloo than face Mother Di during a London Season.

Before he was able to respond, there was a brief knock on the door. Dayton, the butler, entered, followed by William Middleton, the Earl of Windchester and Remington's cousin on his mother's side.

"The Earl of Windchester, sir," Dayton announced, formally bowing.

"Dayton, you've known me since I was a boy, surely you can say William has arrived, and he looks dashing!" Windchester laughed at the look of disdain on the butler's wrinkled face.

"I could never, it would go against my station." Dayton bowed, looking aghast at the mere thought of calling one of his betters by their given name.

"Do not allow him to upset you, Dayton. You know it is all in jest." Remington laughed for the first time since that damned gossip was read.

The butler left the room, with a small smile on his old weathered face.

"What have I missed?" Windchester walked to the sideboard to pour his own glass.

"The Bachelor Duke is in town for the Season," Heartford announced before taking his seat.

Remington shook his head as Windchester's booming laughter echoed off the wall. He did not appreciate the damned title and his popularity.

"I know. The women prattled on incessantly the entire carriage ride from Kent. My mother-in-law wished she could've snatched you up for my wife last Season. I took a cat's sleep from Dartford to London to prevent myself from jumping out of the moving carriage." Windchester huffed as he took a seat on the sofa.

Last Season, Remington found himself pursued by an eager Lady Oakhaven and her only daughter, the honorable Josephine Stint. Viscount Oakhaven amassed a rather large fortune during the Napoleonic wars with his shipping business. When the Viscount died, he bequeathed his entire fortune to his wife, leaving her an extremely wealthy lady. Because of her privilege, the rather vicious and tenacious young woman thought she could seduce Remington into marrying her. Alas, he barely paid her any attention at all.

"A blind man could've seen I was never going to marry the honorable Josephine. The woman is a viper. I'm sorry I did not prevent you from marrying her." Remington tilted his head at Windchester.

"Of course, I am aware. After all, she was caught with Melville with her skirts up and his trousers down." Windchester's loud voice filled the room, causing the other men to chuckle.

"If only you would have allowed me to lend you the funds, you would not have had to marry her." Remington exhaled, wishing he could've stopped his friend from making such a monumental error in judgment.

Their grandfather's estate and properties were ruined by Windchester's father, leaving the coffers empty. When his father died, Windchester inherited a title and a dilapidated estate.

"There was nothing you could do. I decided to be seduced by a pretty face, a large dowry, and an illusion that I would be the man of my household." He shrugged his shoulders nonchalantly. "My wife was lovely then, but now—" Windchester flexed his neck.

"She was also ruined, and possibly carrying someone else's child." Heartford held up his glass in salute.

"Well, we're a fine group." Remington stood and stretched his long limbs.

"Two bachelors and an unhappily married man. One shall never marry, I am in an impossible situation, and what are you, Heartford?" Windchester called out jovially, placing his feet up on the French table.

"I shall go wherever the wind blows. I'm open to anything with the right lady. I, for one, cannot wait for the Earl of Hempstead's ball tomorrow." Heartford looked positively boyish with his bouncing curls and ridiculous smile.

Remington scowled at Windchester. "If you want to act like you were raised in the wild, please do it at your own home." He kicked the earl's outstretched legs in a very ungentlemanly manner, causing the other man to falter slightly at the abruptness.

"He cannot; he's ghastly afraid of his wife and her mother." Heartford chuckled. "Now, as for the ball, I have heard a great deal about Hempstead's wards. I'm rather excited to get a look at them."

"I hope you both enjoy yourselves, because I do not plan to attend at all." Remington relaxed back in his chair.

"What about your friendship with Hempstead? Surely you should attend out of respect for him alone," Heartford reminded him.

Remington did indeed have a friendship with Theodore St. John, the Earl of Hempstead, one formed after fighting for various acts in the House of Lords. They became fast acquaintances last year when the earl's family was in Yorkshire. He often spoke of his daughter and niece and how afraid he was about the girls finding good matches.

Even though he had never met the two young ladies, Remington was in awe of the type of father Hempstead was. If he ever were to have children, he hoped he would be such a father and not at all like the man who had sired him.

"Besides, your mother is sure to be in attendance. If you are not where the eligible young ladies are, she will find you and pull you by your ear like she did when we were boys," Windchester said before downing his drink. "How fares your sister, Heartford?"

"I'm not sure. I was just telling Karrington that I've not heard from her. I suppose I may call on her. I am her real brother, after all." The marquess's tone was more of a question as his brow furrowed in thought.

"Well, the blaggard that is supposed to be her brother, the current Duke of St. Clara, doesn't give a damn about her since she's not his father's legitimate daughter." The anger in Windchester's voice caused Remington to raise a brow. "Not to mention the current Viscount Evers, her stepson, wants nothing to do with her."

Windchester downed the remainder of his drink, then stood, preparing to leave.

"Don't tell me you still have a fancy for her from last Season?" Remington asked, remembering that his friend often tried to converse with Heartford's beautiful sister.

Windchester cleared his throat, his gaze shifting toward the door. "No. I just feel it is all unfair treatment."

Remington surveyed him, his eyes tightening into slits. "Where are you off to? You've just arrived."

"I've only stopped by to see what you two were up to, which is nothing at all. So, I'm off for finer company, now that I'm in town." The earl bowed before he headed to the door.

"You mean finer company that is not your wife?" Heartford raised an eyebrow.

"Of course, she is not my wife. I'm sure my wife is in search of her own entertainment as we speak," Windchester commented before stopping at the door to give his companions one last look. "I shall see you both tomorrow at Hempstead's ball—"

"Not a chance in hell." He glared at the earl.

Remington could think of a thousand other things to do to entertain himself. Attending a ball was not one of them, even if the earl was a close companion.

"He'll be there, or I'll send Mother Di after him." Heartford gave a hearty laugh.

"Good. See you both on the morrow," Windchester bid them goodbye then left.

Remington shook his head, knowing he had no other choice but to attend, or his companions would unleash the wrath of his mother—and no one wanted to face Lady Diana Prescott, the former Duchess of Karrington.

Chapter Two

The debutante ball of ladies J and O St. J will be the event to start the Season. While Lady J is a diamond in the first water, it is said that Lady O is a tad bit buxom.

LADY OLIVIA ST. JOHN LAY ON THE SETTEE IN HER SITTING room with her book open, trying to enjoy the one solitary moment of peace she had received in hours. A lone blonde curl dangled free from the intricate chignon her maid created that morning. Every time she was engrossed in her reading, her cousin would come and demand her attention. If she had to look at one more dress, she would absolutely scream.

Whenever Julia appeared, Livie tried desperately not to roll her eyes. According to her mother, it was very unladylike behavior to roll one's eyes to the back of one's head.

Livie took a delicate nibble of a biscuit and savored the buttery taste in her mouth. She did enjoy Cook's cooking, maybe a little too much judging by the looks she received when out in town. Her eyes closed as she took another bite, letting out a satisfied moan.

She tried not to think about how everything would change if she, or rather *when*, she wed. The probability of her finding a match her very first London Season was nearly unfathomable, but her parents had high hopes that she and her cousin would make advantageous matches. Livie, however, did not share their optimism.

She understood their desperation to find them both husbands as her father had no heir. The difficulty with her parents' plan was that she was considered larger than the average miss and her cousin Julia was spoiled and wild. At an early age, Julia found that she would be allowed liberties since her parents perished when she was very young. The earl and countess felt the need to bring the young girl joy. Julia capitalized on this opportunity constantly and found she rather liked doing things to cause her aunt and uncle grief.

"Livie ... Livie! You're gathering wool again," Julia interrupted, tapping her slippered feet against the plush carpet.

Livie took in her cousin's petite frame, dark brown hair, and blue eyes. Julia had always been the slim one between them, never favoring Cook's delicious sweets. Livie envied her cousin for being small and petite. No one stared at her bosom in polite society.

Unlike her cousin's small delicate stature, Livie was taller than the average lady. Standing at five feet and six inches, her hips were prominent, bottom rounder, and her bosom larger than most. While others of her acquaintance were still developing at the age of twelve years, she had filled out at a surprisingly alarming rate. It was so shocking that when she was only fourteen, the Marquees of Lynbrook offered for her, causing her father to threaten a duel.

The unwanted and aggressive attention of the marquess gave her caution when around any gentleman.

Livie focused on her cousin's more delicate frame and blinked. "It is not gathering wool; the term is woolgathering." She knew perfectly well that Julia knew the correct term.

"I rather like it my way," Julia retorted defiantly. "Now, what do you think?"

Livie continued nibbling on her biscuit as she eyed what was either the fifth or sixth gown her cousin had tried on. She really could not tell the difference between this one and the others.

"It's yellow." Her voice was matter of fact.

Julia eyed her cousin angrily with her hands on her hips. At barely five feet three inches, she was not threatening at all, but she had a temper about her that Livie tried very hard not to be on the other end of.

"I know it's *yellow*. How do I look?" Julia demanded, turning to look in the floor-length mirror.

Livie surveyed her cousin for a moment. A single curl obstructed her view of Julia. A fact that she was thankful for as the dress was obnoxiously bright.

"Bright," Livie replied, a smile forming at the corner of her lips.

Julia turned to face Livie. Her blue eyes narrowed. They were really more like sisters than cousins, having grown up together since Julia's parents perished in a carriage accident when she was only seven years of age.

Without saying a word, Julia walked over to the settee, took an embroidered pillow in her hands, and flung it at her cousin.

Livie sat up in mock outrage clutching the pillow before throwing it back. She laughed as the pillow hit Julia in the face.

The door opened, and Abigail, Livie's maid, walked in, her arms full of packages.

"If you two do not stop, Lady Hempstead will come and scold us all, and why should I get in trouble when I've just arrived." She strolled into the adjoining bedchamber.

Livie reached up, trying to defend herself as her cousin threatened her with the pillow. Abigail returned just as a figure entered the room.

"What's going on in here?" Lady Lenora, the Countess of Hempstead, questioned, her gaze moving from her daughter to her niece.

Julia rose, dropping the pillow on the floor. "It's Livie's fault, Aunt Len. She said I looked bright in this gown."

Lady Hempstead closed the door behind her, her keen gray eyes analyzing her niece. "It is rather bright, dear."

Livie gave a very unladylike snort, slapping her hands together in a manner more suited for a child than a woman who had been presented at court. "I was right. The dress is bright," she said, giggling at her jest.

"You're not funny." Julia glared at her.

"Whatever is wrong with the dress we commissioned for the ball?" Lady Hempstead asked. Julia was known to have a flair for the dramatic.

"I felt it rather bland, so I had Helena take out some of my other gowns so that Livie could help me choose one, but she has been no help at all." Julia took a seat.

"I have been helpful. I informed you it was bright. Do you want to meet your future husband looking bright? If so, please wear it." Livie sat up to glare at her then reached for another biscuit.

"Livie, please, no more biscuits, it will go straight to your bottom. We've been here less than a sennight, and I've already had a row with Lady Jameson over your figure. The nerve of that woman, calling you plump!" Lady Hempstead huffed out in irritation.

Livie dropped the biscuit as if she had been burned.

Upon the family's arrival to their London townhome, her mother had visited with the neighbors she hadn't seen in years. In their time away, their closest neighbor, Lady Jameson, had become an elite member of the gentry, and the lady gave her opinion freely.

Apparently, the conversation had become more vexing for her

mother when the lady felt the need to comment on Livie's weight. Not appreciating the comments, her mother kindly thanked the woman for her opinion and returned home. Upon her return, she had not stopped speaking of the fallout with Lady Jameson. Livie had heard the story at least three times since the argument, but her mother would not let the topic rest.

Livie knew she was plump, the size of her rump and bosom was evidence of that. She tried not to care what Lady Jameson and society thought of her, but it was rather hard to ignore.

"Mother, please calm your nerves. Even you must admit I'm not the size of most ladies who have their first London Season." Livie smiled at her mother.

Her parents were her biggest advocates in life, and for that, she loved them greatly. Neither one ridiculed her about her weight or her fondness for books. They doted on her every need, never once treating her cruelly or being judgmental. They were the kindest people. They raised Julia after her parents died and saved Abigail from the workhouse when she was just a girl of sixteen years. In Livie's eyes, her parents were wonderful, and she greatly appreciated her mother practically coming to fisticuffs on her behalf.

"I, for one, would love your shape. There's just so much more of you. Besides, if I had those, I'd be married in a fortnight." Julia laughed, pointing at Livie's bosom.

"Julia St. John, please behave! My nerves are in an uproar as your uncle is sending a personal invitation to the Duke of Karrington. I do not need your behavior adding to them." Lady Hempstead placed her hand to her forehead. "Julia, please wear the gown that was commissioned. Livie, please, no more biscuits until after the ball. Abigail, do keep the ladies in hand."

Lady Hempstead turned to leave. "I have a million things to do before the ball, and now this!"

"Mother, why on earth would father invite the Duke of Karrington?" Livie's voice shook with nerves, her fingers tapping nervously at her side.

Of course, she knew who he was, everyone knew the Bachelor Duke, but it made no logical sense whatsoever why her father wanted to invite him to the ball.

"Last Season, while we were all in Yorkshire, your father and the duke became very friendly in the House of Lords. Your father feels he is not at all what the gossips make him out to be." Her mother sighed before leaving the room.

"This changes everything!" Julia squealed in excitement.

Livie eyed her questioningly, wondering why the news of the Bachelor Duke had her cousin so excited. She was sure a man that had vowed to never marry would have nothing to do with either of the St. John girls—especially one with a fondness for too many biscuits.

"How does the appearance of the Duke of Karrington have anything to do with us?" Livie acted bored with the conversation, but inside butterflies danced in her belly.

"He's all society talks about. I heard his name several times when I was at the modiste," Abigail murmured before taking a biscuit and sitting next to Livie.

Although Abigail was technically Livie's lady's maid, she was more like a sister to the girls as they were raised closely together. Being only four years older than Livie and Julia, who were only months apart, it was rather difficult for Abigail not to be close to them.

"It has everything to do with us. Either he will want to marry us for our great wits and beauty, or other gentlemen will take notice because he has attended our ball. This changes everything," Julia's voice was filled with confidence. "I must try on my original gown again, and I suggest you do the same."

Julia rushed out of the room, leaving both Livie and Abigail staring at each other.

"If she believes that the Bachelor Duke will marry me, then she's more unhinged than usual." Livie stood, wanting nothing more than to finish her book but knowing that she must try on her gown.

She just hoped that she hadn't gained any more weight in the two days it'd been since she tried on her dress last.

Abigail gave her a cheeky grin. "Really, Livie, you never know what could happen."

Livie laughed, not believing for a moment that she would ever have a chance to marry the Duke of Karrington. Regardless of the impossibility, excitement ran through her veins at the thought of meeting the Bachelor Duke.

Chapter Three

The Bachelor Duke was spotted at the Earl of H's ball.
Is our beloved bachelor in want of a wife at last?

EMINGTON'S CARRIAGE BOUNCED THROUGH THE
uneven streets of London. After he received a personal
request from his friend, the Earl of Hempstead, there
was absolutely nothing he could do but attend the ball.

He was fairly confident he could've appeased his mother
someway, but ignoring a personal invitation was simply imper-
tinent. So, he found himself dressed in his finest black tailcoat,
prepared for an evening of mindless conversation and a constant
stream of silly girls all in want of a husband.

Lord Hempstead was a true gentleman, a man of honor and
worth, everything Remington's father never was. These qualities
led to a relationship that went beyond the House of Lords. It
included the occasional drink at O'Brien's Gentleman's Club discussing the older man's affection for his family.

Remington knew without a shadow of a doubt that his appearance at the ball would have tongues wagging. No doubt, they
would believe he was finally in want of a wife.

He, however, was not and never would be.

Remington watched out the open window as the carriage
came to a stop and the guests turned to see who the new arrival

was. Upon seeing the Karrington family crest, whispers ensued, filling the cool night. A rapping on the door alerted Remington to collect himself in preparation for the onslaught of preening misses.

When the door opened, he disembarked with his usual air of importance and walked through the parting crowd. As he passed, he was greeted repeatedly with "Your Grace" and "Karrington." The entrance hall seemed to stretch endlessly ahead of him.

Eyeing the queue into the townhome and having no patience for lines, he decided to use his title and rank to his advantage. He strolled ahead of the waiting guests to find the earl and his wife smiling amenably.

"Your Grace," the Earl of Hempstead called jovially as Remington approached. "What a wonderful surprise." The earl was a tall, stocky, older gentleman with brown hair speckled with gray.

"Come now, Hempstead, none of this 'Your Grace' nonsense, we are friends after all." Remington bowed before he turned to the countess.

The Countess of Hempstead was a beauty of a woman with dark flaxen hair and a kind countenance.

"Allow me to introduce my wife, Lady Hempstead," the earl said, pride evident in his voice. Love and admiration gleamed in his brown eyes as he looked adoringly at his wife. Remington felt as if he were intruding on an intimate moment. The look that passed between husband and wife caused a deep unknown part of Remington to ache for what he vowed he would never have.

The Countess of Hempstead placed a delicately gloved hand out for Remington, who took it in his own and bowed. "It is a pleasure to make your acquaintance, my lady. I cannot dare believe you have a daughter old enough to be out in society."

Unlike her husband, Lady Hempstead's hair was free from gray, and her skin was nearly flawless. She was blessed with minor lines. There was a twinkle in her gray eyes as she gave him a genuine smile.

Giggling gracefully, Lady Hempstead placed her hand against her chest. "Your Grace, you are too kind, but I assure you, once you set eyes upon Lady Olivia and Lady Julia, you will know the true definition of youth and beauty."

Remington could hear the sincerity and love in her voice as she described her daughter and niece. Unlike most mothers of the aristocracy, it implied that Lady Hempstead was not trying to force her daughter or niece upon him. She was simply very fond of the girls. He liked her immediately.

"With you as their example, I am sure both ladies are a vision. The earl is truly blessed." He smiled widely before giving the couple a final bow.

"You old rake. I'm starting to believe the rumors." Hempstead winked at his friend.

Leaving the happy couple, Remington sauntered through the ballroom, deliberately avoiding several people who wished to engage him in conversation. His gaze roamed the crowded room in search of his relations, hoping to avoid eager mothers and daughters.

He took in the general splendor of the house as he followed the throng of guests into the ballroom. Two crystal chandeliers draped with candles lit the room in a romantic glow to encourage dancing.

Gold trim on the walls and ceilings displayed the family's wealth and standing in society. Painted scenes of heavenly angels lounging on white clouds decorated the ceiling, adding to the elegant decor. It was a beautiful townhome, albeit a great deal smaller than his own, but he was pleased that the earl provided for his family in such a way. It was a shame that he had no heir of his own to keep his wife, daughter, and niece in the lavish lifestyle they were used to.

As Remington passed a circle of gentlemen, he saw Lady Windchester in the center of their attention with Baron Bromswell beside her. Anger filled him, causing his back to stiffen at the sight of the other man.

Remington watched as Lady Windchester flirted readily, batting her blonde eyelashes as she laughed at something Bromswell said. Remington moved on, not wanting to engage the lady in conversation or be anywhere near the detestable Bromswell.

"Good heavens, Heartford, have my eyes failed me? I do believe the Duke of Karrington has made an appearance." Windchester's loud, boisterous voice rung out in the ballroom.

Guests looked upon their group in shock. Whispered voices followed Remington to where Windchester and the others stood. The earl was having too much fun at his expense.

"I see you took my threat seriously," Heartford joked before drinking the glass of iced champagne in his hand.

"I could've appeased my mother, but I could not refuse a personal invitation from Hempstead. It would've been rude not to attend." Remington took a glass of champagne from a passing servant.

His gaze swept the room in search of his mother, knowing she would think more of his appearance than it really was. He prepared himself for her excitement at the mere prospect of gaining a daughter-in-law.

His mother was a great number of things. She was kind, gentle, witty, a grand lady, but most of all, she was forever a doting mother. Her greatest mission in life was for her son to make a love match, as she had done with her second marriage. Not able to birth children, she had always treated Remington as if he were her own.

Unable to locate her amongst the sea of guests, he turned his attention back to his companions.

"Careful, the eligible ladies and their eager mamas may think you are in want of a wife." Heartford's eyes danced with mischief.

Remington followed his gaze, noticing that several ladies were staring at him with their heads together. Even he knew his appearance was a rare sight at a ball.

"Let them believe whatever they want. I am only here at the invitation of a friend." His words were interrupted by the sudden silence that surged through the room.

Two angelic creatures standing in the center of the dance floor had stolen everyone's attention. Remington's gaze was fixated on the blonde-haired, curvaceous woman. Her gray eyes, wide and captivating, surveyed the room as if she could see through the very soul of each person. Her gaze locked with his, causing his breath to catch in his throat like a boy, not a fully-grown man. He returned the stare, feeling an odd sensation take over his body. For a fleeting moment, he felt as if for once in his life, he was whole.

Time passed as Remington, unknowingly to anyone else, played a game of cat and mouse. Tracking the breathtaking blonde became his sole purpose. He made every attempt to focus his attention elsewhere. Yet no matter how determined he was not to look for her, it seemed his eyes sought out the lady on their own accord.

He, however, did not know which one of Hempstead's wards she was—his daughter or his niece. All Remington knew was that the sight of her unnerved him, and he had no idea why.

Finding refuge behind a very large pillar, he watched as she stood dutifully next to the earl and his wife. She was no petite miss. Her curves were in all the places a man desired most. He wanted to know more about her, to discover what lay beneath the prim demeanor she presented to society, to discover the passion she hid from prying eyes. He knew that to do that, to uncover the delectable creature in front of him, he would have to lose a part of himself.

A part of himself that he vowed he would never give up no matter what. He had to avoid the stunning creature at all costs.

Livie took a much-needed breath as her dance with Lord Carmichael ended. He was a dreadfully jovial fellow who spoke incessantly. Even when they were in mid-turn, Carmichael continued the conversation as if they had never left each other's side. She found it difficult to keep up with the topic. His new barouche and the finer details of carriages did not hold her interest.

Lord Carmichael was a short, slightly rotund gentleman, whose eyes twinkled with hope every time he gazed at her. She, however, wanted nothing more than to leave his presence and never have a conversation about carriages again.

He escorted her to her father, who was in conversation with a handsome gentleman she was unfamiliar with. He was a perfect specimen of male vitality. His large body stood over her father. It wasn't just his build but his height that commanded everyone to look up to him.

"I do hope you will save me space on your dance card. You know we really must stick together," Lord Carmichael said before presenting her to her father.

Livie pondered his comment over and over as he began conversing with the handsome but brooding stranger and her father. Her eyes narrowed and her lips thinned as she glared at the clueless Lord Carmichael.

"Karrington, what a wonderful surprise to find you at a ball," Lord Carmichael muttered in awe.

Livie schooled her features as she took in the Duke of Karrington. Of course, a man so commanding and suave would be the Bachelor Duke.

"Yes, well, there are more wonderful surprises in the world than a duke at a ball," the Duke of Karrington replied, causing Livie to giggle.

She tried to cover her response by placing a gloved hand to her lips, but to no avail, as all three men turned to look at her.

"Ah, well, if you all will excuse me. Thank you for the dance, Lady Olivia." Lord Carmichael made a hasty exit, obviously not wanting to be in the duke's presence.

"Your Grace may I present my daughter, Lady Olivia St. John." Her father smiled proudly, as if she was his greatest treasure.

The duke took her presented hand and bowed over it. Livie's heart pounded. Her breath caught in her throat. He was indeed the most handsome man she'd ever seen with jet-black hair and deep blue eyes that unnerved her and caused her skin to tingle. A thick dark band surrounded a crisp blue iris ensnaring her attention. New and exciting feelings flowed through her as she struggled to control herself.

Livie shifted her gaze away from the impressive specimen in front of her, afraid she would reveal the effect he was having on her.

"Lady Olivia, it is an honor to make your acquaintance." His

25

smile was tight, his shoulders rigid as if he wanted to be anywhere but standing in front of her

Although they had never met, his behavior was disconcert-
ing as she had done nothing to offend him. Perhaps he thought
she was like the other ladies, wanting to snare him into matrimony. She shifted and spotted several eyes on them, all eager
misses. Her eyes scanned over their thin shapeless forms, seeing
their judgment. Heads pressed together as beady eyes followed
her every step, each one hating her for capturing his attention,
finding her lacking to gain his regard.

"Thank you, Your Grace. I am delighted you were able to
join us." Her smile was forced, the perfect mask to hide her growing discomfort with most of society's eyes on her.

The current set came to a close with polite applause as couples departed from the dance floor. Livie prepared to take leave
of her father and the brooding duke but her father's happy voice
interrupted her.

"Karrington, would you do me the honor of escorting Lady
Olivia in the next set?" Her father seemed oblivious to the horror
on her face.

The duke pondered the request for a moment, his jaw tense,
eyes crinkled as if he were in deep thought, before he gave her a
pleasant smile. "If the lady agrees, it would be my pleasure." In
one smooth motion, he took her dance card and scribbled down
his name.

Livie blinked several times, trying to compose herself, but
was acutely aware that the duke was waiting for an answer.

"Of course, Your Grace," she replied hoarsely. He took her
by the elbow and escorted her to the dance floor.

As they passed, the crowd parted for them as if they were
royalty. Livie held her head high, trying to ignore the whispers

that now surrounded her. She froze for a moment, unaccustomed to the attention she was garnering from being with such a gentleman. Although, she had stood beside her parents and Julia in front of the same crowd, it was now as if every eye judged her every move.

"Ignore them. They have nothing better to do than whisper about the Bachelor Duke," he whispered conspiratorially, making her feel as if they were sharing their very own secret.

Livie let out a giggle, surprised he had the audacity to joke about his very famous title by using the nickname.

"You are very popular, Your Grace." She tilted her head in his direction, trying to overcome the shock at speaking with the most eligible bachelor in society.

Walking beside him gave her a sense of superiority, and Livie found she held her head up higher while by his side.

His candor about his situation, his attractiveness, and the ease of their conversation disarmed her.

Reaching the dance floor, they took their places toe to toe in preparation for a waltz. Livie stared up into the handsome face towering over her. Heat ran through her veins at his power and dominance.

For once in her life, she was acutely aware of the male form. Her body heated all over as her gaze roamed over him. His shoulders were powerful, his grip commanded her to his will. Livie could feel her body respond to him and hoped there was enough material covering her bosom. She wondered what it would be like to be with such a man—intimately.

The thought was fleeting, yet she chastised herself for being another one of his admirers. She had only been in his presence mere minutes.

"*He couldn't possibly want her.*" The cruel words were

whispered by a passing woman, causing her steps to falter. They were correct of course. There was no doubt that Lord Carmichael was the sort of man that would want to marry her, not the Adonis before her.

"You are mistaken. I believe they are taken by your beauty, my lady." The duke's voice was low and teasing, sending shivers down her spine like molten chocolate.

Swallowing, she stared into his deep blue eyes. Before she was able to respond, he firmly placed his hand in the center of her back, rendering her a puppet and he the puppeteer. When their palms pressed together, it was as if the fabric of her gloves was on fire.

As he led her every step, sensations raced through her body, the feeling like nothing she'd ever experienced. His stoic and unfathomable gaze never left hers.

She matched his every step, trying to hide the confusion she felt. His comment on her beauty was surprising and had disarmed her. Surely this Zeus of society did not think her beautiful. He held her securely in his arms, but it felt more like a dream than reality.

Feeling a slow, tortuous movement at the palm of her hand, her gaze shifted to where they were connected. His thumb circled her palm, and she was momentarily shocked that he was doing such a personal and erotic act. Her heart pounded at the thought of allowing something so forward, so forbidden. Although her hands were covered, it was as if she was bare before him, his touch searing her soul, branding her as his.

The set ended. His hands stilled, his grip firm and unmoving, his gaze holding her captive until the mundane clapping of the other guests released them from the spell that only seemed to affect her and the duke.

Livie relinquished a breath as he took hold of her elbow, leading her off the dance floor. A feeling of dread crept up her spine as she realized her time with him had come to an end.

"Your Grace, you are an excellent partner," she commented as they made their way to where her father was waiting.

"You pay me a great honor, but your beauty and poise only motivates me," the duke replied smoothly, catching her unaware. Surely a man such as him would not find her attractive, especially when he could have any lady in the ballroom.

Once they reached the Earl of Hempstead, the duke released her and bowed stiffly. "Thank you, my lady. It was most enjoyable."

She was unable to reply, taken back by how formal and polite he was after he had been so personal. Before she could respond, a tall, dashing gentleman with golden hair strode over with an air of contempt that belonged on a peer of higher ranking. Livie forced a smile on her face recalling that Baron Bromswell had claimed the quadrille on her dance card.

"Karrington, how kind of you to keep my partner warm for me." Baron Bromswell slapped the duke on the back.

Livie's eyes widened as the duke glared at Baron Bromswell as if he wanted to do him bodily harm.

Taking her from the duke, the baron took her by the elbow, causing a shiver to run down her spine. Unlike the duke's touch, this one made her skin crawl as if tiny bugs were roaming her body freely. The duke's gaze narrowed onto the baron's hand upon her elbow. His face turned hard and unyielding.

"Shall we make our way to the dance floor, Lady Olivia?" Baron Bromswell's sugary sweet voice made the fine hairs on her arm stand at attention.

Smiling tightly at him, Livie tried to hide her discomfort at his smug look and eagerness. He surveyed her as if she were a prize stallion. No doubt her dowry of twenty thousand pounds was the reason for his special attention.

She understood she needed to marry. Her parents could not provide for her forever. But there was something in the baron's manner that put her on alert as if she should run as fast as she could from him.

"If you will excuse me." The duke made a hasty exit.

The emptiness she felt threatened to consume her. Livie hadn't the slightest idea why she cared. It was no secret that he would never marry, and she needed to marry in order to be looked after once her father was gone. She must forget all thoughts of the Bachelor Duke.

Chapter Four

*Has this Season's plump miss landed the attention of the
highly sought-after Bachelor Duke?*

REMINGTON TOOK A VERY UNGENTLEMANLY GULP OF his champagne, determined not to let Bromswell's behavior affect his mood. He scanned the dance floor, his gaze landing on Lady Olivia and her companion. Bile rose in his throat as he thought of the last young lady who received the baron's attention.

An image flashed through his mind, causing his heart to speed up and sweat to bead on his forehead. His mind raced back to that long-ago night, when a young duke was friends with a young baron. Composing himself, he watched closely as Baron Bromswell eyed Lady Olivia as if she were a meal to be enjoyed and devoured. Fear gripped him like never before at the thought that she could fall prey to the baron. Remington warred with himself on if he should allow such an exquisite creature to fall victim to the blaggard.

As he scrutinized the unsuspecting lady, he thought back on when he had first met the young Bromswell. They became fast friends, both young and titled for the first time in their lives. But unlike Remington, Bromswell had no fortune and eagerly latched on to the wealthier man, much like a leech to fresh skin.

It was not long until the young baron's intentions were clear, and his behavior rather abominable. Only Remington's mother was able to save him from the turmoil.

"There you are, my darling," his mother said, catching Remington unaware.

Turning to face her, he tried to calm himself. He gave her a soft smile that showed his love and respect for this woman who had loved him most of his life. Breathing deeply, he let his anger and fear for Lady Olivia subside and focused on his mother.

He took in her neat appearance, noticing how impeccable she looked. Her light brown hair was swept up in an intricate hairstyle revealing very little gray, concealing her true age.

"Mother Di, what a pleasant surprise." He bent to place a kiss on her cheek.

She smiled at the use of the name he'd called her since he was a small boy. The moment she had met the child of her friend, she had loved him as if he were her very own.

Mother Di gave him a brilliant smile as if she'd unlocked a secret. "My darling boy, the pleasure is all mine as my prayers have finally been answered." Remington braced himself, knowing that somehow her prayers included him and Lady Olivia St. John. "What is surprising me is the attention you are showing a certain lady." Her voice was filled with excitement as her eyes lit up like a child receiving gifts.

"It was just a dance, Mother Di. Please do not get too excited," Remington warned, his eyebrows crinkling in thought before offering her his arm.

They began taking a turn around the expansive room. He tried to distract her from her very obvious observation of him being enamored with Lady Olivia. Numerous guests stared at them, following their every step as if they were animals in an exhibit. Society was always so taken by the Warren family, so aware of everything they did since Mother Di married her best friend's husband less than a year after her death.

Remington remembered what it was like for him as a young heir subjected to the whispers and gossips of society like their words were a suffocating duvet.

He loved how his mother ignored the whispers. She seemed so accustomed to it, taking their words and questioning looks like they were a second skin. Mother Di was more acquainted with society and all that was required to be a part of it than he ever would be. Tongues had always wagged in her direction ever since she was a single lady staying with a duke and his wife, until the day she became his duchess herself.

She turned toward Remington as they widened the berth between them and the gossip. "Do not brood, Remington. I saw how you looked upon her."

"Mother Di, I do not think this is an appropriate topic—"

"Do not tell me what is appropriate. I raised you. Have you forgotten?" The glare that followed made him feel as if he was a young boy again. "Duke or not, you're still my son, and I don't want you to miss an opportunity to have something far greater than titles or money." Placing a gloved hand on his cheek, she gave him a warm motherly smile.

"It was just a dance. I assure you it will not happen again. I do not want you to wish for something that will never come to pass. You know I will never marry." His words were final. He took a deep breath to compose himself.

His mind shifted back to creamy skin and storming gray eyes that threatened to sweep him away in a tornado.

"Ah, I should've known it was you who stole my wife," David Prescott interrupted and handed Mother Di a glass of iced champagne.

David's eyes twinkled as he took in his wife and Remington. He was a single bachelor when he first came across Remington's mother in the road. One of the wheels on her carriage had come off nearly causing a horrible accident that would have caused Remington to lose a third parent. It seemed as if luck and love were upon them both as Prescott was out for a ride on one of his prize horses not far from their ancestral home in Norwich.

It surprised Remington that after being a widow for nearly five years, his mother formed an instant attraction to Prescott. It was one that saw past rank and society. At first, Remington believed that Prescott was after her fortune, as Mother Di received a substantial allowance from the Karrington estate. There were a number of fortune hunters pursuing the widow, once the appropriate amount of mourning time was up. Remington confronted a bewildered Prescott, believing that he was another gentleman in want of an heiress. Prescott simply stated that all he wanted was to love her. After such an amiable declaration, he became one of Remington's closest friends and confidants. Becoming more of a father figure to him than his own father ever had been.

"Prescott, I see Mother Di has forced you to yet another ball. How are you faring, old boy?" Remington tilted his head in the other man's direction.

"I can't complain about such things with such a lovely companion as your mother." He smiled lovingly at his wife, as if she was the single best thing in his life.

The whispers grew at the word mother. Society was so enamored with the fact that Remington was so close to Mother Di.

He scanned the room, spotting Heartford and Windchester. Turning to the happy older couple, he gave Mother Di a warm smile. "Mother Di, Prescott, I must bid you farewell." He gave them a stiff bow and turned to leave.

"Surely, you would not leave without partaking in another dance with a certain lady?" Mother Di asked with a hopeful tone.

"Now, Mother Di, do not try your hands at matchmaking. You know how I detest it. Besides, it would be improper for me to dance with a lady I am not acquainted with twice, would it not?" He awarded her with a knowing look.

"Who has time for the rules of society? Besides, you are friends with her father, are you not?" She challenged him.

They stared at each other, both waiting for the other to withdraw, but neither moved until Remington broke. He berated himself that even after all these years, he couldn't stare her down.

David patted him on the back. "You know your mother always gets her way. Why don't you do what she's asking now to make it easier?"

"I'm glad someone in this family knows the rules." Mother Di took her husband's hand affectionately.

"Yes, well, he has to listen to you. I, on the other hand, do not. Good night, Mother Di." Remington bowed one last time before rushing off to find his companions.

He moved quickly, afraid she would try to interfere with his attempt to avoid the lady in question. There had been other eligible young ladies that Mother Di hoped would catch his special attention, but none did.

Until now.

Remington found Heartford and Windchester speaking to the young lady who entered with Lady Olivia. He could only assume that it was Lady Julia St. John. Her brown hair was up in an elaborate style that framed a pretty face.

She stared up at Heartford with awe and wonder. Her

likeness to her cousin was very slight, but Remington could see the familial resemblance in the shape of their eyes and their mannerisms.

"Ahh, Karrington, allow me to introduce you to Lady Julia St. John." Heartford's gaze never left Lady Julia.

She dipped into a small curtsey. "Your Grace, it is an honor to have your presence in our home." Her smile was kind as she awaited his reply.

Giving her a nod, Remington gave her a welcoming grin. "Lady Julia, it is I who am honored to be invited to such an event. Congratulations on your coming out."

"Do not let him deceive you. We practically had to twist his arm to attend." Heartford leaned toward her conspiratorially.

Before another word was spoken, Bromswell and Lady Olivia joined the small group. Remington's entire body stiffened as Lady Olivia stood beside him. The heat from her body engulfed him. Her sweet scent—a mixture of lavender, rose water, and what seemed to be a light touch of citrus—took over his senses.

He found himself wanting to take hold of her and bury his nose in the sweet swell of her breasts. The effect that she was having on him unnerved him to the point that he desperately needed to escape her very presence.

Images from a long-ago night invaded his thoughts, but instead of rich red hair, he saw beautiful blonde. Gray eyes replaced blue. His heart seized within his chest. He took a deep breath, clearing his head so that he could speak.

Turning to Heartford and Windchester, Remington gave them a stiff bow. "I shall take my leave." He turned to the two ladies. "Ladies, if you will excuse me. Please accept my congratulations on your coming out."

He left abruptly, striding from the ballroom, not daring another glance at Lady Olivia and her companion. He couldn't save her from herself if Bromswell was the type of person she wished for a husband. She was of no concern of his. Her fate was her own.

Livie watched as the Duke of Karrington left the ball. The muscles in his back flexed through his waistcoat as he walked briskly away. Her lower abdomen felt as if it was tied in knots. The sense of dread returned. It seemed that every time he departed from her presence, she was filled with trepidation at the thought that it would be the last time.

Staring at the exit, she tried to plaster a smile on her face as Baron Bromswell spoke of his estate in Rochester as if it were a royal palace. She turned and tried to give him her full attention, knowing she should be happy he had sought her out. Yet, something dark lurked behind his happy disposition, the sneer at the corner of his lips never formed a complete smile.

"May I call on you tomorrow, Lady Olivia?" Baron Bromswell's gaze roamed her body solicitously. His predatory eyes held something unnerving within them that made her want to protect herself from him.

Her face was tight as she tried to hide her revulsion at the obvious perusing of her person.

"Thank you, Lord Bromswell, that will be lovely." She feigned politeness while wanting nothing more than to flee from him.

To deny him outright would be rude, so she gave him her best smile, the one her mother taught her to give despite how she was feeling. Although, she was aware that she was in want of a husband, she knew, without a doubt, that she would not accept Baron Bromswell. Indeed, she believed she had been ruined for any eligible gentleman for the foreseeable future, all because of one meeting with the Duke of Karrington.

Taking a deep breath, she tried to center herself, knowing that any future with the duke was futile. She placed a welcoming smile on her face, one that said she was willing and open for a husband. She knew she couldn't outright refuse the baron, especially with no other real prospects. Perhaps she was mistaken about him and passing judgment too quickly.

She stood beside Julia who happily conversed with Lord Heartford, enraptured in his every word. Livie noticed several gentlemen now openly staring at her. It made her fidget nervously. She rushed to straighten her dress to make sure she was presentable. Her father walked toward her with the Earl of Chamberlain. Tucking in her tummy, she held her head high, trying to be more inviting.

Focusing on the conversation around her, she turned to the jovial Earl of Windchester. She took note of his large size, but his friendly charm made her feel as if she'd known him her entire life.

"How has Hempstead kept you two lovely creatures from town all these years?" Windchester gave Olivia and Julia a questioning look filled with curiosity.

Julia perked up, happy to answer. "I wanted to come out last Season, but Livie broke her foot by falling off her horse, and we had to delay an entire year."

Livie withstood the urge to roll her eyes. It wasn't as if she had fallen on purpose. She had not enjoyed being an invalid for nearly four months. At the end, she was happy to delay being paraded around like a bright peacock and having people analyze her on her looks alone.

"Lady Olivia, may I introduce Lord Chamberlain." Her father's voice interrupted her internal thoughts and the need to throttle her cousin for sounding so selfish.

"My lady, it would be an honor to sign my name to your dance card." Lord Chamberlain bowed swiftly, a little too eager to be her partner. He bounced on the soles of his feet, always in constant movement. His speech was rushed, the boyish gleam in his eyes danced with expectation.

Livie held out her arm dutifully allowing him to scribble his name in one of the remaining slots on her card. She wanted to forget about a certain blue-eyed duke, and the only way for that to happen was to find herself more suitors. Preferably not Baron Bromswell, as she would prefer someone who did not make her feel so fearful.

The current set ended, and she found herself escorted to the vacant dance floor by Lord Chamberlain. He was young and the same height as she was. In fact, she seemed slightly taller than him as they danced in a quadrille.

When the set finally came to an end, Livie was happy to be free of the young gentleman and that the end of the night was near. Lord Chamberlain escorted her to her father, who was in conversation with two other gentlemen, who both signed their names to her dance card.

She was caught unprepared for all of the attention and wondered briefly why and how she was garnering so much of it. After each dance, there were several eligible men waiting to sign their names on her dance card. She was now occupied with dances the remainder of the night.

After a dance with a particularly rotund viscount, Livie stood beside her mother, drinking iced champagne. Her gaze wandered around the ballroom in search of Julia. She found her on the dance floor once again with the Marquess of Heartford.

Livie smiled knowingly to herself. She could tell that Julia and the marquess were instantly attracted to each other. She was both happy and envious of her cousin.

When Julia's father, the previous Earl of Hempstead, and his lady wife died in a dreadful carriage accident, they were both little girls, still playing with their handmade dolls, always together—cousins by blood, but sisters in their hearts.

"Pardon me, Lady Hempstead, may I please have a word with your daughter?" Lady Diana asked, her eyes sparkling with mischief.

Lady Hempstead surveyed Lady Diana suspiciously before gracing her with a slight nod of her head. "Of course, my lady, it will be an honor."

Livie excused herself from the group of older women to take a turn around the room beside Lady Diana. The older woman slid her arm through Livie's as they strolled for several moments without saying a word. The crowd seemingly parted and stared as if they were fine art in a museum, taking great interest in the fact that the duke's mother was finding Livie worth her time.

Lady Diana was always at the forefront of society's attention. Julia had regaled Livie with details of every prominent member of society in their carriage ride to town. Apparently, the lady became friends with the former Duchess of Karrington, and upon her death, married the late duke a shocking three months after his first wife's death.

Once they passed the gawking onlookers, Livie gave the lady a quizzical glance. "You do me a great honor, my lady. May I inquire why you sought me out as a companion?"

Lady Diana chuckled lightly. "I see that you and I will get along splendidly." She patted Livie's gloved hand. "My dear, I could not help but notice that you danced with my son earlier."

Livie stopped, shocked by the lady's forwardness. "Indeed, he was simply doing a favor for my father."

"A favor that seems to have captured his special attention. I know my son, Lady Olivia, and as his only living mother, I must tell you it brought me great joy to witness." Her smile was sincere, eyes sparkling with delight.

Flustered and caught unaware by her assumptions, Livie placed her free hand to her chest to calm her racing heart. "My lady, I can assure you there is no understanding. It was only a dance."

"My dear, I know what I witnessed. I would encourage you not to allow anything to deter you. He is dear to me, but I do know the gossips and society do not paint him in a favorable light. I urge you to see past the mask he has in place for society. I am sure you will be surprised at what you will uncover." She raised an encouraging eyebrow at Livie.

"Darling, are you ready to take our leave?" Her husband interrupted their private conversation.

"Yes, of course. Mr. David Prescott, please allow me to introduce Lady Olivia St. John." She said warmly, her gaze traveling from her husband to Livie. "Lady Olivia, my husband, Mr. David Prescott."

Livie gave a short curtsey and smiled warmly at the gentleman. "Thank you both for attending."

She began to walk away but was stopped by the matron. "It was our pleasure, and please do not forget my advice, dear."

Livie nodded before leaving the older couple. As she walked back to her family, she could not help but notice most of the guests watching her every move.

The morning after the ball, Livie prepared for the day. Her mind and heart were still filled with thoughts of the ball and the duke. It was a foolish girl's dream to hope that his mother was correct in her assumptions. She refused to hope that the duchess's words were true.

The door barged open, interrupting the quiet in the room. Julia came bustling in, out of breath and full of excitement, holding the gossips.

"Olivia! You will never believe what has happened!" She laid down on the settee in the room, her legs sprawled out in front of her in a very unladylike fashion.

"Julia, whatever is the matter? Is it the Marquess of Heartford?" Livie asked in concern.

Julia sat up wide-eyed. "It has nothing to do with either the marquess or me and everything to do with you and the Bachelor Duke!" she yelled, holding up the sheet.

Abigail abandoned her duties to sit beside Julia and read the gossip. Livie stared at both of them in shock.

"Me? I don't understand," she muttered, bewildered.

Julia, walked over, and stood in front of Livie and began reading at a rapid rate. "The Duke of Karrington is the most sought-after gentlemen in society. Any available lady would set her sights on him, but is it too late for hopeful debutantes? As a man that never partakes in the menial task of dancing or even attending balls, it seems our duke has finally found someone he feels is worthy of him. Has the plump daughter of an earl captured the Bachelor Duke's eye?"

Silence filled the room as the three women let the words of the gossip sheet wash over them. Livie couldn't believe what she just heard. Was the rest of society mad? She knew what she wished would happen, but the possibility of her wildest dreams coming true was nigh impossible.

She was aware that the duke only danced with her to appease

her father, but that did not stop her foolish heart from hoping the papers, his mother, and her dreams were right.

"Livie! You are the talk of society. Everyone is in an uproar about you and the duke."

"How dare they call you plump for all of London to read!" Abigail shouted, outraged on Livie's behalf. She was another one of Livie's fierce protectors, always coming to her aid. Sometimes she wondered what she ever did to earn such loyalty out of a person.

"You did not tell me you danced, and that the duke's mother took you for a turn around the ballroom?" Abigail's eyes were as wide as tea saucers, her mouth agape in a perfect circle.

"I-I did not think it at all important … besides, Julia was there, and nothing happened." Livie defended herself, not comfortable with both Abigail and Julia questioning her about the duke. She did not want to share anything about the ball, for fear it did not happen at all.

"I was too mesmerized by the marquess to notice! I am sure the duke will call on you. Perhaps he will come with the marquess!" Julia could barely contain her excitement.

"There is no understanding between the Duke of Karrington and myself. Now, tell me all about the marquess as we walk down to breakfast." Livie took her cousin's arm.

Julia's face lit up. She began to retell every detail of her encounter with the Marquess of Heartford. Every dance they partook, every turn around the ballroom, every glance he sent her way.

As Julia prattled on and on, Livie tried to listen, but her mind continued to wander to intense blue eyes, dark hair, and strong arms that commanded her body to do whatever he willed it to. Her heart beat rapidly as she recalled his strong chiseled jaw. Every part of him was magnificent. She couldn't help but hope that she would see more of the Duke of Karrington.

Before she could spend her time analyzing their dance and how he made her feel, her mother rushed from the breakfast room, nearly colliding with them. Her hands were filled with calling cards, her eyes wide like a child who had won a game.

"There you are! Quickly, you must eat, you have several gentlemen callers stopping by today!" her mother yelled, her voice squeaky and high.

"What gentlemen callers?" Livie questioned, looking at her mother as if she'd gone mad. "I believe only Baron Bromswell asked to call on me."

She tried very hard not to show her apprehension to such a man calling on her. She knew that at her size, she should be happy with any husband, but she could not escape the feeling that something sinister was within the baron.

"Baron Bromswell, Lord Chamberlain, Lord Carmichael, and the Duke of Summerset have all sent their cards to secure an afternoon visit," her mother said rather proudly as if she was announcing the Prince Regent.

"The Duke of Summerset is older than you and Uncle!" Julia called out, outraged.

Livie vaguely remembered dancing with the older gentleman near the end of the night, but she thought it was only a friendly gesture as they spoke no words.

"Yes, he is a little older, but you will mind your manners. The Marquess of Heartford has sent a card for you. Now come we must hurry!" Her mother clapped her hands together, excited that the ladies both had callers.

Livie watched her mother, noting how her shoulders seemed less stiff with the prospects of suitors and the girls being cared for once her husband no longer was an earl.

Chapter Five

Missing: One tall and handsome duke.
The Bachelor Duke has not been seen out in society since the Earl of
H's ball. I'm sure Lady O hasn't noticed his absence as she has had a
line of suitors from here to the Americas.

I T HAD ONLY BEEN A SENNIGHT SINCE HE'D LAID EYES ON the most beautiful woman he had ever had the pleasure to behold. Because of that one simple fact, Remington found himself avoiding all events and outings where the fairer sex would be in attendance. He tried indulging himself in one of his usual activities, but nothing kept his mind off of Lady Olivia St. John. Fencing turned dangerous for him, even when wearing protective gear. His mind was not on the task at hand, but a pair of stormy gray eyes.

Hiding out at O'Brien's Gentlemen's Club became a normal occurrence if he wasn't at home in his study, diligently going over his estate ledgers. He found the club rather enjoyable in the evenings when other gentlemen were attending social functions. He took comfort in the easy conversation of the establishment owner Flynn O'Brien, a man old enough to be his father.

O'Brien was a tough as nails Irishman whose father was the third son of the former Duke of Summerset. One would never know his English heritage upon speaking with the man as he spent most of his life in Ireland, until he moved his family to London nearly twenty years ago. A proud man, O'Brien wanted no connection between himself and the Summerset title, as his father's family allowed his family to starve in Ireland.

Over the years, O'Brien and Remington became friends. He found it strange that he was friends with most older gentlemen but could barely occupy the same home with his father when he was alive.

The establishment had small alcoves lining the far walls. Dark burgundy drapes, upholstered chairs, and sturdy tables made the room elegant enough for Remington's tastes. It wasn't as glamorous as White's, but it was more suited for a younger aristocrat that enjoyed boisterous, lively conversation. It wasn't a gaming hell or a brothel; however, if one wanted those services, a word to a footman could lead to other entertainments.

Most younger gentlemen admired O'Brien's work ethic and refusal to acknowledge his connection to the Summerset title. On the outside he was an Irishman, but he was also of English nobility.

Remington took a sip of his brandy. He had one mission on his mind—avoiding Lady Olivia St. John until the end of the Season. It would prevent him from doing something rash, like claiming her in front of all of society by ravishing her plump lips and curvaceous body.

"There you are! Have a drink with me. I'm celebrating!" Heartford announced, too boisterous for Remington's mood.

"And what exactly are we celebrating?" He eyed his friend suspiciously, as one of the young O'Brien boys came over to serve them.

Heartford raised his glass. "A toast to Lady Julia St. John—"

"What are we celebrating?" The Earl of Windchester demanded as he pulled out a chair and joined them.

"Lady Julia St. John for some apparent reason." Remington had an idea of what Heartford planned to announce.

"Before you interrupted me, I was going to toast to my intended. I have asked to enter into a courtship with Lady Julia." Heartford raised his glass then took a hearty drink.

"Well, congratulations are in order!" Windchester raised his arm to signal for a drink.

Griffin O'Brien walked over and poured another glass of brandy for Windchester.

Remington raised his drink, taking in his friend's happy disposition and the twinkle in his eye. The man even sat up a little straighter than normal. In that instant, he envied Heartford, especially since he was able to do the one thing that Remington had vowed to himself that he would never do.

Commit himself to another person.

"Well done. I am surprised you wasted no time." Remington tipped his head toward Heartford.

"She captured me from the start. I saw no need to delay my life another second without her in it," Heartford answered joyfully.

Remington felt a pang of jealousy, for Heartford knew exactly what he wanted in life—Lady Julia St. John.

"Here's to your courtship, and may your marriage be better than mine." Windchester took a hearty sip of his drink.

"Well, that shouldn't be too difficult," Remington replied, causing both men to laugh.

"It should not. Tell me, have you heard from your sister?" Windchester inquired in a casual tone.

"I received a letter from Lady Evers stating that she was enjoying a long holiday in France and shall return within a month," Heartford said.

"No doubt she has company. I know she's your sister but choosing to openly bed whomever she pleases isn't the smartest idea." Remington shook his head, not understanding how someone would want to be the talk of society.

Windchester scowled openly at him, taking Remington by surprise. "What do you expect? She married a man old enough to be her father. Her real father never acknowledged her." Windchester listed off each point on his fingers.

"To be honest, he barely acknowledged me, and I was his heir." Heartford interrupted the long list to add his opinion.

"Yes, well at least you inherited everything, she has nothing but a widow's jointure." Windchester gave him a look of disdain. There was no trace of his usual jovial disposition. "Not to mention the fact that the man that she was told was her father simply ignored her and his precious heir disowned her in front of all of society. Now her stepson practically ignores her like the plague." Windchester glared at his friends, his cheeks heated with anger.

"Good Lord, man, I didn't know you felt so passionately about the lady." Remington raised an eyebrow at his friend.

"I do not. I was only stating the cruelty of her situation." Windchester ignored the questioning looks.

"There you are, Karrington. I wanted to check for myself that the rumors aren't true." Baron Bromswell interrupted the group friends.

Remington took a deep breath, not wanting to acknowledge Bromswell's existence. His hand tightened around his glass, and his jaw clenched. He felt a throbbing in his head at the effort he was using to ignore the baron. Any time they were in each other's presence Remington wanted nothing more than to pummel the man bloody.

"What rumors would that be, Bromswell?" Remington finally spoke, his words coming out clipped.

"Do not pretend with me! You know perfectly well I am speaking of the rumors about you and Lady Olivia. Tell me now, do you plan to court her?" the pompous Bromswell demanded, always believing that he was higher than his station.

Remington eyed the man with disgust. The events from that dark night long ago entered his mind again, and his distaste deepened. Bromswell removed his gloves, glaring down at Remington as if he were the duke and Remington the baron.

Bromswell came from a family rich in history. Two of his ancestors served in the court of Henry VIII, a fact that he constantly reminded anyone that would listen.

Taking a sip of his brandy, Remington fought the urge to punch Bromswell in the jaw in front of every gentleman in the club. "My plans are of no concern of yours. I suggest you find another heiress to unleash your cruelty upon."

Bromswell let out a sinister laugh that caused Remington's blood to boil. Visions from that long-buried night assaulted him, but instead of long, flowing red hair, the lifeless body had flowing blonde hair and luscious curves.

"You call it cruelty. I call it sport." Bromswell shrugged his shoulders carelessly. "I have plans for the lady and her dowry, so I suggest you put an end to the endless chatter and do not approach her again. At any rate, I plan to make an offer to her father."

Remington stood to face the other man, his body looming over Bromswell's much smaller, thinner frame. "You have no say if I approach her or not—"

"I will very much have a say, as she will be my intended. I plan to court her, and I will make my intentions known tonight at the Ratchford Ball, so do not approach Lady Olivia again." He eyed Remington for a moment before turning and leaving.

His body shook with the revelation that Baron Bromswell planned to court Lady Olivia. He should be happy that she would no longer be a distraction for him, but what fate would she have as Bromswell's wife?

Taking his seat, he tried to ignore the nagging feeling in the pit of his abdomen at the news that Bromswell may soon have Lady Olivia St. John. Remington rubbed his chest, his mind running with wild with the choice he needed to make.

"Why do you always tolerate that ass of a man?" Windchester questioned, shifting his large body forward.

Remington licked his now dry lips, sweat beading at the nape of his neck. He had never revealed to his friends the worst part of himself. A secret that only Bromswell and Mother Di knew.

"Tolerating him is better than running him through with my sword." Remington forced a laugh at his own joke.

"It may be best to run him through than for us to have to deal with him." Heartford countered, nodding his head in Remington's direction.

Windchester's eyes shifted to Remington suspiciously. "Tell us what in bloody hell was that about now?"

Remington shrugged his shoulders. "Bromswell has it in his mind that I will come between him and Lady Olivia's courtship."

"Well, he obviously does not know that the Bachelor Duke will never marry." Heartford tapped the table, causing Windchester to laugh with him.

Remington's smile was tight, a mask to hide his true emotions. His thoughts focused not on the loathsome title but on Bromswell's true intentions. How could he save another innocent from his cruelty?

Livie painted on a smile, remembering to be welcoming and charming as she entered the townhome of Lord and Lady Ratchford. Her parents conversed with the older couple. Lord Ratchford and her father were old acquaintances that went to Eton together. They greeted each other fondly with hearty laughs and handshakes.

Ratchford House was one of the grandest homes in London occupying an entire block. Livie eagerly took in her surroundings as they were escorted to a lavish ballroom. She had heard great things about Lord Ratchford's library and the infamous chess games her father partook in. Having beaten her father repeatedly in chess, she longed for another opponent. She wished she could take on the cheating Lord Ratchford.

Smoothing out the dark purple gown, Livie tried to calm her nerves, both hoping and dreading that the Duke of Karrington would be in attendance. Beside her, Julia shined in a dark blue gown. The guests turned to stare at the young ladies who had become the talk of the Season. Livie's steps faltered under the weight of their attention. The whispers and glares made her throat tighten, and she found herself swallowing repeatedly.

"I have promised Henry the first dance." Julia stopped behind Livie's parents as they conversed with another couple.

"Try to remember yourself, you mustn't call him Henry while we're out in society." Livie was happy that her cousin had entered into a courtship with the marquess, but one really must remember propriety.

Livie and Julia walked deeper into the ballroom in search of refreshments, leaving her parents to converse with their friends.

"I will remember myself around others, but only you can hear me," Julia whispered the last part much quieter for emphasis as they made their way to the champagne table. "Besides, there is word that the Duke of Karrington will attend, although he hasn't been to a function since our ball. Perhaps there is still hope for you two?" Julia's gaze swept around the room looking for the marquess.

Livie sighed, trying not to think of the Duke of Karrington. After all, it had been a sennight since had she first laid eyes on him, and seven days seemed like an eternity. Although, she tried to be welcoming to other gentlemen by accepting their visits, she found that none of them were who she wanted them to be. Every gentleman that did not have dark hair, blue eyes, and the ability to unnerve her with one glance was of no interest to her.

She knew that she could not be too selective, but Lord Carmichael was a total bore and constantly made remarks about how fortunate she was to have so much male attention. Lord Chamberlain was desperate to marry an heiress in order to save his family lands from ruin. The Duke of Summerset was in dire need for a young wife in which he could produce an heir. He went on and on about how his family's estate and title were in fear of going to an Irish relative if he did not marry and produce a son. After two of his sons perished in Waterloo and the third died suddenly in the winter, it seemed the duke's situation was rather urgent.

Out of all the gentlemen, no one was worse than Baron Bromswell. He unnerved her, and she constantly found herself trying not to be left alone with him for even a few seconds.

With every caller, she could not help but wish that they were the Duke of Karrington.

"There is no hope, dear." Livie wanted to say more on the subject, but before she could continue, her parents walked toward her with Baron Bromswell.

"Lady Olivia, you look enchanting this evening." He bowed low.

Giving him a forced smile, she looked at both of her parents noticing her father's encouraging look.

Livie resisted the urge to roll her eyes at her father's behavior, but she understood that he wanted his family to be taken care of in the event of his untimely death. Like his brother before him. It still annoyed her that he was unable to see past what she thought was Baron Bromswell's façade. Her father's only thought was that the gentleman was a suitable match, but Livie felt differently every time his beady eyes gazed upon her.

"Thank you. It is most kind of you to say." Feigning politeness, she couldn't escape the uneasy feeling the baron gave her.

"May I have the first set?" he asked, ever the gentleman. However, she felt his kind words were nothing but tiny sharp knives pricking her skin.

"Of course." She held out her arm so he could write his name on her dance card.

A series of hushed whispers swept over the ballroom, and all eyes gravitated towards the entrance. Livie's gaze followed, and her heart stopped in her chest. Standing in all his glory beside the Marquess of Heartford was the Duke of Karrington.

"Oh, finally, the marquess is here. Uncle, please get his attention," Julia said excitedly, watching her intended as he entered beside the duke.

"Do calm yourself, Julia," Lady Hemstead reprimanded.

Livie noticed Baron Bromswell's body stiffen as he watched the duke and marquess weave through the crowd. The closer they came to where she stood, the faster her heart raced within the confines of her chest. The palms of her hands began to sweat inside her gloves. She tried to pull at the fabric to ease her discomfort, but it was to no avail.

"Good evening, Lord Hempstead, Lady Hempstead," the Marquess of Heartford greeted as he joined them.

"Good evening, Heartford," Lord Hempstead returned before shifting his eyes to Remington. "Ahh, Karrington, it's good to see you at another ball." Lord Hempstead eyed the men fondly.

"Hempstead, I found an incentive to attend more functions." The duke stared directly at Livie, causing her lips to part as she let out the breath she was holding. "Lady Olivia, may I have the first dance?" He ignored Baron Bromswell altogether.

"Lady Olivia has agreed to dance the first set with me." Bromswell sneered at him.

The tension was so thick that Livie's gaze shifted uncomfortably between the group to see if she was the only one who felt it. She caught her mother's questioning eye and knew she, too, could feel the animosity between the gentlemen.

"The second set then, if you will be so kind." The duke's voice was like honey, creating tingles down her spine. She longed to bathe in his voice as his piercing blue eyes held her captive.

"Of course." She held out her arm so that he could write his name on her dance card below the baron's. She wished that the duke's name was at the top of her dance list, but she could not outright refuse the other man in front of society. The baron stood beside her, glaring at the duke.

She wondered what the duke had done to earn such a look. At her debutante ball, they were very hostile towards each other, and now they could barely be in the other's presence. What had happened between them?

Livie studied the duke's features, aware of the heat of his body. The sweet woody scent of sandalwood assaulted her nostrils, and she wished she could bury her nose in his hair.

"If you all will excuse me. Lady Olivia, I will find you when the set begins," the baron murmured. "Lord Hempstead, would you be available to have a brandy with me at O'Brien's tomorrow evening?" He kept his gaze on Remington.

The duke stiffened as Baron Bromswell continued to speak to her father, his eyes like daggers aimed at the baron.

"Ahh, yes of course." The earl's gaze shifted from Baron Bromswell to his daughter, then to his wife.

Her father straightened his jacket, his head perked up at the thought of securing another match. Livie knew that her father was proud to have the marquess courting Julia, as it was his constant worry that his brother's child would not make a good match. Now with the baron inquiring about Livie, she was sure by the way her father's lips widened into a broad smile that he was happy for his daughter as well.

Livie felt it was rather rude for the baron to bring the subject up in front of others. Her father however seemed to believe Baron Bromswell was a suitable match, but she knew like her, he'd hoped the duke was taking a fancy toward her.

The baron gave a curt but victorious bow, looking extremely smug and pleased with himself before leaving them.

"Are you well, Lady Olivia?" Remington asked, concern etched in his handsome face.

"I am well, Your Grace. I-I just felt a chill." She blinked rapidly, trying to ignore the pain in her chest, the absolute dread she felt at the very thought of an offer from Baron Bromswell.

Remington began unbuttoning his tailcoat. She stared at his long perfect fingers as they released each button from its confines. With every freed button, Livie's heart pounded faster. The constant rhythm felt as if it was moving her body closer to him with each fierce beat.

"Please, allow me." He started to remove the garment. Her

eyes widened at the sight of his powerful upper body prominently displayed through his shirt and vest.

Livie licked her dry lips as she tried not to stare at the virile specimen of a man in front of her. She was hot all over and resisted the urge to take her fan out of her reticule, surely that would alert the others to the effect he had on her.

"Oh, heavens, I cannot. I assure you I am fine now," she protested, noticing all eyes were on her and the duke's exchange. The whispers were deafening. His coat was halfway off his large frame, and her gaze traveled the length of his arm where his muscles threatened to burst out of the sleeve.

She wondered what activities he partook in to be so well-built.

"Nonsense, you look as if you are freezing. What sort of gentleman would I be if I let you catch your death?" His face was serious, but his voice was teasing. His blue eyes twinkled mischievously.

She blushed furiously. A wide smile broke through the mask that she desperately tried to keep in place in front of society. He filled her with hope and a playfulness she found she rather enjoyed. Fun, carefree, and teasing her as if they had known each other longer than a sennight.

"She's fine, Karrington, for God's sake put your jacket back on. People are staring," the earl's gruff voice interrupted the moment.

"It is most kind of you." Her voice quivered as she tried to erase the image of his taut muscles. A picture of him only in shirtsleeves and a vest was forever engraved in her mind. She knew she would always have it even if she did not have him. But from the way his eyes seemed to focus on her, the way his mouth curved at the corner when he teased her, all caused her girlish heart to flutter.

Should she dare hope?

Chapter Six

He lives!
The Bachelor Duke finally graced us with his presence at Lord
and Lady R's ball. It appears that he may have his eyes set on a
certain plump miss. Will Lady O do what no other miss was able
to do and capture the heart of the Bachelor Duke?

R EMINGTON HID IN THE LIBRARY, DRINKING WITH
Hempstead, Lord Ratchford, and others. The beginning
chords of the first set began filling the old townhome
with music. He knew he could not stay in the same room as Lady
Olivia and Bromswell as they danced with the other couples to
La Polka.

It took every ounce of will not to seek out Lady Olivia to ensure her safety. If Remington knew anything about Bromswell, it
was that the man would never harm a woman in front of society.
He prided himself on keeping his gentlemanly mask up, so the
aristocracy would trust him around their daughters and wives.

With Lady Olivia safe at the moment, Remington tried
to focus on the conversation surrounding him as he took slow,
steady sips of brandy.

"I think Bromswell would be an excellent match for your
daughter, Hempstead," the Earl of Allendale said. "After all, at
her size, you can't expect a better one."

"I don't see what her size has to do with anything. She shines brighter than any diamond. There's no need for her to settle for Bromswell." Remington spit the words out with venom. He'd never cared for Allendale, but the man's comments only increased his disdain for the portly gentleman.

The men all glanced from Remington to Allendale, who shifted uncomfortably from the cold tight stare he was receiving.

"Yes … well, there have been some rumors throughout the years," Lord Ratchford announced matter of factly, trying to change the subject.

The current subject change caused Remington's back to stiffen.

If there were rumors associated with Bromswell, there very well could be rumors about him. Although, Remington knew his station and title saved him, the thought of being the subject of negative gossip, like his father, made him sick to his stomach.

"There are always rumors with men such as us." The Duke of Melville took a rather large gulp of brandy.

"What sort of rumors?" Hempstead questioned, curiously. He obviously wanted to know more about the man showing his daughter affection.

"It seems he likes to have a bit of sport with the light skirts, but I'm sure your daughter will be perfectly safe as his wife," Allendale replied cheerfully.

The music stopped, alerting Remington to the end of the first set. It was now time for his dance with Lady Olivia. He drank the rest of his drink in one ungentlemanly gulp.

"Yes, because we all know wives are safe with their husbands." Remington's voice was harsh and bitter, causing the other men to stare as he walked past them and out of the library.

Taking long strides down the hall, he passed century-old

paintings and artwork. The townhome reminded him more of a museum than a home. Reaching the entrance to the ballroom, he scanned the crowded space for his dance partner. He found her easily, a dutiful smile on her face, her womanly curves begging for all to gaze upon her.

Making his way to her, he watched as she politely dismissed the baron and perused the room as if she were searching for someone. Her gaze locked with Remington's, causing him to stumble slightly from the very weight of it.

He reached her, ignoring the increase in chatter surrounding them. He gave her a curt bow, rose, and offered her his hand. "Shall we?" She rewarded him with a smile as bright as the sun.

"Yes." Her voice was breathy as if she had run a mile around Hyde Park.

"That is a lovely color on you," he replied, trying not to devour her with his eyes. The gown shaped her body wonderfully, and he found himself stirring.

Once again, the crowd parted for them as they joined the other couples in line for an English country dance. Eyeing his partner appreciatively, he found he did not mind dancing when he was able to glance at such beauty.

The music began, and his gaze never left Lady Olivia's. He placed his hand on top of hers. The same feelings he had the last time he danced with her washed over him, causing him to curse himself for even trying to stay away. Her touch felt like fresh sunshine warming his face after days of darkness. A small part of him wanted her light to guide him out of the dark hole he had created for himself.

He was safe alone in the dark but standing there in front of her had him longing for her sunlight.

A sennight, seven miserable days, he had tried to forget her and leave her to her fate with Bromswell. Lady Olivia haunted the back of his mind. Every time he closed his eyes, he was captured by her stormy gray eyes. Bromswell confronting him at O'Brien's was all Remington needed to make a decision. His heart thumped wildly at the thought of Lady Olivia in the hands of the cold-hearted bastard. He knew he must do everything in his power to prevent history from repeating itself.

They followed the other couples in the long queue, happily smiling and laughing.

"You seem different, Your Grace," Lady Olivia commented as he twirled her around.

"I feel different." His reply was short as they spun around the couple beside them.

Her teeth caught the corner of her bottom lip in their grasp. Color rose to her cheeks, and her eyes avoided all contact with him. Remington loved seeing the effects his words had on her. He wanted her to know it was all because of her, this new him who went to balls and faced off with blaggards.

When they reached the head of the queue of couples, he took her hand in his.

"I'm glad you feel different, you were rather rude a sennight ago." Her lips quirked slightly upward to match the teasing sparkle in her eyes.

"I did not mean to be rude … I was caught unaware by … something." He didn't want to elaborate or admit the deep emotions she bought out of him.

Remington wished she was the cure he needed to end a family history of cruelty to women, but he did not think even the magnificent creature in front of him had that much power.

He wanted the dance to last for hours but knew soon, he would have to return her to the safety of her parents. Remington was aware they were the object of everyone's attention, but he ignored the onlookers, focusing on the smile on his partner's face, how her eyes twinkled with delight, how her lips had a rosy hue to them, as if begging to be kissed not by any gentleman—by him.

When they finished the last set, he escorted her to a server for refreshments.

"Thank you, Your Grace. I do enjoy a country dance … it is delightful." Her cheeks were flushed, and her bosom heaved as she tried to catch her breath from their rigorous dancing.

"I find it is only delightful with the right partner." His voice was deep and steady, as his gaze locked with hers, making it clear who the right partner was.

"Yes, well, that could be said for any activity, even conversation," she challenged, meeting his gaze.

"And do you feel I am the right partner?" he questioned, the corner of his mouth twitching.

"That remains to be seen. I've only been in your company on one other occasion, and then you were very much silent and brooding." Her gaze scanned the area, and he knew she was aware that the entire room was focused on them.

"Well, I do apologize. I find it difficult to be at ease in front of certain company." His jaw tensed as he tried to hide his anger. Since the incident so many years ago, it was always difficult for Remington to be in the vicinity of Bromswell.

"Is the gentleman a friend of yours?" she inquired.

"He is not, and Lady Olivia, excuse my boldness, but I do not believe Baron Bromswell is the sort of gentleman you want to associate with." Remington reached out for her gloved hand but immediately stopped as the whispers increased around them.

Lady Olivia took a step back as if she had been struck. "I do not see why that is any concern of yours." The harshness in her voice was evident while her small hands balled up in fists. Her eyes turned into tiny slits as she glared at him.

Remington drew in a calming breath, trying to control himself. She was breathtaking when upset. He found that he wanted her just so he could watch the rise and fall of her bosom. The tightness at the corner of her mouth caused her lips to protrude slightly.

Shaking his head of all thoughts about how delectable her anger was, he tried to convey to her the dangers that marriage to Baron Bromswell would bring. "I do not mean to offend you. I only mean that you should not encourage him. He is a fortune hunter, among other things, that I do not think your delicate sensibilities could handle."

They stared at each other, both not saying a word until Lady Olivia broke the tension surrounding them. "I thank you for your concern, Your Grace, but I can assure you it is not needed. Please excuse me, I see my mother." She gave him a hasty curtsey before turning to walk away.

Grabbing her gloved hand in his, he stopped her retreat. "Lady Olivia …" He searched her beautiful face, visions of the past swam in his mind, and there was only one thing he could say. "May I call on you tomorrow?" He asked desperately trying to recapture the closeness he felt during their dance. Remington couldn't allow her to be with Bromswell or any other, and because of that simple thought, he knew what he had to do.

Livie blinked several times, aware that the Duke of Karrington still held her hand. She could feel the stares on her, hear the hushed whispers discussing the impropriety of it all, but she couldn't move even if her very life depended on it.

"Will you do me the honor?" he asked again, giving her a rather dazzling smile. It transformed his entire face, making him even more handsome. It rendered her even more speechless, if it were at all possible.

Gazing up at him, she gave him a questioning look. "You want to call on me?" She must have misunderstood him.

"Yes, very much so, if you will have me." His voice was barely a whisper, but she heard him perfectly.

She took several breaths, trying to compose herself. Licking her lips, she peered up at him through her lashes. She was perplexed by his warning about Baron Bromswell. Livie wondered what reason the duke had to keep her for himself. Was it her large dowry, or was he truly attracted to her as she was to him? Livie knew she was pretty, beautiful even, but her one flaw was something that the gossips and the whispers constantly reminded her of.

She exhaled, feeling the tightness of her gown, wishing she would've allowed Abigail to let out the bosom.

"Karrington." Her father's deep voice interrupted their moment, causing the duke to release her gloved hand and take a much-needed step back. Finally, she could breathe and collect her thoughts.

"Hempstead, I was just asking Lady Olivia for permission to call on her tomorrow, if you are agreeable?" Remington's smooth voice was loud enough for their audience to take in his every word.

"Yes, yes, of course, if Lady Olivia has no objections." Her father's voice was now overly friendly as he looked from his daughter to the duke.

Aware that both her father and the duke were waiting on an answer, Livie nodded her agreement.

"I look forward to seeing you," she whispered, trying to find the bravado she had earlier when he tried to warn her against the baron. But for some reason, she found she had no courage, because she wanted him more than anything.

Taking her father's arm, he escorted her over to where her mother and Julia chatted happily.

"There you two are. Darling, how was your dance with the duke?" her mother asked, her voice hopeful.

"I'd say it went rather well. He has asked to call on her to-morrow," her father declared as if she was unable to answer for herself.

Livie watched him in amusement, glad that the news of the Duke of Karrington wanting to call on her had erased all thoughts of Baron Bromswell.

Beside her, Julia clutched at her arms, leaning into her excitedly. "I knew there was hope!"

"Oh my! Olivia, that is very exciting news, indeed," her mother exclaimed.

"Mother, please, I'm sure nothing will come of it." Livie prayed that she was wrong. She couldn't deny that she wanted him to desire her. He plagued her dreams at night and during the day. Yet, doubt crept in her mind as she remembered the gossip sheets and the whispered words of society about her size. Perhaps he required her dowry, like so many others.

The Bachelor Duke could have any available lady he liked, so why choose Livie?

"Lady Olivia, may I sign your dance card?" a deep voice interrupted her inner musings, causing her entire family to look at the interloper.

Livie took a deep breath as she saw not one but five gentlemen all waiting to sign their name to her card. One glance from the Bachelor Duke had thrust her into the minds of every eligible gentleman. No more a wallflower, she plastered on a tight smile as she dutifully held out her arm.

Viscount Wallace signed his name, followed by Lord Hargrove, the Duke of Summerset once again put his name down followed by a stiff bow. Then came Lord Carmichael and the Duke of St. Clara. All eligible gentleman, all in want or need of a wealthy wife. Not a single one could erase the fact that the Duke of Karrington was calling on her tomorrow.

Livie looked over to find Julia also had suitors signing her dance card but not as many as herself.

The extremely tall and rail-thin Viscount Wallace led Livie to the dance floor. The viscount was in want of a third wife to care for his four girls and hopefully produce a male heir. Livie smiled and asked questions about his girls, but she knew she would never agree to marry him.

The next set was with Lord Hargrove. He was handsome, and he knew it. In fact, he commented several times on how many likenesses he had of himself. Livie found him rather too touchy with a grip that was tighter than she would have liked in a partner.

When she finally took the dance floor with the last name on her card, she hoped no other gentleman would come anywhere near her or her dance card. Her feet hurt, and she could hardly take a sip of champagne before the next partner requested her company.

The Duke of St. Clara was everything one would think a duke would be. He was handsome with rich brown hair and round chocolate eyes. His eyelashes rivaled any lady's, his nose was as perfect as if it was carved by Michelangelo himself. His one flaw, which to Livie discarded all his other qualities, was that he was absolutely aware of just how handsome he was.

"You've certainly become the bell of the Season." The Duke of St. Clara stood across from her, waiting for the orchestra to begin.

"I'm not sure if that is a compliment or not, Your Grace." Livie smiled but resisted the urge to roll her eyes at him.

"It is surprising, usually a flower of the Season would not be so …" He trailed off and appeared to be searching for the correct word. "Exotic."

Livie's eyebrows crinkled in concentration, not finding herself at all exotic. The most exotic thing about her was the annoying cluster of freckles on the side of her neck. Relief filled her once the set finally ended and he led her back to her waiting family.

Unlike the Duke of Karrington, the Duke of St. Clara was annoying, conceited, and rude at times. His sense of self-worth shone through every action.

They weaved through the crowd. Livie was sure to keep her dance card hidden from view in fear that another gentleman would want a dance. She was terribly exhausted; her feet were killing her and none of her partners was the one she wanted.

"Ah, it seems as if Karrington really is obsessed with you," the duke sneered, causing Livie to follow his gaze.

Livie glared sideways at the Duke of St. Clara, his comment causing her to stiffen. "Surely one shouldn't believe everything they read in the gossips."

He surveyed her coolly. "No, they shouldn't."

Livie smiled triumphantly remembering the tales Julia read about the duke's gambling.

The Duke of Karrington stood amongst her family, chatting amicably with her mother and father while Lord Heartford and Julia whispered to each other.

"Here she is." Her father beamed at her proudly.

Livie was pleased that her father was happy about all the attention she was receiving from the Duke of Karrington and a host of other eligible bachelors. Knowing how her father fretted over who would provide for his family if he were to perish like his brother.

The Duke of Karrington offered her his arm. She stumbled briefly in her rush to abandon her dance partner for the object of her dreams.

The duke looked down at her, his blue eyes dancing a waltz at the sight of her. The look of joy at her now being back in his grasp unnerved her, because it was exactly how she felt inside.

"Thank you for returning Lady Olivia to us, St. Clara." The Duke of Karrington's voice was smooth, but there was an underlining firmness to it that made Livie shiver in need.

It made her feel like he wanted her. She couldn't help but notice that the entire ballroom had taken note of his silent declaration by the single act of offering her his arm while she was beside another man.

"Of course, Karrington. Lady Olivia, it's been enlightening." The Duke of St. Clara gave her a curt nod before his eyes shifted coldly to the marquess. "Heartford."

"St. Clara." Lord Heartford's boyish features contorted slightly, revealing his disdain for the other gentleman.

Without another word, St. Clara left the small group. Livie tried to catch Julia's eye but she was too enamored with the marquess to care about the scene unfolding in front of them.

Livie let out a tiresome sigh, shifting from foot to foot trying to alleviate the pain.

"Would you like to sit for a moment while I get you some refreshments?" the Duke of Karrington asked, concern crinkling at the corner of his eyes.

She felt she should be embarrassed that he noticed her discomfort, but really, she had been dancing the entire ball and needed a reprieve.

"Yes, I would enjoy that very much. I feel I need to rest before the next onslaught of gentlemen." Her mother passed her the reticule she was keeping secure as she danced with multiple partners.

The Duke of Karrington escorted her through the crowded room. She resisted the urge to cling to him in fear, not liking being the center of attention.

Livie fisted her free hand in her gown, trying to hide the shaking that threatened to reveal just how affected she was by their stares and whispers. Each step toward the empty chairs in the corner of the room felt like she was walking to a guillotine.

Her throat tightened at the thought. The whispers surrounding Livie were as loud as screams in her mind.

"I'm sure it's just a passing fancy."

"It must be because of her dowry, what else could he see in her?"

"You have to admit she is pretty, but her size."

The dull sound of voices and the irate stares of eligible ladies and their mothers followed them. They reached the chairs untouched by society, although their venomous whispers felt like lashes against her skin. Her only comfort was the strong presence of the gentleman beside her.

"Don't run off with another gentleman while I'm gone." He gave her a playful wink that caused some of the fear she was feeling to ease slightly.

Livie faked indignation, glaring at him, her eyes tightening into what Julia called her cat-like stare. "I'll try, but you never know when another dashing duke will come to sweep me away. You must hurry."

"I'm the only dashing duke that will sweep you away." His crooked smirk inflamed her body despite the spectators.

She licked her dry lips watching him in confusion as her body felt as if she was on fire. Her gown felt hot, heat crawled up her spine to her scalp. She quickly took her fan out of her reticule to fan herself. Remington left her and she watched him move through the crowd, admiring his form.

Setting her reticule down on the chair beside her, she utilized the fan like a shield, fanning her face rapidly.

The duke returned with two glasses of champagne and sat down beside her.

"Thank you, Your Grace. I fear that all the dancing has worn me out immensely." She took a proffered glass, then a sip of the chilled drink.

"I'm sad to hear it as Heartford and I had hoped to add our names to your and Lady Julia's dance cards." He leaned toward her, brushing her shoulder with his.

"For Lord Heartford, I may be convinced," she teased him, pushing him back with her shoulder.

They sat in silence drinking their champagne.

"Do you ever get used to their stares?" Livie gave him a sideways glance before discreetly tilting her head toward their gawkers.

A low chuckle left his lips, and he shook his head, causing a strand of rich dark hair to fall on his forehead. The lone lock transformed his usual brooding features into a carefree one, that she had never seen on his handsome face. "I've become an expert at ignoring them. You will, too, one day."

"There you two are. I was hoping that I could sign my name on your card, Lady Olivia?" Lord Heartford asked, giving her a bow.

"Yes, yes, of course, my lord." She smiled brightly, his happy disposition and charm so different than that of her companion.

The duke addressed Julia from where he stood beside her. "Lady Julia, may I have the next set?"

"Yes, we can't let Lady Olivia and Lord Heartford have all the fun, Your Grace." Julia smiled widely, glancing from Livie to the duke.

Livie finished her drink before standing to be escorted to the dance floor by Lord Heartford. She had a permanent smile on her face as she danced the waltz with Lord Heartford. He was witty, kind, and talkative. She could see why he and her cousin suited each other so well. Where Julia was fierce and wild, he was patient and understanding.

Unlike her waltz with the duke, this one felt as if Livie was dancing with a close friend. She enjoyed how easy it was to be near him and know that he had no interest in her.

"Are you in town alone?" Livie followed his steps across the dance floor.

"No, my uncle and mother are in town with me. My mother, however, refused to come tonight because of a three-year disagreement with Lady Ratchford, and my uncle usually agrees with whatever Mother says." He shook his head, causing his boyish white-blonde curls to glimmer in the candlelight.

"They have disagreed for three years. Whatever for?" Livie asked, bewildered at his mother's behavior.

Lord Heartford laughed heartily. "I cannot recall the reason but once you meet my mother you will see that she can hold a grudge for a very long time." He led them past a talkative Julia and a stoic-looking duke. "I suspect Lady Julia is demanding to know Karrington's intentions with you."

Livie looked over to find her cousin's mouth moving rapidly. "Should I demand to know your intentions?" She raised an eyebrow at Lord Heartford, one side of her mouth quirked in a sly smile.

He cleared his throat before answering. "My intentions with Lady Julia are to make her every dream come true."

"Good." Livie smiled brightly as her heart filled with joy. He would suit her cousin well. Julia loved when someone doted on her, and it seemed that Lord Heartford was no different.

The guests were slowly exiting the Ratchford's ball in the early hours of the morning when Livie realized she did not have her reticule.

"I left my reticule somewhere. I will meet you all at the carriage," Livie said to Julia as her parents bid goodnight to their host and hostess.

The moonlight shined through the windows of the now-empty ballroom as Livie tried to locate her missing handbag. Panic filled her as she realized she may have lost her grandmother's handkerchief for good. The keepsake was nestled inside the silk material.

It was one of the only heirlooms she received from her maternal grandmother, who wasn't the most affectionate woman to anyone except Livie. Her mother always thought it was odd that her mother loathed her but adored her daughter. She gifted Livie a necklace and a handkerchief, informing her very sternly that a lady should always have a handkerchief at the ready.

Seeing the tiny, dark purple reticule, Livie began walking across the room to the small chair it sat upon, remembering she'd placed it there before her dance with Lord Heartford.

"Ahh, finally, I have you alone," a cold voice said, causing her to turn around abruptly.

She came face to face with none other than Baron Bromswell. He stalked over to her, causing her to take several steps back. The look on his face was cold and harsh compared to the facade he usually had in place.

"Baron Bromswell, what a surprise. I only came in to retrieve my reticule. I'm sure my father is waiting." She gave him a tight smile.

"I wanted to make my intentions clear to you before I spoke to your father. I intend to court you," he informed her in a clipped tone. His gaze slowly traveled down her form in a snake-like fashion.

She clutched her bag tighter to her chest, the fabric providing her some small strength. "And do I have any say in the matter?"

"No, not unless you wish to be a spinster, depending on the kindness of your parents for the rest of your life. I'm sure at your size, one can't afford to be picky." He stepped closer to her, invading her personal space, increasing the panic she felt since he stalked toward her. "Besides all these other suitors will soon flee once Karrington is done with this little game."

"Game? What game?" Panic and worry crawled up her chest threatening to choke her. She feared that the duke did not want her, that all the whispers and gossips were correct.

Bromswell laughed heartlessly. "Did you really think he was interested in you? He has vowed to never marry. I don't see you changing his mind."

Livie tried to compose herself, not wanting to show any weakness to the vile man, but the fear was crawling underneath her mask and she wanted nothing more than to run. "I thank you for your honesty. I would rather take my chances on spinsterhood than marry a man who would trap a lady alone and demand marriage. As for the duke's intentions, that is no concern of yours." Having nothing else to say to him, she turned around and tried to walk away.

He grabbed her roughly by the arm and spun her around to face him. She gasped at the tightness of his grip. Panic and worry ran through her at his ungentlemanly behavior.

Baron Bromswell grabbed her by the chin yanking her forward to face him. Her eyes widened, frantically searching for anyone to save her. No one was around, just the two of them.

"I do not believe I'm giving you a choice. You will marry me, or I will ruin you. With any luck, someone will discover us shortly."

"Get your damn hands off her!" The duke pulled Bromswell away roughly, causing Livie to stumble and nearly fall. She caught her balance and placed her hand to her stomach, trying to center herself.

"She is no concern of yours," the baron hissed at the other man.

Taking a step toward Bromswell, the duke let out a dark chuckle. "She is my intended, and as such, that makes her very much my concern. So, I suggest you find another lady to play with before I make your life miserable."

The two men stared at each other for what seemed like an eternity before the baron took a step back. His gaze shifted from the duke to Livie, a cat-like smile on his face. It made her shiver in fear, and she wanted to grab the duke and flee the room

"Oh, Karrington, you know I like misery." The baron stalked away, leaving them alone in the ballroom.

Walking over to her, the duke's gloved hand palmed her cheek. "Are you all right?" His tone was soft, unlike the baron's rough demands. The duke was so overwhelmingly sincere that she was momentarily stunned by his kindness and care for her.

"I-I am well. Just startled by his behavior." She stared up at him, their lips a whisper apart as he inched closer to her, his hand still on her arm.

"I promise he will not bother you again." He inched forward and wrapped his free hand around her waist, pulling her against his hard body.

"You did not have to lie." She searched his handsome face, wondering if what the baron said was correct.

Livie averted her gaze, not wanting to show him how devastated she was by the fact that he did not want her as she wanted him. The events earlier in the evening had given her hope that maybe there was a chance for them. Now, she knew that he was just being kind to her. Any gentleman would surely intercede if a lady was being attacked the way the baron had accosted her.

"I did not lie." The duke's voice was soft, his breath massaging her lips, causing a shiver to run through her.

Her breathing increased, and her eyes fluttered close in anticipation of his lips against hers.

"Livie! Uncle is waiting—" Julia's loud voice caused them to break apart hastily.

"Coming!" Livie called out before walking to her cousin, who raised an eyebrow at her.

Ignoring Julia's knowing glances, Livie remembered her manners and turned back toward the duke. "Goodnight, Your Grace."

"Goodnight, Lady Olivia. I shall see you tomorrow."

Livie watched as the duke walked past them and stopped in front of Lady Ratchford. Her lips tingled at the thought that he almost kissed her.

"What was that about!" Julia asked quietly, as they walked toward their host. "Did you kiss him?"

"No! Of course not," Livie protested as she smiled tightly as they neared Lady Ratchford.

"It looked like he wanted to," Julia whispered-yelled before they stopped in front of Lady Ratchford.

"Ladies, I thought everyone had left the ballroom." Lady Ratchford looked shocked to find them still in her home. Her cool gaze surveyed Livie with no interest. Livie knew that the woman wasn't very amiable, as she had spent time in Lady Ratchford's company. She always appeared to be comparing other ladies to herself.

Livie felt uncomfortable and cleared her throat before she spoke. "We apologize, my lady. I left my reticule and went in search of it. Thank you for a lovely evening." She dipped a curtsey before she pulled Julia along toward the door of the home.

"You kissed him, didn't you? Tell me, Livie!" Julia insisted as they passed the Ratchford's butler.

"Julia!" Livie hissed turning to her cousin as they walked out into the early morning air. "I-I did not kiss him. He was assisting me with Baron Bromswell."

"What happened with Baron Bromswell?" Julia wondered as they walked toward the waiting carriage.

"Will you keep your voice down." Livie scowled at her cousin. "He was rather rude, but the duke interrupted him, that is all. Nothing else happened."

Julia's eyes closed to tiny slits, and her lips thinned into a straight line. "Fine, but this isn't over, dear cousin, and I am convinced more than ever that he wants you after what I saw in the ballroom."

"Girls, what is taking so long?" her mother called from the carriage.

"Coming Mother." Livie pulled Julia to the carriage, her mind on one thing and one thing only—nearly kissing the Duke of Karrington.

Chapter Seven

The gauntlet has been thrown and the Bachelor Duke has declared himself to Lady O. Surely, we should not take out our handkerchiefs yet.

LIVIE LOOKED AT THE ANTIQUE GRANDFATHER CLOCK ON the wall for the hundredth time. Only five minutes had passed since she last checked, but it felt like a lifetime to her. It was near four-thirty, and there was still no sign of the duke.

Although there were still nearly two hours remaining for the appropriate time for social calls. She desperately tried not to fret. Unlike the Duke of Summerset, Lord Chamberlain, and the Marquess of Heartford, the Duke of Karrington did not grace her with his presence at exactly three o'clock.

Beside her, Julia smiled openly at the marquess, who sat in an armchair, while the other gentlemen sat on opposite ends of the sofa. Her mother sat in a lovely upholstered chair in the center between the chaise lounge and the men.

"Lord Chamberlain, when will your sisters come out?" Lady Hempstead asked.

"My father wanted them both to come out this Season, but my mother insisted he wait another year." Lord Chamberlain spoke swiftly, eyeing the room, his hands fisted.

"How old are your sisters?" Livie asked, trying not to be rude and look at the clock once more.

The duke was not coming. She knew it had been too good to be true, for him to want her. She took a deep breath wanting to make the most of the gentlemen who still found her interesting.

It seemed as if Baron Bromswell was correct. The duke had indeed tired of her.

"Fifteen and fourteen." Lord Chamberlain shrugged his shoulders as if their ages did not matter.

"They are young, are they not?" Livie tried to conceal her horror, as she remembered what it was like to have a man interested in her at such a young age.

She couldn't imagine being forced to marry so young. She was happy that her parents allowed both her and Julia to wait until they were a bit older.

"It seems rather harsh, but everyone must contribute to save the family. If I do not marry by the end of this Season, we may be destitute by next Season." Lord Chamberlain relaxed back, his short legs stretched out in front of him.

"Yes, it is rather awful what we gentlemen must do to save our families." The Duke of Summerset's voice was clipped, his jaw tight.

"Yes, being a gentleman is rather difficult, I imagine." Livie smiled widely, trying to keep her eyes from rolling.

The Duke of Summerset rose. "I must be going, more ladies to call upon. Lady Olivia, as usual, you are a vision. I do hope to dance with you at Lady Booth's ball."

"Of course, I will save a spot on my dance card," Livie agreed kindly.

"I really should be going as well. Lady Olivia, a great honor for you to allow me to call." Lord Chamberlain stood.

"Of course. Thank you both for coming." Livie stood as the two gentlemen walked out of the parlor.

Livie sat down in her seat beside Julia, who quickly took her hand and squeezed it. She eyed her cousin, noticing how excited she was that Lord Heartford remained. Julia's cheeks were a deep rosy red, her eyes dancing.

"Tell us, Lord Heartford, have you known the Duke of Karrington very long?" The countess turned her full attention to the marquess.

Livie eyed her skeptically, knowing very well that her mother was eager to know how strong their connection was.

"I've known him my entire life. Our fathers were very close, which also made our mothers friends. We're practically brothers. It's always been Karrington, Windchester, and myself." His cheery voice was filled with fondness.

"How wonderful to have such friends. I am glad that Lady Olivia has always had Lady Julia. They were closer than cousins, even before her parents perished. Whenever we would visit, they would disappear, their heads together, and wouldn't separate, even when it was time for us to leave. Once, Lord Hempstead and his brother had to pull the two apart!" She chuckled.

Julia moved her hand from Livie's to take her by the arm. "I can't dare part with her now. I do not know how we will manage being separated by marriage."

"I'm sure that will not be a problem, as we will often visit Hemsworth Place—" The marquess stopped speaking abruptly, aware of his insinuation on both accounts.

Livie stared at both her cousin and Lord Heartford in shock. Not only did her cousin's words make it sound as if they were in need of husbands, but the marquess insinuated that she would marry the Duke of Karrington.

"I was going to suggest we all take a walk to Hyde Park, but now that the other gentlemen are gone, perhaps I can escort both ladies?" Lord Heartford asked before there was a knock on the door signaling another visitor. Everyone stood to welcome the newcomer as their butler, Thomas, entered with none other than …

"The Duke of Karrington, my lady."

Although she was very much hoping he would come as he had said, seeing the duke in her parlor was still a jolt. His presence caused her to let out an audible gasp, causing all eyes to turn to her.

Her mother raised a perfect eyebrow before turning to welcome her new guest. "Your Grace, what a pleasant surprise. The marquess was just telling us of your acquaintance."

"Ah, yes, I've had the unfortunate pleasure of being one of his closest companions," the duke said, causing all the ladies, except Livie, to giggle.

The marquess laughed. "Here I thought I was the unfortunate one."

Livie stared at the two old friends, astonished by their camaraderie. She noticed how relaxed the duke was in his company compared to how he acted in front of Baron Bromswell and the rest of society.

A shiver ran through her at the thought of the baron and the previous night's incident. Her upper right arm had a bruise where the baron grabbed her roughly. No matter how she tried not to think of it, it still haunted her. She was only happy that the duke came along when he did.

"Please be seated." Her mother waved to the only available seat, which was the chair closest to Livie's side of the chaise.

"Lady Hempstead, your parlor is lovely." The duke's voice was sincere as he looked around the room.

Livie followed his gaze, feeling a sense of pride in her home. It was theirs before her father had become the earl. She had spent the first seven years of her life running around the townhome free and happy. Her parents didn't have a care, her father happy as a solicitor. He enjoyed handling all of the legal matters for their ancestral home, and that way, there was no fear that someone would take advantage of the estate.

"Thank you. We've had this townhome since we were first married. It's where Lady Olivia was raised until we moved back to Yorkshire." Her mother looked over at her tenderly, her voice full of love.

"How splendid to have such memories," the duke stated before turning his blue eyes to Livie. "And how are you today, Lady Olivia?"

The room became unbearably hotter with his attentions focused on her. Livie cheeks flamed against her will at the memory of their near kiss filled her mind.

Her mother cleared her throat rather loudly, causing Livie to jump. Looking around the room, she noticed that everyone was waiting for her reply. Clearing her own throat, she gazed at the duke. "I-I am well, Your Grace." She smiled gracefully, taking a moment to try and compose herself. "Did you enjoy the ball?"

"I enjoyed it very much. Usually, occasions such as balls and parties rarely hold my attention for long, but I suppose I did not have much of a reason to enjoy them until now." His voice was rich and full of meaning. It transported her back to the night before when he declared himself to her.

She felt so much power in that single moment when he told Baron Bromswell that she was his intended, and then they almost kissed.

"Your Grace, the marquess was going to escort the ladies around Hyde Park. It is lovely out. Perhaps, you would be so inclined to join them," her mother said, giving the duke a pleasant smile.

"Splendid, the fresh air will do me some good. Would you allow me to escort you, Lady Olivia?" He gave her a questioning gaze.

"That would be lovely." Livie stood, followed by Julia.

"We shall return momentarily. We must prepare for the weather." Julia grasped her cousin by the arm smiling at the two gentlemen standing before them.

"I will find Abigail to escort you." Lady Hempstead rose as well. "If you will excuse us."

Livie followed her mother out of the room to Julia's subtle but hard pinches at her side. She discreetly tried to swat her fingers away but to no avail. Once they were out of the parlor and finally alone, Livie swatted at her cousin's hand.

"Will you stop it!" Livie whisper-yelled, still feeling the effects of the last pinch to her side.

"Girls! Do not fuss. Now go prepare." Her mother rushed off, leaving the two alone in the foyer.

"Admit that I was right." Julia crossed her arms, glaring at her cousin.

"I won't give you the satisfaction." Livie turned away and started up the long staircase.

Julia was directly on her heels. "Fine, don't say it, but I was right. He fancies you. The question is, my dear cousin, will you accept him?"

Livie stopped cold, watching as Julia sauntered away to her own room. Would she accept the most sought-after bachelor in all of London?

She exhaled deeply, a tingling sensation running through her, as she considered the question. She knew the answer without a shadow of a doubt.

Absolutely.

"For God's sake, stop staring at me as if I have two heads," Remington snapped, standing up to walk around the room. He knew his friend had never known him to show interest in a lady as a wife.

"I'm wondering if you've gone mad." Heartford followed suit and walked behind him.

"Whatever could you mean?" Remington feigned ignorance.

"Do not play coy. You do know what this looks like?" Heartford retorted, his voice low to avoid being overheard.

"What exactly does it look like?" Remington asked before walking over to the chessboard by the large window. A game was currently in progress.

He momentarily wondered who was playing. One person was clearly winning, two white rooks had become queen and the white king was in a position of checkmate. His fingers itched to make a move.

"It looks as if you plan to marry her. I beg you, if you are playing a game—" Heartford started but stopped.

Remington put the full dukedom behind his glare. "I do not play games, and as my friend, you should know I would never play with a lady's feelings."

The chatter in the hall alerted them that they were no longer alone.

No, Remington did not play cruel games with young ladies, that was what Baron Bromswell did.

"I'm sorry, but I care for Lady Julia, and she loves Lady Olivia as if she were her own sister. I just want to ensure her well-being." Henry's voice was rushed and low.

"I assure you. I only have her well-being in mind—" Before Remington could say more, the ladies reentered the room in their pelisses and bonnets ready for a walk.

"Ladies, you look well prepared for the weather." Henry gave them a dashing smile, causing Lady Julia to giggle.

Remington cleared his throat, trying not to think of the awestruck couple that just left the room. He offered Lady Olivia his arm and raised an eyebrow in question.

Tilting her head, she pondered for a moment before asking, "They're rather sickening, aren't they?" Her lips were twisted to the side in an adorable question.

Unable to help himself, Remington gave a rich hearty laugh. "Indeed, they are."

Lady Olivia giggled, biting her bottom lip as she wrapped her arm around his proffered one. He flexed his muscle, securing her arm.

Looking down at her, their eyes locked. "You can be rather naughty when you want to, can't you?" he questioned teasingly, grinning at her beautiful face.

His heart started beating faster. His hand itched to touch the porcelain skin of her cheek, wanting nothing more than to kiss her like she'd never been kissed before.

Remington watched as she opened and closed her mouth several times. A red bloom spread across Lady Olivia's cheeks until it traveled down her neck.

"I-I want to be naughty," she whispered.

Her words shocked him, and he roughly wrapped his free arm around her waist pulling her closer to him.

"Oh—I'm sorry, I meant, I don't ... don't mean to be ... naughty," she corrected herself quickly, looking around frantically.

Her eyes widened as his grip on her waist increased, and he wanted nothing more than to crush his lips to hers. Having her so close to him was driving him mad with desire. Her power over him was growing by the second.

"Livie! What is taking so long," Julia yelled before coming into the parlor.

Remington released Lady Olivia and took a step back. He tried hard to ignore the fact that he practically accosted the lady in her father's home.

He ran his fingers through his hair, trying to compose himself before he did something that might cause Hempstead to want to duel.

"I'm coming. I was just fixing my bonnet," Lady Olivia informed her cousin as she waited for Remington at the door.

Offering her his arm again, they walked out of the parlor and the short distance to the London streets where Heartford patiently waited for them to join him.

"Ahh, there you two are. Shall we go?" He gave them a cheery smile before Julia accepted his arm, and they began walking.

Following behind the ever-chatting Julia and Heartford, Remington and Olivia were quiet as they walked in the crisp London weather, her maid dutifully behind them, a book in her hand.

"Thank you for last night. I believe the baron may have partaken too much in the offered claret." Lady Olivia's voice wavered, causing him to turn toward her.

"Yes, well, I don't think he will bother you again." His tone was harsh as he remembered the nerve of Bromswell, trying to force himself on her.

Lady Olivia stumbled briefly, and Remington tightened

his arm around her so that she did not fall. The simple stumble made his heart stop. He opened and closed his fist several times to calm himself.

"Why would he not?" Her voice was timid, so unlike her behavior in the parlor.

Stopping to let a carriage pass, he faced her and was mesmerized by her gray eyes.

"Because you will be mine."

Chapter Eight

The Bachelor Duke and Lady O were seen strolling arm in arm
through Hyde Park. Is this the end of our beloved bachelor?
Say it isn't so.

HER MIND SWIRLED LIKE SHE WAS IN A CARRIAGE
moving at an ungodly speed, wondering what it would
be like to be his? Would she feel this yearning if she
was indeed his?

Could this perfect specimen of a gentleman really want her,
the declared plump miss of society? Baron Bromswell's words
came flooding back. "*Once Karrington is done with his game.*"
Doubt crept back in, squashing the momentary joy.

A cluster of women whispered behind their parasols, glancing back as they moved toward the park. Their snickers only increased her insecurity.

"How do you know I wish to be yours?" She glanced at the
duke slyly.

He let out a hearty chuckle, amusement in his blue eyes.
The bright reflection of the sun shined on his handsome face and
threatened to take away her breath, if she would allow it.

He considered the question for a moment as they entered
the northwest enclosure of the park from Grosvenor Street.
The park wall, Kensington Garden, and the Serpentine River

surrounded the northwest enclosure. A gate separated horse riders and carriages from walkers.

A pleasant breeze swept around them as they leisurely followed behind Julia and the marquess. There was a copious amount of distance between them, allowing private conversation.

The duke turned to look over his shoulder at Abigail, before he leaned in and whispered at the shell of her ear, "Don't you?" His cool breath fanned the sensitive flesh, sending a delightful shiver through her body like bolts of lightning. An unfamiliar sensation danced a waltz in her belly, causing her to squeeze her abdomen muscles as her womanhood pulsed with need—for him.

"I haven't decided yet?" she whispered, gazing ahead at the splendor of Hyde Park.

A devilish smirk graced his full, pink lips, and at that moment, she desperately wanted to feel them on hers. "That is a fair answer, but you must know that I want you to be mine … most ardently."

At his declaration, she stopped walking momentarily, so affected by his admission. From the moment she saw him at her ball, she wanted nothing more than to be *his*. But she didn't dare hope, she believed the gossips and the whispers that she was too plump. So much so that she'd avoided Cook's wonderful biscuits since then.

But could it really be so simple? Could he really want her, for her and not her dowry to save his estate or because he needed an heir? Did he want her?

Side eyeing his tall physique, she wondered what sort of husband he would be. Although he had been brooding and oftentimes quiet when he'd been in her presence. He was never unkind toward her or ever made her feel uncomfortable like Baron

Bromswell and Lord Lynbrook had. She had heard horror stories of wives in the peerage. Both Abigail and Julia took delight in retelling what they overheard from housemaids or gossip.

Livie had never witnessed anything but love and devotion between her parents.

The thought that her husband could be cruel to her was unfathomable. She wanted the type of relationship that her parents had, but she knew that the probability of that happening was low. The only gentleman that she had any desire for had vowed to never marry, and yet here he was standing beside her.

"Will you speak with my father today?" She glanced nervously at him, unable to stop her thoughts from telling her that it was not true. The tightness of her gown across her middle had her doubting his intentions.

"Yes, only if you are agreeable to the courtship." Glancing around, he tentatively reached out to take her gloved hand in his, caressing it with his thumb.

Warmth spread through her as thoughts of children with the same dark hair and blue eyes filled her mind. The color of his eyes reminded her of the sea in Scarborough, where her family spent their summers.

"Livie! Look, deer!" Julia shouted very unladylike toward her.

Livie closed her eyes briefly. Julia never cared for propriety, since Livie's parents doted on her cousin's every need and allowed her wildness. She often misbehaved. Livie had hoped it would end once they were in town. Trying to hide the embarrassment of her cousin using her nickname in front of the duke and marquess, Livie walked closer to watch the deer as they grazed near the river.

There was one large deer that looked to be the mother of

the two fawns beside her. Their rich brown coat gleamed in the sunlight. The speckles of white added to their beauty.

"I do wish I had something to feed them, perhaps carrots?" Livie kept her voice low, not wanting to disturb the deer.

The duke let out a small chuckle, glancing at her. "Carrots would not be a good choice. They prefer acorns or corn, but I find it is not wise to feed them."

"Why ever not?" she asked. The two smaller deer started playing with each other.

"It's not wise to feed them our food. They become bothersome once fed. They tend to want it again and will return for more."

"Really? I suppose if something I've never had before was presented to me for the first time, and I liked it, I would want to try it again and again. It's like being presented with sweets, one will always want more." She smiled wide, knowing perfectly well she could never give up sweets.

The duke laughed, his face transformed in front of her eyes. He looked younger in that moment. "Precisely. Once granted the forbidden, one cannot help but want it, especially if it tastes so sweet." His gaze lingered on her mouth, causing her to nervously bite the corner of her bottom lip.

A slight breeze caused the sides of his hair to blow beneath his hat, and she wondered what it would feel like to run her fingers through the strands and inhale his spicy, masculine scent.

Nervously shifting from one foot to the other, Livie let out a shaky breath, trying to control herself. He unnerved her a great deal, the way his eyes seemed to look through her, the way his sinewy body towered over her much smaller one, making her feel safe and protected.

"How are you so knowledgeable about the eating habits of

deer?" she asked, hoping to steer the conversation back to safer topics, one that would not have her thinking she was the forbidden fruit of which he spoke.

"There are a great many on the grounds of my ancestral home, Hemsworth Place. When I was a boy, I loved nothing more than to sneak them the occasional unwanted vegetable. They would often come close to the estate in hopes of receiving more ..." He trailed off not finishing his sentence as a shadow overtook his countenance. His eyes darkened and his hands gripped into fists at his side, as if he was fighting a bad memory.

Noticing that his mood had become mercurial, she quickly filled the silence. "We only have a small number at Hill Manor, and they tend to live more in the woods. Julia and I are always excited when we see deer, especially ones so close."

A fawn wobbled to them, away from its mother. Tentatively, she reached out a small gloved hand only to remove it swiftly when the creature's head jerked suddenly at her proximity.

The duke bent slightly, placing his larger, stronger hand on top of hers. Her breath hitched as he pulled her closer to him, a closeness that surely looked improper to onlookers.

Entwining his fingers with hers, he extended their connected arms toward the small deer. Her breathing increased as his warmth engulfed her.

The animal considered the two of them before inching forward. Slowly, the duke lowered their combined hands, placing hers on top of the fawn. Her fingers moved hesitantly over the small head. She smiled and felt triumphant at the small accomplishment of petting a deer.

Slowly removing their hands, the duke released her. He lengthened the space between them, and it was then that Livie realized the intimacy of their closeness.

"Thank you." Her voice was filled with wonder. She watched the fawn run back to its mother, forgetting them instantly.

"You were so eager to touch it; I did not want you to miss the opportunity. Usually, I would not suggest touching a wild deer, but I saw no harm in it since these are so accustomed to people being in the park." He gazed around, and his shoulders relaxed. "Earlier you mentioned your home, Hill Manor. I remember your father telling me that it sits at the very top of a hill?"

"It does indeed! It is rather bothersome really. Though it isn't that far above the rest of Richmond, it has always stood out. When we were girls, Julia and I would roll down the back of the house until we were exhausted, or her maid, Helena, would march us inside for a bath." She laughed at the memory.

"You two seem very close. How long has she lived with you?"

They began walking slowly, finding Julia and the marquess perched on a bench ahead of them.

"Since we were girls of seven years. We were born only three months apart at Hill Manor. My mother often jests that we were inseparable at birth, and when we left to return to London, both of us apparently cried until we were reunited again. But sometimes my mother has a tendency to exaggerate."

He chuckled at her, a teasing smile on his lips. "Mothers tend to enjoy over exaggerating. My mother does the same to me. It is rather unnerving as I'm a man of eight and twenty, and a duke!" It was obvious by his smirk that he was very fond of the former Duchess of Karrington.

"If I may ask, how long has Lady Diana been in your family?" Livie's voice was gentle as she waited for his reaction. Unlike Julia, she wasn't abreast to all of society's gossip and was curious about the relationship between stepmother and son.

Contemplating her question, he gestured toward the

available bench so that she could take a seat. Dutifully obeying his silent request, she sat before briefly turning to eye Julia as she explained something to the marquess. Her hands moved above her head in an animated expression, causing him to laugh loudly at her antics.

Turning toward Abigail, Livie caught her raised eyebrow and the cheeky grin on her lips from the bench across from where she sat. Livie rolled her eyes and turned back toward her companion once she was assured that all of her acquaintances were occupied. The duke took the empty seat beside her, his back straight and shoulders rigid.

The duke gave her a hesitant look before taking a deep breath. "My mother, Eliza, died in childbirth when I was eight. She and my sister did not survive." His voice was filled with sorrow, and he took a moment to compose himself. "My father refused to name the child, but my stepmother insisted that my mother wanted to name her Claudia, and so that is the name we gave her."

Tears blurred Livie's vision as she tried to fathom the idea of someone not wanting to name an innocent child that had perished. Before she could stop them, tears fell her cheeks for the loss of his loved ones. The thought of him as a little boy, who lost his mother and sister on the same day all alone with a cruel father, caused a deep melancholy to fill her.

Gently placing one of his gloved hands on her cheek, he wiped away her tears with his thumb. His touch scorched her very soul, and she craved more of it.

"Do not cry for me, Livie," he whispered her name as reverently as a prayer in the middle of a lightning storm.

"How can I not? To experience such loss at a young age seems unimaginable to me." She placed her hand on top of his.

"It was. However, I had Mother Di, who has always treated me as if I was her own son." His voice was full of love for the woman who raised him.

"Mother Di?" she asked curiously.

"Yes, it's what I called her when I was a boy after she married my father. The name hasn't changed over the years."

She smiled at him. It filled her heart with joy knowing that he had Lady Diana as a mother figure.

Their eyes remained locked until a loud cough interrupted them. Removing her hand quickly, Livie looked over at Abigail, who hastily looked away trying to avoid eye contact.

"You must forgive Abigail. She's under strict orders from Mother to be a dutiful chaperone." Livie gave her maid a stern glare before turning back to the duke. She understood that Abigail was doing what her mother instructed, but really, coughing was a bit much.

"I understand. Your mother will be happy to know she is effective," he teased, leaning closer to Livie.

"Yes, because there is much mischief we can get into out in the open with half of society around us." She scanned the large park, noticing several gazes on them, as usual.

"One can always find ways to be mischievous if they wish." He placed his hand over hers where it was hidden from watchful eyes.

She gave him a coy smile. "Perhaps you are the naughty one."

His eyes sparkled as he leaned into her again. "I definitely am, my Livie."

Chapter Nine

It's official the Bachelor Duke is in a courtship with one Lady O.
Oh my.

FOLLOWING BEHIND A GIGGLING HEARTFORD AND LADY
Julia, Remington and Lady Olivia walked the path back to
her townhome in comfortable silence.

The maid trailed behind the group, not paying any attention
to them. Remington made a note to speak with Heartford about
their deportment while out in plain view of society's ever-watchful eye.

It seemed that neither him nor his friend could control
themselves around the St. John ladies.

And while his own inscrutable behavior in Hyde Park
would surely cause tongues to wag, Remington could not be
ashamed of his time spent with Lady Olivia—Livie. Seeing the
color that formed on her cheeks when he called her by the name
only her family was at liberty to use, caused passion to stir inside
of him. He longed to spend his life whispering it against the soft
expanse of her neck while being buried deep inside of her.

It was a strange feeling for him to enjoy her presence so immensely when he was certain he was only willing to court her for
one reason—to protect her from Baron Bromswell.

But now his motives seemed rather glib, the reason behind

wanting to protect her now seemed superficial to him. He couldn't deny he wanted her, wanted to know every part of her, to spend his nights discovering her passion in ways only a husband would know.

A husband. He wasn't sure if he could be a husband to her. The only thing that he knew for certain was that he could not allow Baron Bromswell anywhere near her.

"Pray tell, Your Grace—"

"Remington. Please call me Remington when we are alone, Livie," he whispered her name as if he was meant to say it for the rest of eternity.

"I'm sure we will never be alone, Your Grace. Between my mother and father, we're sure to always have Abigail with us." She gave him a cheeky look, a smile on her plump lips.

"Ahh, but we are practically alone now, my Livie. All of our companions are engrossed in their own entertainment." he teased her, enjoying the reddening of her cheeks.

To prove his point, he tilted his head toward the couple in front of them and then he turned his head to glance back at Abigail. Livie followed his movements.

Giving her a knowing smile, he shrugged his shoulders. "See, practically alone."

"Very well … Remington." Her mellifluous voice caused pleasure to run through him, straight to a certain part of his anatomy.

"Thank you, Livie," he said, enjoying the redness in her cheek that reminded him of roses in the spring.

Clearing her throat, she glanced up at him. "Tell me more about Hemsworth Place. The marquess was telling us that you all have been friends since childhood, and he often visited."

"When we were younger, he and Windchester would often

spend entire summers there while our parents were off gallivant-
ing around England. There is not a single room we all do not
know as if it were our very own," he said as they grew closer to
her townhome.

They grew closer to her home, causing nerves to fill him
at the thought of speaking to Hempstead about courting his
only daughter; after all, he was known as the Bachelor Duke.
Remington knew that Hempstead was a private man and, like
him, abhorred the gossip. So, allowing his only daughter in a
courtship with a man, who was at the forefront of society's gossip, would be a hardship.

"Do you spend more time at Hemsworth Place or in
town—" Her question was abruptly interrupted when a small
child barreled between them causing Livie to release his arm.

He turned to reach out for her but was stopped by the
child's nursemaid running after the wayward child. "I do apologize!" she called behind her without stopping her hurried pace.

His heart stopped as Livie lost her balance and tumbled toward the fairway where a carriage was coming toward her at a
fast pace. Without thinking of his own safety, Remington dashed
toward her. He thought of nothing or no one but saving her. His
muscles ached with the quickness of his movements. When he
reached her, he could see the carriage coming toward them, feel
the horses' breath on his face.

Wrapping his arm around her waist, he took hold of her
and wrenched her out of harm's way. The carriage hurried past
them sending dirt and dust their way.

"Oh, dear lord." Livie's voice was frantic. She clung to
Remington, who held her around the waist and close to his chest.

She rested her head on his chest, her shoulders heaving in
exhaustion. Her bonnet was now skewed on top of her head.

Remington rubbed his hands up and down her back trying to soothe her nerves. "Are you well?" he asked urgently, his face buried in her hair, his hands still safely around her.

"Yes … yes, thank you—" Her words were interrupted by Abigail and Lady Julia running to her.

"Livie, are you alright! You could've been killed." Lady Julia shouted and clutched at her chest as she ran over to her cousin.

"Well done, Karrington." Heartford slapped his back in appreciation, quirking a brow at him.

Remington realized that his arms were still firmly wrapped around Livie. Finally, he released her into the care of her cousin and maid.

His heart wouldn't slow, and he felt as if he was going to be sick at the thought of her nearly dying. The thought that he could have lost her caused sheer terror to fill him. He couldn't lose someone else like he lost his mother. He wanted to keep Livie close to him and never let her leave his side.

He relaxed marginally as the ladies fussed over Livie. He focused on the fact that she was alive and well. His hungry eyes roamed her, looking for any sign of injury.

Breathing in deeply, he let the panic he felt moments ago leave him, taking comfort in the fact that he was able to reach her in time. Livie looked over at him momentarily, catching him in her stormy gaze, and he knew that he would risk himself a thousand times if it meant saving her.

"Lady Olivia, are you alright?" Her maid brushed the dirt off of Livie's pelisse.

"How utterly terrifying you must have been," Lady Julia said, holding on to her cousin's hand.

"I am fine, just a little shaken." She gave everyone a forced smile and blinked repeatedly.

Remington saw her distress and took her by the arm. "Let's get you home, so that you can rest."

"Yes, I fear after that excitement, I am eager to sit." She straightened out her bonnet before she draped her arm around his.

"Of course." He took her by the elbow and escorted her away from everyone. They walked in front of their small group, leading the way to her townhome.

"Finish telling me about Hemsworth Place. I fear I need something to distract my mind from almost being trampled." Her voice quivered slightly.

"Of course, whatever will help." He squeezed her elbow.

Exhaling loudly, he tried to ignore the melancholy that had taken over him. "Currently, the estate is going through renovations. I have just hired a new head gardener who plans to expand the gardens and add a conservatory."

He was proud of the modifications he was overseeing at his home. Growing up, the ancestral estate was a constant reminder of his father's cruelty. As the years went by, new memories replaced older, more horrific ones. Looking over at his Livie, he hoped and prayed he would not be like his father.

If she ever became his wife, he would cherish her but how could he force himself to marry her knowing the cruelty of his past. But God help him, he wanted her, of that he was certain.

"That sounds divine, Remington. Do you miss it terribly?" She gripped his forearm with her free hand.

"I do. It gives me great joy to work on my estate. I cannot wait to share every acre with you—" He stopped abruptly at his blunder.

They finally reached her home, a three-story white mansion with casement windows that were hinged to the side and opened outward.

"I would love nothing more." Lady Olivia's smile was spell-binding as she stared up at him, momentarily rendering him unable to form words.

The door opened, and the aged butler greeted them. Not wanting to delay, Remington faced him, heedless of propriety. "Where may I find Lord Hempstead?"

"He is in his study," the butler answered briskly.

"Lady Olivia come let's get you cleaned up." Her maid took Livie by the hand, leading her away.

"This way, please, Your Grace." The butler walked down the hall.

Remington adjusted his waistcoat, taking in the art that lined the hallway. A painting of Hempstead, Lady Hempstead, and a young Lady Olivia, sat in the middle of a lavish wall.

Stopping, Remington observed the younger Lady Olivia, taking in her bright gray eyes, long blonde hair, and full lips. She was a vision, even as a child. He smiled at the image of a little girl with his dark hair and her gray eyes. Quickly, he shook his head, trying to compose himself.

"Your Grace?" The butler stood by a large, walnut door with dark patterns woven in the aged wood.

Taking a deep breath, Remington walked toward the door, allowing the butler to open it and announce him. Walking into the office, he took in the masculine décor, dark blue drapes hung to the floor, shelves and shelves of books and figurines surrounded the room, and a large, old grandfather clock stood proudly in the corner. The desk was covered with ledgers, and a small miniature likeness of Lady Hempstead sat on the edge of the desk, perfectly placed so her husband could gaze at her periodically.

The office was so unlike what his father's office was or even Remington's current one. A jolt of longing filled him, as his gaze stayed glued on Lady Hempstead's likeness, so much like her daughter's.

From behind the large desk, Hempstead stood to greet him. "Karrington. I'm pleasantly surprised that you are willing to give up your bachelorhood."

Remington avoided eye contact. He had never wanted to be a bachelor—he had to be, but no more. "That makes two of us, but she has beguiled me, and I find myself in strange territory."

He felt like a green boy, instead of one of the most powerful dukes in England, all because of stormy gray eyes and round hips. He had no choice but to protect her from Bromswell, she did not deserve the cruelty he would bestow upon her.

Remington could not deny the undeniable pull he had to her. The beauty she possessed captivated him every single time he was in her presence. That alone gave him cause to protect her from the dangers of being the baron's wife.

When he was friends with Bromswell all those years ago, the young baron had a preference for beautiful, flawless women. Remington learned early on that his former friend liked to leave his mark. It was no secret that his coffers were empty, making Lady Olivia a prime target.

"You wish to court Lady Olivia?" the earl asked, as if he wanted to reassure himself of Remington's intentions.

"I do. I would also like to be her only suitor." Remington's gaze never left the earl's. He wanted to be sure that no other man would be in the same vicinity as his Livie. She was his now, and he would make sure that everyone knew.

"I see. And is she agreeable?" Hempstead stood and walked to the sideboard to pour two glasses of cognac.

His shoulders were tense as Remington watched his associate closely. Although, Hempstead was a great many years his elder, he did consider the man a friend and knew this wasn't easy for him. She was his only daughter.

"She is agreeable to the courtship." Remington took the offered glass of cognac. "Thank you."

Hempstead took a hearty drink then sat back at his desk. "I will not object if this is what she wants, but I must know. Why her? You could have anyone."

Remington shifted uncomfortably under the concerned father's watchful gaze.

"I do not want anyone else." The statement was said simply, but Remington was surprised at how true it felt. From the moment he laid eyes on her, he hadn't wanted anyone else. The reality of the statement shook him to his very core.

"I will not object if this is what Lady Olivia wants. I'm just concerned about the gossips and society's obsession with you."

"I have no control over that. It has long been my cross to bear." The annoying gossips had been a constant in his life since he was a small boy. He had never become accustomed to them.

"I understand that. However, I will ask one thing of you." The earl's voice was firm.

"Of course." Remington maintained eye contact, although sitting across from the earl made him feel like a small boy again in trouble in his father's office. No matter how small his actions were, they always resulted in a beating.

"Do not hurt her."

The words hung in the air between them, alerting Remington to the fact that it was a warning, not between two friends, but between a father and the man who wanted to court his most precious daughter.

And he knew not to take it lightly.

"I would not dare."

He would do everything in his power not to.

Everything.

Chapter Ten

Have we finally lost the Bachelor Duke? I'm sure mothers and daughters are crying all over England. Do not give up just yet ladies, Lady O may not be worthy. Time will tell.

LIVIE SAT AT THE CHESSBOARD ANALYZING HER FATHER'S latest move. She'd bested him twice in a row, and now it would be a third time as she made her move to capture his king. After she placed the king dutifully on her side, she smirked.

She enjoyed playing chess a great deal. The strategy and concentration necessary to best an opponent exhilarated her. Her father began teaching her the intricate game when she was only four years of age, and since then, they'd played frequently. The years had only made them more competitive, and she quickly became more of an opponent. So much that he no longer allowed her to win.

Once in town, their schedules prevented them from finishing a game together. They made their moves as time allowed, often with the other not in the room.

She stood, walked over to the settee, and picked up the book she was reading, pleased with herself. Turning the page, she found the sonnet, always loving the magic and pure poetry of Shakespeare's writing.

Reading the same line over and over, she tried not to think

about the conversation her father was having in his study at that very moment. To think that she would be in a courtship with the Duke of Karrington was almost unimaginable.

She giggled to herself, remembering the rumors that circled him. *"He will never marry."* It seemed that society was wrong after all.

It was foolish to still doubt him, but a part of her could not help but wonder, like the rest of society, why he chose her.

"Ah, there you are, Lady Olivia." Her father's voice interrupted her thoughts as he came into the room with the duke behind him.

Her father walked over to the chessboard, examining the pieces.

"Lady Olivia, am I disturbing you?" Remington's deep velvety voice asked.

"Of course not, Your Grace," she said sweetly, watching her father closely.

"When did you make this move. I thought I had you this time!" her father practically shouted, causing Remington to turn and walk over to the game.

"I wondered who you were playing with. I didn't know you played?" Remington questioned, looking over at her.

"Yes, I've played for years. If you play, I'm in desperate need of better competition." She held back a laugh at her father's scowl.

"I'm going to beat you again … one of these days." Her father turned away from the chessboard.

"I'm certain you will, Father," she said seriously, trying to hide the smirk on her lips.

He let out a huff and walked toward the door. "I'll go and fetch your mother. Do you know where she is?"

"Yes, she had to rest after hearing about my near accident—"

"What accident?" Her father turned to look at her.

Livie started fidgeting with her hands, her head down. "It was nothing really, and Lady Julia should not have informed her."

"Lady Olivia," her father chastised.

"Fine. A child came running and bumped into the duke and myself. I ended up in the fairway, but fortunately, the duke was able to assist me before a carriage came," she rushed out.

"I assure you, had the nursemaid not ran past me, I would've reached her sooner, and for that I am sorry, Hempstead." Remington's voice was grave, his eyes downcast.

"Nonsense, Karrington. Thank you for assisting my daughter. You should've mentioned it in my office." Her father's voice was insistent.

"I'm sorry, it actually slipped my mind at the time," Remington replied.

"No, of course. I'm happy you were able to help her. Thank you, Karrington." Her father turned to her. "Please try to be careful."

"I will, Father. Please do not worry." Livie walked over to him, took him by the hands, and squeezed.

"Good, I'll go fetch your mother," he said before leaving them alone.

"Are you well, Livie?" Remington walked over to her and rubbed his hands up and down her arms intimately.

Hearing him call her by the pet name her family used sent a jolt of pleasure through her body. She wished to hear it from his lips until she was old and gray. Livie turned in his arms, needing him to stop touching her, before she did something bold, like throw herself at him and demand he kiss her.

"I am fine, Your Grace—"

"Remington, please. After all, we are alone, although I am not sure for how long." His gaze traveled over her, causing her cheeks to heat. She could feel the warmth travel down her neck to the valley of her exposed bosom, and she desperately wanted to fan herself.

"Remington, please do sit." She waved a hand to the adjoining sofa, trying to compose herself. "I believe mother wasn't feeling well and may be resting."

In truth, her mother said the excitement of having a duke courting her daughter and said daughter nearly being trampled by a carriage was too much. She feared that she might swoon. So, she had locked herself in her rooms for an afternoon nap.

Livie walked over to the sofa with the duke following behind. He waited for her to sit before taking the spot beside her. He then rose abruptly, pulling the small book from beneath him.

"Oh, I'm so sorry." She reached for the discarded book in his hand.

Turning it over, he read the title. "Ahh, *Shakespeare's Sonnets.* A favorite from my childhood."

"Really? I have never known a gentleman who loves Shakespeare." She smiled fondly at him, happy that they had something in common.

Setting the book beside him, he took her gloved hands in his and stared intently into her eyes.

"O me! What eyes hath love put in my head,
Which have no correspondence with true sight,
Or if they have, where is my judgment fled,
That censures falsely what they see aright?"

His free hand moved to her cheek. His fingers caressed her soft skin, causing her breathing to increase. Her heart beat as if it were an African drum, like the one she saw in an encyclopedia she'd seen some time ago. It felt as if her heart was trying to be heard around London.

Cupping her face with his other hand, he continued,
"If that be fair whereon my false eyes dote,
What means the world to say it is not so?
If it be not, then love doth well denote,
Love's eye is not so true as all men's: no,
How can it? O how can love's eye be true,"

Excitement filled her as she stared at him, wide-eyed. Her breathing came out in shallow breaths as she intertwined her fingers with his. Shakespeare had never sounded so seductive. Desire filled her as she watched his lips curve around each syllable.

He took a deep breath before continuing, his voice full of want and need. The realization sent a shock of ecstasy running through her. She bit her lip, trying to hold back the wanton moan that threatened to escape her.

"That is vexed with watching and with tears?
No marvel then though I mistake my view,
The sun itself sees not, till heaven clears.
O cunning love, with tears thou keep'st me blind,
Lest eyes well-seeing thy foul faults should find."

Tilting his head, he leaned in closer. His gaze never left hers. She closed her eyes and held her breath as she waited for his lips to touch hers—finally.

Something bumped in the hall, and they jumped apart, both looking toward the door.

Livie blinked several times. Remington stared at her, a teasing smile on his lips. Removing her hands from his, she straightened, embarrassed by his closeness.

"T-That was wonderful Remington," she stammered, trying to gather her senses. "How ever did you learn Shakespeare's sonnets by memory?"

"Mother Di would have me recite them over and over

whenever I misbehaved, which was quite often, I'm afraid." He laughed lightly at the memory.

"I had the privilege of speaking with your mother at our ball. She was entertaining and correct, it seems." She gave him a flirtatious smile, so happy the older woman was correct in her observation of her stepson.

"Ahh, I wondered how long it would take for Mother Di to pounce on you. Tell me, what was she correct about?" He sounded slightly annoyed. His lips formed a straight line, as he tilted his head toward her in question.

"You," she stated simply.

"Yes, she was rather adamant about my feelings for you after we danced." He took her hand in his, caressing it with his thumb, his lips relaxing into a smile.

The motion was intimate, transfixing her gaze. "If I may ask, what are your feelings for me?" She gazed down at their joined hands, fearing the answer.

Lifting her chin, his gaze fell to her lips and then back to her eyes. "I hoped the conversation I've had with your father would make my feelings clear to you and all of society."

"What was the outcome of the conversation with father?" Her voice was small. She barely recognized the sound over the pounding of her heart.

"Your father agreed to the courtship." His fingertip traced the swell of her cheek.

Livie couldn't find her voice to form words. She was now in a courtship with the Duke of Karrington—the Bachelor Duke.

Her hand gripped the cushion beside her as she tried to steady her nerves. She suddenly became hot all over.

"I did ask one thing of him." His voice was serious, as he avoided eye contact with her.

She bristled, while she waited for whatever the request was. "What did you ask?"

"I asked that you do not accept any other suitors while I am courting you." His hand took hold of hers. His body was rigid as he waited for her to react.

At first, Livie was happy that he would ask for such a bold commitment from her. It made her feel wanted. Or, maybe he thought of her like property, something to be bought and used as he pleased.

Her mind transported back to a long-ago day. She was reading in her favorite spot in the library when the Marquess of Lynbrook came upon her after a meeting with her father. The portly man grabbed her roughly, trying to force himself on her. It made her feel like she was nothing. She never wanted to experience that feeling again, no matter how her heart reacted in his presence.

Removing her hand from Remington's hold, she stood abruptly and turned her back on him.

"Why did you feel the need to even ask that of me? What exactly do you think I would do with another suitor?" She turned to glare at him, her arms crossed over her chest.

Standing, Remington rushed over to place his hands on her tense shoulders.

"Sweetheart, it is not you who I am worried about. It is the other gentlemen, one in particular." He stroked her shoulders trying to soothe her, which she both loved and hated. Loved the warmth and feel of his strong fingers but hated how easily she melted beneath his touch.

"I will agree if you, also, will not court anyone else." Her body softened under his tender caresses, her skin on fire from the simplest of touches.

"I do not want anyone else," he whispered. His gaze lingered on her lips.

She didn't dare move. He leaned in. His lips were a breath away from her own. She'd never wanted anyone as much as she wanted the Duke of Karrington.

Just as his lips scorched hers, causing sparks of pleasure to course through her body, pooling in the apex of her thighs, footsteps in the hall caught their attention.

Remington hastily stepped back just as her mother's voice sounded from the hall. Livie blinked several times, feeling like cold water had been poured over her head.

"Oh my, I do hope I didn't keep the duke waiting!" Distress filled her mother's voice.

Livie watched as Remington took another step away from her, turning toward the door just as her mother entered, looking as flustered as she felt.

"Your Grace, please forgive my tardiness. I lost track of time, and Abigail accompanied Lady Julia to the modiste, she insisted she had to find another ribbon for Lady Wilcox's ball. I hope you do not take offense to our lack of propriety," her mother said in one breath.

"Indeed not, my lady. I thank you and Lady Olivia for your hospitality, but I must bid you farewell." His smile was soft as he looked from mother to daughter.

"Thank you for coming, Your Grace." Livie sighed, wishing they hadn't been interrupted.

"It was my greatest pleasure." He branded her with the intensity of his gaze.

It filled her with warmth all over, and she bit the inside of her lip trying to not focus on the strange feelings that coursed through her body. A million sensations prickled through her, all leading to the apex of her thighs.

Lady Hempstead cleared her throat. "Yes, you must join us for dinner soon, and please bring your mother."

"Thank you for the invitation. I'm sure my mother would enjoy that greatly. I shall wait expectantly for the invitation. Good day, ladies."

Livie watched as the duke exited, taking in his strong form. She wanted him to stay and complete their kiss. Once he disappeared out the door, she turned to focus on her mother.

"Well, that must have been some visit. I cannot believe my daughter is courting a duke!" Lady Hempstead fanned herself frantically with her hand.

Taking a much-needed seat, Livie traced her bottom lip with her fingertips. Her first kiss had been with Remington. The brief moment that his lips touched hers awakened a need inside of her. His lips were full and soft against hers, and she wanted to feel them against hers as much as humanly possible.

Livie took another much-needed breath, trying to calm her racing pulse. She counted down the seconds until she would finally feel his lips against hers—without interruption.

Chapter Eleven

She's back!
While we all would like to focus on the Bachelor Duke's obsession with one
Lady O. What we really want to know is ... where has Lady E been?

THE DARK LIQUID SOOTHED REMINGTON'S FRAZZLED nerves. He had done what he vowed to never do. He had entered into a courtship with a lady. A very smart, beautiful, outspoken woman.

Although he was in position of one of the most powerful dukedoms, he found he did not know the first thing about courting a lady. A part of him wanted to end the farce, but to do that would allow Bromswell to have her. And Remington would never allow that to happen.

His mind was filled with her, nothing could stop him from thinking about her hair, her eyes, her intelligence. Loud conversation and an annoyingly happy friend did nothing to steer Remington's mind from constantly focusing on one thing and one thing only—his courtship with one, Lady Olivia St. John.

Remington's mind wandered to his afternoon spent in the presence of the most extraordinary human he'd ever known. He enjoyed their easy conversation, how she asked questions about him and did not solely focus on herself, like the small number of women he had conversed with. Walking to Hyde Park, they spoke as if they'd known each other for a lifetime and not a fort-night. Brushing his lips briefly against hers had set his entire being afire with desire. Her soft lush body pressed against his stirred a hunger deep inside of him, as if he were a starving man left alone on an island for months and she was his last salvation.

There was no excuse for the animal that took hold of him whenever he was in her presence, or the need to possess and pro-tect her from anyone who would cause her harm. Livie had given him a gift, permitting him to court and eventually marry her. There was one thing perfectly clear to Remington—he would not disappoint her. He would be a dutiful husband until his dy-ing day.

Now, he had to go about the delicate dance of courting a lady. He stared down into his drink, searching for answers. He wished he could end it while he still had time, while Livie could still be saved from a scandal, but the very idea of not being able to be near her, to stare into her deep gray eyes brought a pain to his heart like he had never felt before.

"I need a drink," Windchester said wearily as he took the empty chair next to Heartford.

He looked forlorn and withdrawn. Before Remington could inquire about his friend's disposition, Baron Bromswell strolled over to their table, sneering down at him in disdain. His stature was stiff, his eyes void of any compassion, revealing how heartless he truly was.

"Karrington, I know you were not interested in the little cow until I made my intentions toward her clear. Come now, back out so that Lady Olivia and her twenty thousand pounds can belong to me." His voice was cold and condescending.

Remington stood to face the vile creature. It took every ounce of his being to not pummel the man. "I will warn you only once, Bromswell. Not under any condition are you to refer to my intended as a *cow*. In fact, never refer to her at all. She will not be one of your conquests and fall prey to someone such as you. Stay away from Lady Olivia—"

"Or what? We both know you do not have the bollocks to do anything." Bromswell took a step back, a smirk on his smug face.

Stepping closer, Remington took hold of the baron's lapel. "Try me, and you will find out just how big my bollocks are."

The baron's eyes grew wide with fear as the other patrons of the establishment began staring at the two gentlemen. Remington released him, knowing that Bromswell was only a threat to those he felt were weaker than him—women. He straightened his now wrinkled jacket with a devious smile of his own.

"This will not be the last time you hear from me." The baron gave him one last look before leaving.

Remington sat only to find both his companions looking at him.

"Would someone tell me what the bloody hell is going on?" Windchester demanded.

"Is everything all right, gentlemen? I noticed the little confrontation with the baron." Flynn O'Brien walked to their table. His broad shoulders hunched over with old age, bright red hair streaked with gray.

"Everything's fine, just a misunderstanding over a young lady." Remington smiled.

"Our duke here has gone and found himself courting one, Lady Olivia St. John." Heartford patted Remington on the back.

"Surely you jest. When did this happen, and how did I miss it?" Windchester gawked openly at his friend, utterly perplexed by the news.

"Aye, it's all everyone is talkin' about today. Where ha' you been hiding, lad?" O'Brien's teased the younger man in his thick Irish brogue.

"That is an excellent question, Mr. O'Brien. I was just wondering that myself?" Remington tilted his head at Windchester.

Chuckling, Mr. O'Brien patted Remington on the back. "I'll leave you to your interrogation. Congratulations, lad. Havin' a wife to cherish is a fine thing indeed."

"She hasn't agreed to be my wife just yet, but if she does, I'll be a very lucky man." Remington raised his glass to the older man. He would be lucky, but would he finally break a history of abuse that ran through the Warren line?

Remington couldn't be like his father, a man that would hit a child for spilling his tea, or a woman for saying it was *"no bother."*

O'Brien squeezed his shoulder, taking him out of his dark thoughts. "If you keep thinkin' like that, she'll be yours sooner than ya think." Laughing, O'Brien left the three men alone to enjoy their brandy.

Turning back to face his friend, Remington eyed Windchester curiously. He had been uncommonly missing as of late. While he understood the man did not wish to be around his wife or her mother, disappearing on one's closest friends was unusual.

"Are you going to reveal who she is?" Remington's voice was cool as he swirled the brandy in his glass.

A brief smile took over Windchester's face, causing him to look younger, before it morphed into one of pain and sadness.

"Well, I'm sure Lady Oakhaven is going to be heartbroken over the news that Karrington is now in a courtship." Heartford changed the subject, apparently noticing his friend's discomfort.

"I am afraid there are other matters that will disturb my

mother-in-law's delicate sensibilities." Windchester took a gulp of his brandy, ignoring his friend's questioning look.

Sitting up, Remington leaned on the table, his gaze intense. "Such as?

"I do not wish to burden you." Hunching his shoulders in defeat, Windchester shook his head, before looking up and signaling Flynn O'Brien. "Come, let's celebrate. The Bachelor Duke is in a courtship! God save the dear girl!" He slammed down his hand, causing his friends to laugh.

In a million years, Livie never dreamed that she would be the center of attention at Lady Wilcox's annual ball. The popularity of the event was known even in the far reaches of Yorkshire. Now she found herself under intense scrutiny as she arrived on the arm of the Duke of Karrington. She plastered a smile on her face, trying to ignore the usual looks of disdain and judgment. They had only been courting a day, and she still could not believe that he chose her.

Livie watched as her parents moved through the crowded ballroom greeting acquaintances. Lady Wilcox, a robust and buoyant widow, blocked Livie's and Remington's way. She was so overwhelmed that the Duke of Karrington was present at her ball that she could not contain her excitement.

"Upon my word! You pay me the highest of honors! Now tell me the truth, Your Grace, are we to expect wedding bells soon? You and Lady Olivia are the talk of the town, and they say it is so." Lady Wilcox rambled on without taking a breath.

Livie gasped at the lady's bold question, wanting nothing more than to pull Remington away from the intrusive woman.

She could feel the heat of embarrassment rise up to her décolletage, and once again, she felt a seed of doubt growing in her mind.

Bowing his head graciously, Remington replied smoothly, "You will be the second to know, my lady. If you will excuse us, I spot my acquaintances." Taking Livie by the elbow, he led her away from the prying yet friendly woman.

"I am glad you were able to plot our escape. I feared she would swoon if she did not take a breath." Livie leaned into him so only he could hear her.

His answering laugh was a pleasant surprise. One she wished she could hear more of. "Livie, you are a wicked little thing," he whispered seductively before a fan hit his shoulder rather roughly.

They turned to find his mother glaring at him coldly.

"Is there something you wish to inform me of?" Tapping her slippered foot, she waited a second before continuing as if she had not asked him a question. "Imagine having to learn about your own son's courtship from the gossips. It is an outrage, Remington. I have never felt such disappointment from you. Not to mention the sheer embarrassment of others congratulating me, and I have no clue what they are speaking of!" She blotted at unshed tears with her handkerchief.

"Mother Di, please do not be cross with me. I assure you our courtship has just begun. In truth, I was waiting for you to return from the country with Mr. Prescott. If I had known you had returned, I would've informed you immediately," Remington rushed, his voice wavering under her scrutiny.

Livie smirked at his nervousness, enjoying the banter between surrogate mother and son.

"Fine, I guess the sight of this beautiful creature on your arm can thaw my cold heart to forgive you this one time." His mother crossed her arms looking fierce. "But I warn you, if I have to learn of an engagement from the ton, I shall challenge you to a duel. My darling girl, how happy I am to see you." Lady Diana took Livie's arm, officially freeing her from Remington.

"Lady Diana, it is wonderful to see you again."

"Please, Lady Olivia, you must call me Mother Di." She winked at Remington, causing Livie to laugh. She tried to hide it with her gloved hand but was unable to.

Livie wanted to be cross with Mother Di, for like Lady Wilcox, she, too, was making assumptions about the possibility of marriage. But Livie knew that older women took joy in the marriage of younger women. Though, she did feel it was a bit premature to assume they would marry. They'd only been courting less than a sennight.

"Ah, Remington, I'm surprised to find you alive. Your mother has been very upset with you," Mr. Prescott's jovial voice called out. "Lady Olivia, you are a vision tonight. I do hope this rake is treating you properly." His playful wink made her giggle.

"He is indeed. He does try to misbehave, but I can handle his impertinence."

"You most certainly can, and if he gives you any trouble, you are to send for me straight away." Lady Diana wagged a silk-gloved finger at her.

"You all do realize I am right here," Remington said.

Heartford, Lady Julia, Windchester, and his wife joined the small group. The countess eyed Livie skeptically, her cold eyes scanned her person and found her wanting. Lady Windchester's beauty was profound and bold, the type of lady that poems were written about if it wasn't for the permanent scowl she possessed.

Shifting uncomfortably, Livie tried to give the lady a pleasant look noticing the countess' disdain for her.

"Another ball, Karrington?" Windchester gave Remington a questioning gaze.

"Yes, I now find balls much more entertaining." Remington avoided looking at Livie, but she felt him move closer to her side.

Gooseflesh rippled across her skin as his sleeve brushed against the thin muslin of her gown. It excited her that he seemed to need a connection with her.

"I must admit, Lady Olivia, it is an honor to meet the one who has secured the special attention of our duke. You must confide in me how you succeeded in such a task." Lady Windchester's voice was sweet with an underlying edge to it.

"She did absolutely nothing but grace him with her charm and beauty. I, for one, am very happy for the both of you." Windchester's joy for them was evident in his voice as he lifted his glass toward them.

His wife took a deep sip from her champagne glass and narrowed her eyes at Lord Windchester. She looked around the ballroom as if searching for someone other than the man beside her.

Livie and Julia exchanged glances at her behavior. Perhaps their marriage was less than happy.

"Thank you, my friend. I am among the happiest of men, due to this lovely creature beside me." Remington's eyes met Livie's, causing butterflies to dance in her belly and heat to rise in her cheeks.

The gentlemen continued to converse about Mr. Prescott's horses, while the ladies discussed their favorite modiste in town. Madam Beaumont had only been in London for two years but had become the most popular dressmaker.

Lady Windchester excused herself from their company to speak with a group of gentlemen across the room, including

Baron Bromswell. Shocked at the woman's boldness, Livie was both happy the cold woman was gone but sad that the earl had such an unhappy marriage. He was such an amiable man.

The earl, however, ignored his wife, continuing on with his conversation.

The room went suddenly silent before a mass of whispers were heard throughout the room. Livie turned to see who the new focus of society's scrutiny was. A tall, slender, beautiful woman with silky hair so light that it shined in the candlelight stood at the entrance of the ballroom, ignoring the attention. There were dark circles under her eyes, and she looked as if she hadn't slept in days.

The occupants in the room began whispering madly as questions circled the newcomer with every step she took. A hint of sadness took over Livie, for she knew exactly what it was like to be the talk of society. It was daunting to be at the center of attention and one of the things that frightened her about coming out this Season.

"Where has she been?"

"There are only a few things that a lady goes to France for."

"Ah, it seems your sister has returned from France." Remington's voice was teasing as he leaned closer to Heartford.

Livie's gaze shifted from the Marquess of Heartford to Julia, who looked equally as surprised by the news that the marquess had a sister. Which was surprising, as Julia prided herself on uncovering secrets. The lady in question glided through the crowd, her eyes focused on Livie's small group.

"Karrington, Heartford … Windchester, I see you three are inseparable as usual." The woman smiled at the three gentlemen. Her eyes lingered first on Lord Windchester then Remington for longer than Livie thought appropriate.

For a lady to look at a single man in such a way, let alone a married one, seemed a bit forward to Livie. The look of familiarity was one she did not like the woman having towards Remington at all.

"I see you've returned safely from your travels, though you do look a little under the weather. Was it not a pleasant journey?" Heartford bent to place a kiss on her cheek.

This simple act caused a chorus of whispers to travel throughout the room.

"I see you still have no clue what to say to a lady, dear brother," she teased, patting his arm.

The resemblance between brother and sister was uncanny. Standing side by side, one would think they were twins if it was not for their age difference. The lady seemed to be only a few years older than Livie, although the way she carried herself said she was someone who had experienced a great deal in her young life.

"Lady Evers, it is a pleasure to see you. You know my mother, and her husband, of course." Remington waved a hand to Mother Di and Mr. Prescott. "May I also introduce you to Lady Olivia and Lady Julia St. John."

"Yes. I've heard so much about you both in Heartford's last missive. Lady Julia, he did not do your beauty justice in his last letter." Lady Evers tipped her head at Julia, her green eyes piercing, as if she could see through her.

Lady Evers's beauty and poise caused Livie to feel a hint of jealousy at the thin and beautiful woman that shined under society's scrutiny. Unlike her, who nearly crumbled every time she had to face the ton.

"How surprising, as he has never mentioned you in my presence. Why did you not ever mention you had a sister?" Julia's voice was petulant as she glared at Lord Heartford.

Her arms were crossed over her small chest, and her right foot tapped insistently, a sign that she was extremely upset. Julia's lips thinned, her eyes closed into tiny slits, and her nostrils flared. Livie wanted to warn the earl of the monster that could be Julia St. John, but he would soon discover the truth.

He stammered nervously. "I-I admit I had failed to mention Lady Evers. We've only become acquainted as siblings last year. And besides, it is a very delicate subject; after all, we do not share the same mother."

"It *was* one of the biggest scandals, larger than when I married my best friend's husband shortly after she passed." Mother Di said as she turned to Lady Evers. "Everyone wondered why your mother, the late duchess, hid you for so many years."

"Lady Diana, I've always admired your ability to be truthful. It is a quality that most people of our station lack." Lady Evers gave Mother Di a smooth smile that transformed her pretty face.

"Yes, well, it's one of my few qualities I refuse to change." Mother Di turned to Livie and took her by the hand. "Have you ever seen a more beautiful girl than our Olivia here? She is a perfect match for His Grace, is she not?"

Lady Evers blinked several times. "I had no idea. Heartford only mentioned both ladies, paying special attention to Lady Julia. He failed to mention Karrington was in a courtship."

"In my own defense, Karrington only recently decided to get his head out of his—" Heartford began.

Remington cut the marquess off before he could say the crude word. "I am very glad my life entertains you all. It is true, the Bachelor Duke will soon be no more." He gave a dramatic bow.

Livie tried to contain her joy.

"Have you been well, Lady Evers?" Windchester stared intently at the woman.

"Yes. I see your wife is doing well." Lady Evers's voice was strained. Lady Windchester was busy conversing with several gentlemen, her hand stroking one of their arms in open flirtation.

Windchester was momentarily at a loss for words, looking uncomfortable at the lady's observation.

"I believe this next set is mine. Is it not?" Remington held his hand out to Livie when the current dance set ended.

Livie lifted her arm and made a show of eyeing her dance card. "Yes, it seems it is, Your Grace." Her voice was low and needy to her ears, and she could feel the heat on her cheeks. She placed her hand in his to be escorted to the dance floor with the other couples.

Livie let out a shuddering breath as Remington pulled her close to his body. This waltz, although familiar, was nothing like the first time she danced with him. This time she was acutely aware of her body awakening every time she was in his presence. He gazed down at her as he commanded her body where he wanted it to go, and she found that she would follow wherever he led.

She licked her dry lips as she stared at his, longing for when he would press them against hers again. Taking her lip captive between her teeth, she was shocked when Remington missed a step causing them to stumble lightly. She looked up to find him staring at her mouth. She released it from the hold she had on it. Her tongue darted out to wet them lightly.

Remington bent down, his hot breath near her ear. "You're bewitching me, Livie."

She swallowed loudly. "Good." Her voice was small, but inside she felt triumphant, because just maybe she was affecting the Bachelor Duke as much as he was affecting her.

Chapter Twelve

Everyone is talking about the Bachelor Duke and Lady O. Will dinner with the parents change everything or is our duke one step closer to matrimony?

LIVIE STOOD IN HER DRESSING ROOM AS ABIGAIL LACED the stays of her corset. Her breasts lifted, practically spilling out. Breathing in and out, Livie pressed her hand to her abdomen directly over her petticoat, wishing she could make it tighter.

"Stop touching your tummy. You are going to look very lovely for dinner tonight," Abigail's voice stuttered with emotion as she held the green evening gown out for Livie to step into.

Livie tucked a loose curl in place, her nerves knotted in anticipation. Her parents were hosting the dinner party in celebration of both her and Julia's courtships.

"I haven't had one of Cook's sweets since my courtship with the duke began. Mother is being relentless. Not to mention I'm sure I have not lost a single stone." Livie huffed in response, scanning her own body critically.

She wanted the night to be a success. It would be the first occasion that she actually spent time with Lady Diana and her husband out from under the ever-watchful eye of society. If she were to marry Remington, she wanted to get to know his family as well. Livie was a ball of nerves, and she desperately wanted something sweet.

She walked over to her dressing table, took out her paternal grandmother's gold necklace, and handed it to Abigail. The intricate flowers held tiny emeralds to perfectly match the dress.

Fastening the necklace, Abigail smiled at Livie's reflection in the mirror. "You are a vision. You will indeed take the duke's breath away."

Before Livie could answer, Julia rushed into the room. She was wearing a dark blue gown with leg o'mutton style sleeves and a fitted bodice. She announced dramatically, "Livie, we must hurry before our guests arrive."

"I'm coming." Livie rolled her eyes. She stood and followed her out of the room and down the stairs, listening to her cousin prattle on.

"Do you think his mother and uncle will like me? What if they forbid him to marry me? I couldn't bear it. To think of my life without Henry is unbearable." Julia barely took a breath.

"I'm sure it will be fine. How can they not love you?" Livie questioned as they reached her parents at the bottom of the stairs, ready to welcome their dinner guests.

"You're right, everyone loves me, it's impossible not to. Even his sister seemed rather agreeable, don't you think?" Julia fluffed her skirts, a nervous habit she had.

"Yes," Livie answered shortly, not knowing what to think of Lady Evers. She was a beautiful, slender lady, who was very acquainted with Remington and his friends.

It unnerved her that the lady was so comfortable in his presence and so pretty and thin—very thin. How could Livie compete with the beautiful, slender woman?

Livie took her place beside her parents with Julia standing beside her. Her father gave the butler a brief nod. He opened the door just as the Marquess of Heartford, his lady mother, and uncle walked up the steps and into the house. Lady Heartford's dark hair was vastly different from her son's golden curls. Her disposition was nothing like the always jovial marquess.

Before the marquess could pass his hat to the waiting butler, Julia gave him a breathtaking smile and took a step forward. "I am so pleased you were able to join us," she gushed, ignoring the rules of propriety.

Looking up at her, his face lit up. "I would not have missed it if my very life depended on it." Bowing to her, he ignored the others, having eyes only for Julia.

Beside him, his mother cleared her throat rather gruffly for such an elegant looking lady. "Excuse me, may I present my mother, Lady Heartford and my uncle, Mr. Livingstone." He waved his hand to the family of four in front of him. "Lord Hempstead, Lady Hempstead, Lady Olivia, and this lovely creature is Lady Julia."

Julia bobbed a curtsey, her excitement bubbling out of her as she stared expectantly at the current Lady Heartford, who gave her a curt greeting.

"Ahh, Hempstead, thank you for inviting us. My nephew is quite enraptured," Mr. Livingstone greeted Livie's father cheerfully. His tall, rail-thin frame contrasted sharply with his sister's shorter stature.

"It is an honor to have you all in our home," Livie's father responded, ignoring the latter part of the gentleman's comment.

"Constance will show you into the drawing room." Her mother fanned her hand out, where a maid was waiting diligently to escort them.

The duke, Mother Di, and Mr. Prescott entered next. Remington's gaze fixed on Livie as if she had set every star in the sky.

"Lord and Lady Hempstead, good evening. I was very

pleased to receive the invitation," Mother Di greeted her hosts gracefully.

"It is our pleasure, Lady Diana. We know of the bond between you and His Grace. I dare not exclude his only living mother," Lady Hempstead said.

"You pay me a great honor, Lady Hempstead." Mother Di took the countess's hand and squeezed.

The sight of the two women conversing easily filled Livie with joy.

"Please allow me to escort you to the drawing room, Lady Diana." Her father offered Mother Di his arm while her husband escorted Lady Hempstead.

"Ladies, may I escort you both?" Remington gave both Livie and Julia a dashing smile.

"Thank you, Your Grace, we would be obliged." Julia took his proffered arm as Livie walked to his other side.

Julia peered around the duke to stare at her cousin. "Henry's mother did seem rather odd, did she not, Livie?"

"Mmm, must we discuss this in front of the duke?" Livie's nervously shifted her gaze from her cousin to Remington.

She really didn't want him to see how her and Julia behaved. Surely, they should act with some sort of deportment in his company.

They stopped in front of the drawing room. "His Grace is well acquainted with us. We may speak freely, can we not?" Julia questioned raising a brow at him as they stopped outside of the parlor.

"Of course, you can. Your secrets are safe with me, Lady Julia, and I will always hold Livie's secrets close to my heart." His gaze traveled over Livie's person, causing her breathing to increase as her lips parted in need of air.

"Do not be silly. Livie has no secrets. You've never met a truer person." Julia's voice was sincere as she released his arm and walked into the drawing room.

Livie loved her cousin, but she did think she had some secrets from Julia, and the rest of the world.

Remington leaned down to whisper in her ear, causing her already pounding heart to triple in speed. "If you have no secrets, I shall enjoy creating ones with you."

She giggled. "What shall we do to make these secrets?"

"Oh, darling, leave that up to me—"

"Lady Olivia, Your Grace, the guests are waiting on you," her mother said, interrupting their playful banter.

Straightening, Remington escorted them both into the drawing room where the rest of their party sat, drinking wine.

Mr. Livingstone stood anxiously, wringing his hands, when Remington and Livie entered the room and walked toward them. "Your Grace! I was thrilled when I heard you were courting the lovely Lady Olivia. Having known you all these years, I must say I was quite shocked at the news. Good for you!"

"Thank you, Livingstone." Remington nodded to the older gentleman.

"That makes two of us, Livingstone. I was thrilled my son found someone on which to place his special attention." Mother Di took a sip of her sherry.

"I do wonder how his real mother would feel about such a statement coming from the likes of you." Lady Heartford's voice was cold. Her dark eyes bored into Mother Di's.

Livie looked at each woman, appalled by Lady Heartford's harsh words. The chatter around the room ended, all eyes going from Lady Heartford to Mother Di expectantly. The air in the room now felt heavy. Livie looked over at her mother for some direction on how to steer the conversation. She sat bone straight, her eyes filled with interest, as if she was waiting on a war to happen.

Looking down with a bored expression, Mother Di delicately smoothed out her skirts, a lovely silver color that brought out her eyes, before easing an imaginary stray hair back in place. She plastered a tight-lipped smile on her face and made eye contact with Lady Heartford. "As I was her closest and dearest friend, I can assure you in all honesty that she would be very pleased. After all, it was her dying wish that I care for Remington as if he were my own son."

"Did her dying wish also include you marrying her husband when she was only gone three months?" Lady Heartford spit out with venom, looking as if she wanted to unsheathe a sword and duel the other woman.

"Perhaps we can spare the St. Johns the usual arguments when we're all together," Remington said harshly, interrupting what appeared to be an ancient disagreement between the two ladies. His jaw tightened as if he was trying to prepare himself for the upcoming battle of wills.

Mother Di ignored her son, before inspecting her gloved hands in bored fascination. "Lady Evers was a vision when we saw her at Lady Wilcox's ball. Her resemblance to your husband has always been uncanny—"

"How dare you!" Lady Heartford slapped her hand down on the table, looking as if she wanted to throttle Mother Di.

"That is enough, you two. I suggest that you both find a way to be in each other's company. Especially with both Heartford and I courting Lady Julia and Lady Olivia." Remington's voice rose slightly, putting an end to the feud.

Livie cleared her throat several times, trying to interrupt the argument, thinking that family dinners will be more than interesting in the future with Lady Heartford and Mother Di constantly bickering.

"Mr. Prescott, is it true you raise horses?" Livie asked, trying to alleviate some of the tension in the room while the two ladies continued to glare at each other.

She felt the need to try and make the evening enjoyable, especially for Remington who looked like he wanted to flee in embarrassment. Although, Livie felt that both ladies were in the wrong she couldn't help but believe that Lady Heartford was the main cause of the animosity.

"Yes. My thoroughbreds are descendants from one of the three founding stallions, the Godolphin Barb," Mr. Prescott said proudly, his chest puffing out a little.

"How fares your new thoroughbred?" Heartford asked cheerily, his gaze shifting over to his mother.

"He is a magnificent creature. The Prince Regent himself has inquired about him. I feel I must gift him the horse. He is royalty, after all." Mr. Prescott's demeanor lit up proudly, the evidence that he took pride in his horses clear on his face.

Thomas entered the room, his old eyes searching out Lady Hempstead. "My lady, dinner is served."

Mother Di and Lady Heartford avoided each other's gaze as everyone stood, waiting on their hosts to exit the drawing room. Livie took Remington's proffered arm, staring up at him boldly as they stood waiting on the others leave the room.

"I did not have the opportunity to tell you how absolutely breathtaking you are tonight." Remington's voice tickled her ear, causing delicious tingles to dance down her spine.

"Thank you, Remington." She smiled shyly and avoided eye contact, unaccustomed to compliments.

They followed their party to the dining room, being the last to join. As the guests sat down for dinner, the atmosphere was still charged with animosity. Although the two ladies were on opposite ends of the dining table, they occasionally glared at the other, making the other occupants feel uncomfortable.

Livie felt the need to steer the conversation in a completely different direction, focusing on less contentious topics. Her mother was of no use, being so enamored with Mother Di. Julia was occupied with trying to please who she hoped was her future mother-in-law, but the woman completely ignored her.

"I'm finding that we have so many invitations, I do not know which to choose from," Livie said, her gaze shifting around the table.

"Whichever one you choose, I would be happy to accompany you." Remington captivated her in his strong gaze.

Excitement built in her chest at the thought that he wanted to attend more events with her. Livie could face all of society with him by her side.

"We must visit Vauxhall Gardens, and I would love it if you joined us at the opera. We have a box, of course." Lady Diana took a delicate bite, ignoring Lady Heartford's scowl.

"I would like nothing more, Mother Di." Livie set her fork down, stuffed from the meal.

"Do you have a box Lady Heartford?" Julia asked trying to engage the lady.

Lady Heartford did not acknowledge Julia immediately, but took a sip of her wine as if she had not heard the question.

"We do have one, and we would love for you to attend with us," Heartford answered for his mother. He glared at his mother, but she ignored him.

The woman was abominable. Julia's shoulders slumped, her

usual happy face was now downcast. Livie did not like how the countess treated Julia, especially because she had no reason to be rude.

Once the table was cleared, a chorus of desserts was served: iced pudding, iced oranges, compote of peaches, and dessert biscuits.

Livie's mouth watered seeing Cook's dessert biscuits. The memory of their buttery flakiness had not lessened in the fortnight since she'd had one. As soon as one was on her plate, her mother gave a delicate clearing of her throat, causing Livie to look up at her. Mother and daughter held each other's gazes momentarily until Livie took a dainty bite, her eyes challenging her mother.

Julia giggled, stealing Lady Hempstead's attention away from Livie's dessert.

"I hope the gentlemen don't mind taking our drinks with the ladies. I would like Lady Olivia and Lady Julia to play for us tonight." Lord Hempstead stood and walked over to his wife to take her hand.

"We would be honored, Uncle, wouldn't we Lady Olivia?" Julia asked, challenge in her eyes. She knew how much Livie loathed playing and singing in front of people.

"Indeed, Lady Julia," Livie replied, sweetly.

Once they were escorted back to the drawing room, Livie rushed to the pianoforte, sitting down before Julia, who was too enamored with Lord Heartford.

Since they were small, they often fought over who would play and who would sing. Neither one of them enjoyed singing very much, so soon it became a game of who could reach the pianoforte first.

"Your singing voice is much more pleasant than mine." Livie turned to one of their favorite pieces to play.

"Fine, but next time, you're singing." Julia stomped her foot in defeat.

Livie ignored the small tantrum as her fingers began to move across the silky keys. Her eyes closed of their own accord as Julia started to softly sing *The Three Ravens*. Her beautiful, high soprano voice filled the room. Livie opened her eyes, intending to steal a glance at the marquess to see how he was responding to Julia's voice, only to find her eyes locked with the deep blue of Remington's.

Her fingers kept playing, as she stared openly at him, enjoying the intimate moment. Once the last chord was played, the room stood, clapping at the performance.

Livie stood and bowed alongside Julia. Her gaze found Remington's again. He winked, causing heat to spread across her cheeks.

The slight smirk on his lips informed her that he knew perfectly well the effect he had on her.

Chapter Thirteen

What fun is there to be had at the Opera? Rumor has it that our Bachelor Duke will be in attendance with Lady O. How long will this farce last? Inquiring minds want to know.

THE KING'S THEATER WAS FILLED TO THE SHUTTERS with the wealthiest and most distinguished members of society, all wanting to see the performance of Mozart's *La Clemenza di Tito* opera. As Livie entered on the arm of Remington, she once again found herself the center of attention. They trailed behind his mother and her husband. Through the crowd, Livie tried desperately to focus on the elaborate chandeliers hanging from the painted ceiling and the deep, rich burgundy curtains that covered the windows and not the whispers that followed her.

"*She is too round in the hips.*"

"*I dare say she is wide for a miss.*"

"*What must he see in her?*"

Remington stopped as they passed the small crowd at the entrance, turning to face each one of their onlookers in the eye. His glare was cold as he took her gloved hand in his, pressing her knuckles to his lips. Gasps echoed around the room, but Livie could not care less. Her eyes were locked on the vibrant blues of the man who always knew exactly what she needed.

He returned her gloved hand to his arm, never taking his gaze from hers. They made their way to their box seats, catching up with his mother at the entrance.

"My dears, I'm going to go powder my nose. I feel I'm starting to feel a bit under the weather." Mother Di was pale and a bead of sweat glistened on her brow.

"Would you like me to accompany you?" Livie took a step forward, worried about Mother Di. She had looked a little pale in the carriage earlier but insisted that they still attend the opera.

"No, please take your seats. Mr. Prescott shall escort me. I fear I may be getting a bit of a cold." She daintily patted her nose with a handkerchief as her husband escorted her away.

Remington led Livie into the secluded opera box, drawing the curtain closed behind him. They were utterly alone for the first time. He cupped her cheek and gazed into her eyes. Heat spread throughout her body. Her heart began to beat wildly in her chest. "Livie, I am very sorry you had to be subjected to their gossip."

His hand traveled to the nape of her neck, guiding her head back as he leaned down, their lips a whisper apart. Her tongue wet her dry lips in anticipation. "Let me assure you that I find every single inch of you pleasing, and I cannot wait until the day I may call you mine."

Remington's lips pressed to hers. His free arm encircled her waist and pulled her closer to him. A groan of pleasure escaped him. Livie was excited, knowing she was the one that caused him to react in such a way. He brushed his lips softly against hers, allowing her time to become accustomed. She relaxed in his arms. Her lips parted, releasing a sigh of contentment.

Taking her bottom lip into his own, he sucked gently, before gliding his silky tongue along it. Livie whimpered, the pure ecstasy of his lips touching hers was a feeling she had never felt in her life. His hand spread wide on her lower back branding her through the fabric of her dress.

"Remington," she sighed against his lips, hearing voices all around them. She wanted to stop the madness with all of society just on the other side of the curtain. But she could only grasp his lapels and hold on tight as she opened to him, allowing him the freedom to devour her.

Time stood still while they kissed for what seemed like forever, their lips unable to part, even for something as basic as breathing. The dull sound of voices all around her was drowned out by the rushed beat of her heart. Remington trailed kisses down her neck, and she tilted her head back, gasping for sweet air while new sensations traveled down to the apex of her thighs.

"Livie, my God, Livie," he groaned out before he covered her mouth again with his.

"How wonderful of Lady Hillwood to invite us to dinner." His mother's loud voice pierced the cloud of lust that had taken up residence in Livie's mind.

Remington released his hold on her and took a step back just as his mother and her husband entered the box. Livie took several quick breaths clutching her heaving chest trying to ease her frantic nerves.

"There you two are." Lady Diana's gaze landed on Livie, giving her a knowing look.

"Are you well, Mother Di?" Livie tried to steady her voice but heard it quiver.

"I am, it's just a cold. I'm sure I'll be better in no time at all." Mother Di passed them as she walked toward a seat. "A fine lot they are tonight. I am accustomed to their scrutiny, but how dare they make say such vile things about Lady Olivia." Shaking her head, she sat down with a look of disgust.

"Yes, well, I did not wish to subjugate Lady Olivia to their idiotic behavior a moment longer," Remington voiced coldly.

Livie beamed at him, stunned that he felt the need to protect her from society's cruel words. Although, since she and her family arrived in town there'd been nothing but cruel things said about her. The gossips had been especially ruthless.

"Yes, you were right on that account." Mother Di faced Livie. "Ignore them, Livie, society is always criticizing their betters, and you, my darling, are better than them all".

Livie's affection for the woman grew. "Mother Di, you pay me a great compliment." Remington guided her by the elbow to the empty row in front of the couple.

"Nonsense, it's the truth." Mother Di said. "Besides, every now and again, we need to tip the scale of propriety." She giggled as Livie took a seat in front of her.

Mr. Prescott walked over to the curtain and took it in one of his hands. "Are we ready to put on a mask for London?" His eyes danced with mischief.

"We're always ready. Open the curtain." Mother Di gave her husband a nod.

Pulling the curtain back in one flourish, he turned away from the audience, just as necks stretched to view the occupants of their box.

Livie stiffened when she heard the whispers but was unable to make out what they were discussing. As if feeling her need for reassurance, Remington took her hand that lay between them, intertwining their fingers. She was immediately comforted, her head rising slightly. His attention gave her the strength to face her jury.

He leaned over and whispered in her ear, "Are you well, my darling?"

Tingles ran up her spine at his closeness. The stage curtains opened, and the orchestra began, but Livie could not focus on the opera.

She turned to face him, licking her dry lips. "Very." Their eyes locked. The dark line surrounding his iris made the bright blue more captivating. Her cheeks heated from the memory of their kiss, and she longed for another one, desperately.

"Good." He licked his lips, causing her gaze to dip to them. They were pink and full, and she imagined swiping her tongue against them. Leaning over, Livie inhaled his spicy, sweet scent. She squeezed her thighs together, trying to stop the aching need pulsating madly at her core.

Sitting straighter in his seat, he focused on the performance in front of them. Livie tried to ignore Remington and focus on the opera, but with her hand safely enclosed in both of his as if he were cradling it, she found him difficult to ignore.

When he leaned over again, she could barely contain her need to feel him against her once more. "Do you know Italian, sweetheart?"

Turning toward him, she was overcome by his closeness and struggled with an answer. She could not help but enjoy the terms of endearment that so easily fell from his lips.

"Very little."

He moved closer so that his lips were a breath away from her ear.

"Command me as you will be;
Order my every move.
You are my destiny;
I would do anything for you."

With his last syllable, his lips brushed against her ear. Her body quivered from the intimate touch. She turned toward him, completely under his spell. In that moment, she knew she was his and his alone, and she was irrevocably changed forever.

Their eyes locked, and they stared at each other until a delicate throat cleared. "My dears, I enjoy a good show as much as anyone, but I do believe all of society is enjoying it a little too much."

Both Livie and Remington turned to find every eye in the theater on them. Whispered voices filled the large space, nearly overpowering the singing.

Livie's eyes widened, and panic took over her. Her gaze darted quickly around the theater with only one thought on her mind.

Oh dear.

Remington sat beside Livie as his mother and Mr. Prescott exited the carriage in front of their townhome on South Audrey Street.

"Please apologize to your parents on my behalf. I feel my head will explode if I do not rest. Perhaps you should accompany them, dear?" Mother Di asked her husband as he assisted her out of the carriage.

"Mother Di, I assure you, all will be well. The St. Johns are only on Grosvenor Street. We will be there in no less than fifteen minutes. Please allow Prescott to look after you while I escort Lady Olivia home," Remington assured her.

She nodded once before bidding them a good night. He worried about her, as she was rarely ever sick when he was growing up.

139

The door closed, and Remington rapped on the top of the carriage to signal the driver to move along. They both sat in silence as the carriage bounced through the unpaved streets of London.

Remington felt a heavy weight on his chest from his actions at the opera. They would surely never stop speaking of the incident just to vex him.

Taking her by the hand, he entwined their fingers. "Forgive me for my behavior at the opera. I'm afraid I may have compromised your reputation."

"We did nothing wrong." Livie bit her bottom lip.

He stared at those luscious lips, his body stirring from the simple act.

The carriage shook side to side, jarring Remington out of his lust-filled mind. "That doesn't matter, they will surely wag their tongues about how we are not engaged." His voice shook in anger.

She cupped his face. "Please do not fret. I am sure no one knew we were in the box alone."

"Sweetheart, I've spent my entire life growing up surrounded by society, they will ruin your reputation just to wound me. It is no secret how I have always loathed being in the gossips." He ran his hand through his hair. This was what he never wanted—someone close to him to pay for his acts.

He took a deep breath, knowing what he should do to save her. For it was clear she did not only need saving from Bromswell, she needed saving from Remington as well. "Perhaps we should consider terminating our courtship to spare your reputation and the scrutiny that comes with courting the Bachelor Duke." His voice was grave. There was an aching pain in his chest, a hole grew in the pit of his stomach at his words.

Livie placed her hands on her lap, and Remington noticed how they shook slightly. "If ... If that is what you wish, Your Grace." She turned to stare out the window.

They were nearing her home, giving him little time alone with her. He gazed at her, his heart breaking at the tears that shone in her eyes. Livie blinked, and he watched in horror as a few tears fell on her beautiful face.

"Darling, look at me, please?" he begged as he gently placed his hand on her chin, turning her toward him. He caught her tears with the pads of his thumb, each tear was like a knife in his heart. "I want nothing of the sort, but if it will save your reputation from scandal ... I dare not be selfish."

There was nothing he would not do for her, including releasing her from their arrangement. The realization of how much he had come to care for her shocked him. Wrapping his arms around her, he pulled her to him, needing to feel her in his arms.

"We cannot live our lives afraid of society. The ton will use us if we allow them to." Unshed tears glistened in her eyes. "However ... if your affections for me have changed, that would be reason to end our courtship."

"Never, darling. I want you more than words can describe." Gripping the nape of her neck, he pulled her closer to him as the carriage slowed. "I don't deserve you."

The words were true, but he didn't deserve her, not after all the horrible things he witnessed throughout his life. The mistreatment toward women that he never was able to save. His real mother, Eliza Warren, Mother Di, and another, whose name he could barely think without feeling the failure of his actions.

"You deserve me, and much more," she whispered, her gaze on his lips.

Unable to control himself any longer, he covered her mouth

with his. Her gasp quickly turned into a moan of pleasure. Remington's hands roamed her lush curves, and he could feel her body relax in his embrace. Her arms wrapped around his neck, pulling him closer. It thrilled him that his shy Livie desired him.

His mouth slanted across hers. The sounds she made only spurred him on, increasing his desire to a fevered pitch. He lifted her up onto his lap, feasting on her as if she was the last meal he would ever have in this cruel world. Having her on him drove him wild with desire. He fought against his own restraints to not take her in the carriage.

Livie ran her fingers through his hair, causing him to release a shuddering breath. Her grip was light, but feeling her fingers in his hair had his member twitching eagerly in his breeches. Livie turned her head, a desperate exhale for air escaping her, as Remington's lips hungrily traveled to the base of her neck.

His teeth nipped at the sensitive flesh of her throat as one of his hands caressed a nipple. He groaned out loud, wanting nothing more than to pull her gown down and bury his face in her lush, ripe breasts. She let out a strange sound that filled him with a deeper desire as he pulled her closer, wanting all of her.

Taking her lips again, he nibbled on the sensitive flesh of the bottom one. His tongue slowly swept across it, begging for permission.

Livie scooted up further on his lap. Remington's hands gripped the skirts of her gown, her bottom was now in contact with his hard member. It was the sweetest form of torture, but he knew he must stop it. His head fell back against the seat, and he gripped her hips, imploring her to stay still. If she continued to move, he might spill himself right then and there.

"For the love of God, Livie … you're driving me mad," he

pleaded desperately. Each shift of her body rubbed tantalizingly against him.

"Is that a good or a bad thing?" she asked, innocently with wide stormy eyes.

Remington chuckled, loving her purity. "Both." He took her by the neck and pulled her to him, plundering her mouth.

His tongue glided against hers erotically. Leaning forward, he held her in his arms, cradling her like the precious jewel she was to him.

A sharp rap on the door brought Remington out of his lust. Freeing her lips, he pressed his head against hers. Her eyes danced happily.

"In a moment, Perry." Remington gave Livie one last, chaste kiss before helping her sit beside him.

"It is not Perry."

Chapter Fourteen

There was much more than singing happening at the opera. the Bachelor
Duke and Lady O were caught in a compromising position.
Are wedding bells imminent?

TIME STOOD STILL AS LIVIE STARED HORRIFIED AT the carriage door. To be caught in such a predicament was embarrassing no matter who discovered them. She quickly straightened her dress as Remington arranged his cravat back in order before he opened the door.

Julia stood in the cold evening, bouncing on her toes, her hands rubbing together.

"I came to fetch you! You won't believe what happened?" Julia reached into the carriage and took Livie by the hand.

Livie came out first, followed by Remington.

"Is everything well?" Livie inquired, fear gripping her as she wondered why Julia came out to retrieve her. She turned to Remington, dipping a quick curtsey. "Your Grace, thank you for a lovely evening. Please send my regards to Mother Di. I hope she feels better soon."

"Of course." He bowed. "May I call on you tomorrow?"

"Yes, I would like nothing more." Her eyes locked with his and she licked her lips, remembering their time in the carriage.

"Livie, come!" Julia pulled her cousin away, squeezing her arm. "What was happening in the carriage?"

Before Livie could answer, her father appeared in the doorway, glaring at her and Julia. "Olivia, what was transpiring in the carriage that you were delayed so long?" her father asked as they entered the foyer.

She wrung her hands nervously. "We were discussing the opera and his mother's health."

He gave her a stern look that caused her to shift uncomfortably beneath his intense scrutiny. "You would confide in me if something was amiss?" he asked, ignoring Julia beside her.

"Yes, I would, but I assure you, Father, the duke is always a gentleman in my presence." Livie answered before turning toward an anxious Julia. "What has happened?" she asked, wanting to change the subject from her and Remington.

"Livie! I'm engaged!" Julia flung her small frame against her, encircling her in a grip stronger than one would think her capable of.

Embracing her cousin, Livie smiled. "That is the happiest of news! You must tell me everything."

"It was glorious, but it is not information for Uncle's ears, come!" Julia dragged her away, leading her up the stairs.

Livie was happy for her cousin and hoped that she would be next.

Once in her room, Julia practically pushed her cousin onto the dark rose settee beneath the windows. Her cousin's excitement spilled forth before Livie could even adjust her position.

"Oh, Livie! It was magnificent. Henry knelt down on one knee, looked into my eyes, and admitted that he loved me with a great passion and could not live without me in his life. Can you believe he used those words? A great passion! I cried and said yes, of course, before attacking him and falling into his arms. The kiss was like nothing I've ever felt before. It wasn't the first time we've kissed, but this one felt so entirely different." Julia rambled on, not stopping to breathe in her happiness.

"I'm so happy for you. I know how much you love the marquess, and I know he adores you." Livie hugged her cousin, squeezing her tightly.

"He does adore me as I do him. That is why, while we were alone, I did allow certain liberties. After all, he will be my husband."

"What type of liberties?" Livie thought about her own indiscretion in the carriage. The kiss had awakened parts of her body she had not known existed.

"I-I let him touch me intimately, and I may have touched him as well," Julia whispered. Her cheeks turned bright red. "But I know you are too innocent to think of such things."

Livie glared at her cousin, who could be simply infuriating at times. Growing up together, the two fought viciously before making up and declaring their undying love for one another, forgetting whatever they were fighting about.

"You'd be surprised what I've allowed the duke to do, and I assure you it is much more than holding hands." Livie rolled her eyes at Julia, getting more and more upset by her assumptions.

Julia gave her a quizzical stare, tilting her head to the side as if she was taking inventory of her words. "Are you really going to keep a secret from me? What exactly was happening in the carriage when I knocked?" Julia crossed her arms and smirked.

"Things," Livie said in a singsong voice, her body still on fire from her liaison in the carriage.

"Olivia St. John, if you do not tell me this instant. I will tell Auntie that Cook sends sweets up from the kitchens." Julia challenged, raising her eyebrows.

"You wouldn't dare," Livie said slowly. Cook had sent sweets up since she was a girl.

"Would you like to test that theory?" Julia perched back, a wide grin on her pretty face.

"Let's just say one can do much more in a carriage than riding."

Staring openly at her cousin as if she was a complete stranger, Julia opened and closed her mouth several times. "Livie! I'm absolutely shocked. What did you do in the carriage?"

"He kissed me as if his life depended on it," she whispered, still feeling the weight of his lips, the feel of his hands.

"Oh my, aren't we a pair." Julia tapped a delicate finger to her chin.

The ladies stared at each other before giggling profusely. Livie knew she would miss this when Julia married the marquess, but she hoped they would still see each other often.

"Livie?" Julia asked.

"Yes?"

"Did you feel the kiss everywhere?" Julia asked softly as she stared off whimsically.

Livie's face heated at the memory of Remington's lips, his hands roaming her body, the bite to her neck that caused a pulsating need of desire to course through her.

"Yes."

The following day, a jubilant Remington relaxed in O'Brien's with Heartford. He tried to focus on his friend's happy news, but Remington could not help but replay the events from the previous night in his mind. Everything about Livie called to a part of him he never knew existed.

Heartford, who was now on his fourth glass of brandy, nearly fell out of his chair. He wobbled unsteadily then jerked upright in an effort to steady himself.

"I think you've had enough, old chap. You don't want Hempstead to see you as drunk as David's sow after he's granted you the hand of his niece, do you?" Remington took hold of the glass and moved it out of Heartford's reach.

"I hope I'll never get that drunk!" Heartford sat up straighter. "My God, you don't think Hempstead will change his mind, do you? I shall never be happy without Lady Julia."

"You will never endure such a thing. Hempstead can see as well as any other that you are hopelessly in love with her." Remington raised his arm, calling over a servant. "Now come, let's get you sober before you make a fool of yourself."

"Your Grace?" the boy asked excitedly.

"Ahh, which one are you?" Remington tipped his head, awaiting his answer.

He had been to the O'Briens for dinner last season, when he had assisted O'Brien with a matter concerning his eldest son, Tavish. Remington always thought the man was mad for having so many children near the same age. It seemed as if he and his wife were finally slowing down.

"I'm Finnegan, sir. The second youngest." His voice was proud as he stood tall, his arms clasped behind his back awaiting Remington's request.

"I swear the world will be run by O'Briens one day," he teased, giving the young man a smile. "I think it's time the marquess had some coffee."

"Of course, right away, Your Grace." The boy nearly tripped over his long legs to do Remington's bidding.

Windchester entered, looking haggard and disheveled. His

clothes wrinkled, cravat untied, a sour disposition on his usually friendly face.

"What is the matter?" Remington asked.

Windchester's body sagged in weariness, his hands gripping his hair in distress.

Heartford glared as a steaming cup of coffee was set in front of him. "Windchester, what has been troubling you for days now?"

"I will not lay my burdens upon either of you." Windchester took the decanter of brandy on the table, poured his own glass, and drank as if he needed the strength that only the strong drink could provide. "You are engaged to Lady Julia, and I do believe that wedding bells will soon be in Karrington's future."

Remington swallowed loudly. He exhaled slowly trying to stop the panic that surely would follow after such a revelation, but there was none.

"If you cannot confide in us, your friends since infancy, then to whom can you tell your secrets?" Remington raised a brow at his cousin.

Remington began to say more on the subject, but was interrupted by the Earl of Darby. The older, stocky gentleman was a notable gossip who kept company with none other than the Countess of Windchester.

"Karrington, I've heard the most scandalous news about you and Lady Olivia St. John." He bounced up and down on the heels of his feet, like an anxious child.

"You know the duke does not entertain gossip, Darby," Heartford slurred, pointing an unsteady finger.

"This particular bit of gossip was witnessed at the opera in front of all society and is front page in today's gossip sheets." The man shrugged his shoulders. "It seems you have compromised

Lady Olivia's reputation, and there is now a question of her virtue."

Remington's heart plummeted to the pit of his stomach. Standing, he took Darby by his shirt and pulled him forcefully. "If you ever slander her name again, I shall run you through with a blade." He released the older man. "I must go check on Lady Olivia."

Remington left the club, hoping that Hempstead didn't think badly of him or Livie. He was sure to have heard the rumors circulating about the opera.

"Karrington!" he heard Windchester call after him, but his mind was on one thing.

He scrambled to his carriage, hoping to reach the Hempstead's home before the news. He would do anything to protect Livie.

Anything.

Chapter Fifteen

Is Lady O's reputation destroyed? Will the Bachelor Duke save her, or will he allow her to be ruined for all eternity?

L IVIE WALKED TOWARD THE DOOR IN MADAM Beaumont's dress shop. They had spent nearly two hours looking at wedding gown sketches for Julia. Somehow, they were leaving with sketches picked out for both Julia and Livie.

While Julia chose a more elaborate sketch, Livie's gown was simple and flowing. She tried not to focus on the fact that Madam Beaumont would begin working on the dress right away. The truth was that Livie and Remington weren't engaged, so choosing a gown seemed a little premature to her.

Livie wanted to hope, especially after the opera. She felt safe, secure, and wanted when in Remington's arms. He wanted her, despite what the gossips and society said, and although she found it a little unbelievable, she trusted him.

"I will have both gowns prepared within a fortnight." Madam Beaumont nodded enthusiastically.

The door was pushed open with force, Abigail rushed in holding the gossip sheets. "Lady Olivia, Lady Hempstead, you must come quickly, the earl is beside himself." She held out the paper for Lady Hempstead, who took it in her hands.

"Oh dear, we must hurry."

"What is it?" Mother Di leaned over, looking down at the paper. She had joined them at the dress shop at Livie's mother's invitation.

"*Occupants at The King's Theater witnessed more than Mozart's* La Clemenza di Tito *opera. Our Bachelor Duke and Lady O provided their own entertainment. Was Lady O ruined, will the Earl of H demand our duke marry the lady? Only time will tell.*"

Livie squeezed in and read over Mother Di's shoulder. Her heart stopped as she read that a witness reported she was in the box alone with the duke.

"The earl is in a rage and demanded I come to bring you all home." Abigail wrung her hands together nervously, as her eyes shifted from Livie to Lady Hempstead.

"I assure you I was only gone but a moment. The duke only removed Lady Olivia from the crowd because they were being rather rude," Mother Di said to her mother as they walked out of the boutique beside the countess.

"I'm sure it is not your fault, Di. I shall speak to Lord Hempstead directly. Please do not trouble yourself." She gave the other woman a quick air kiss on the cheek.

"I will come with you all. Perhaps I can help come up with a solution or ease his mind." Mother Di gave her mother a small smile before she went to her own carriage.

Livie stepped inside their carriage and sat down. Her hands fidgeted with her skirts as she tried to prepare for her father's wrath. Nothing could take away the anxious feelings that consumed her.

She could only imagine what her father must be thinking after reading the gossip. There was some truth to what was written in the paper, Remington had ruined her at the opera. Ruined her for anyone else.

The carriage stopped, and she felt fear take over her at facing her father. What could she say to defend herself?

Her mother led them into the house. Livie felt as if she were being escorted to her judgment. Julia took her by the hand and squeezed, providing her some small comfort.

They entered the parlor together finding her father standing beside the sideboard, drinking. His posture was straight while he stared down at the gossip sheet clenched in his other hand.

"Lord Hempstead, you sent Abigail for us?" her mother asked in the sweetest voice.

Her father whirled around. Livie saw the anger in his usually friendly face. The silence was deafening as everyone stood, not saying a word. "Julia, please leave us," he demanded, his voice tight, his eyes trained on Livie, who chewed her bottom lip.

Beside her, Julia squeezed her hand, and Livie was thankful for the support.

"Father, I can explain." Her voice was low and shaky.

Her father ignored her. His eyes were cold, so different from the love and affection she usually saw. She felt sick to her stomach at the thought of disappointing her father. Never in her life had she ever seen such a look upon his face.

"Theodore, I saw the paper, and I assure you they are mistaken—" Lady Hempstead began but was cut off by her husband's angry voice.

"Mistaken? Witnesses say they were practically kissing!" he shouted at his wife, taking Livie by surprise. He never yelled at her mother. "All of society seems very sure that your daughter was alone in the opera box with him as well!" He rushed over to Livie, taking her by the arm in a tight grip.

"Father, you're hurting me!" she pleaded with him, tears in her eyes.

"What happened at the opera?" He stared into her eyes, his face unreadable.

A commotion in the hall was heard, and seconds later, Remington burst through the door unannounced.

"Release her, Hempstead, this instant!" he commanded the older man, rushing over to them.

Her father released her immediately stepping back as if she burned his hand. "Dear God, forgive me, Livie."

Remington went to Livie, gently placing his hand on her shoulders. "Are you all right?" he asked, his voice soft.

She nodded her head, still in shock that her father handled her in such away.

Remington turned back to her father. "Hempstead, if anyone is to blame for their behavior at the opera, it is I."

Her father shook his head adamantly. "I was afraid of this happening. Society is too obsessed with you and now my daughter is ruined!"

"She is not ruined, Hempstead. Nothing untoward happened. I simply was translating the opera for Lady Olivia, perhaps we forgot ourselves for a moment, but you must know I will marry her if she will have me." Remington looked at Livie, and she felt as if all the air had left the room.

She wanted to marry him, of course she did, but not like this. Not by force, she wanted him to crave her so much that he couldn't be without her. She knew that feeling because it was slowing consuming her, seizing her every waking moment.

Livie turned away from his piercing gaze and took a seat on the chaise lounge to steady herself.

"Surely, it has not come to that." Her mother spoke up, being the voice of reason.

Remington sat down beside Livie, taking her hand in his. She felt strange doing something so intimate in front of her parents.

"It doesn't matter, that was always my intention. I don't care if it happens sooner than I planned." Remington's thumb circled her hand, the act and his words causing her to relax. "What do you think, Livie?"

He wanted her as much as she wanted him.

A small smile graced her lips at his use of her nickname in front of her parents. Before she could answer, a knock on the door alerted them to another visitor.

Thomas walked in with Mother Di.

Remington stood to greet her. "Mother Di, what are you doing here?"

"I was on my way home from the dress shop when I had a wonderful idea." Mother Di clapped her hands together.

"What is it, Di?" Her mother asked.

"I was thinking perhaps you and the ladies should come to Essex with me. That way Livie and Remington could have some time apart, which would give society time to find a new topic to discuss." Mother Di took a seat on the sofa, a triumphant smile on her face.

Her father walked around the room, one of his hands on his chin. "I think that's an excellent idea. When would you leave?"

"I believe we can leave at the end of the week. How does that sound Len?" Mother Di asked.

"That would be perfect. We will prepare, some time away from town is exactly what I think we need. Right, Livie?" her mother asked, forgetting all signs of propriety.

"Yes, I can't wait to leave London for a few days. When would we return?" Livie resisted the urge to look at Remington, taking solace in his hand in hers.

"Perhaps you all should stay at least a fortnight." Her father noticeably relaxed.

Livie put on a brave face, placing her hand down between her and Remington. He moved his fingers closer to hers. She sighed at his touch, knowing he felt the same.

How could she be away from him for a fortnight?

Two days after the opera debacle, society was still in an uproar over the gossip papers' tale of Remington and Livie. Walking through the Egyptian Hall, Livie and Remington kept an appropriate amount of distance between them as they perused Giovanni Battista Belzoni's show of the tomb of the Egyptian pharaoh Seti I.

The Valley of the Kings exhibit mesmerized Livie. She gasped as she came face to face with the head of the mummy of Seti I. Remington brushed his finger against hers, taking hold of her pinky finger and hiding their combined hands in the skirts of her light blue day dress.

She gave him a questioning look. "We mustn't get caught doing anything too forward. I don't think Father could take another scandal in the papers."

He released her finger hastily. "Forgive me. Not being able to be near you is agony, especially knowing that you leave in a matter of days for a fortnight."

"For me as well." She glanced around the room, taking note of the watchful eyes.

They neared the end of the exhibit, waiting for Heartford, Julia, and Abigail to near so they could exit the crowded hall. Once the others arrived at the entrance, the jolly group piled into the carriage.

"That was simply amazing!" Julia exclaimed, bouncing in her seat beside the marquess. "To think, he lived hundreds of years ago, can you imagine?"

"Not at all! Did you see his face?" Livie could still see the mummy in her mind.

They chatted happily about the exhibit and all the wonderful things they viewed from the tomb as the carriage jostled side to side.

Across from Livie, Julia and Lord Heartford began whispering to each other, officially ignoring the other couple.

Remington took her by the hand, intertwining their fingers. "I'm going to miss you when you're gone," he whispered.

She could feel her body heat beneath his gaze. Looking away, she eyed the couple on the other side. Their heads were practically touching as if they were the only two people in the world.

"What will you do while I'm at Talbert Abbey?" Her voice sounded small to her own ears. She feared that he would entertain other ladies while she was gone, eventually replacing her.

Remington turned toward her, pulling her hand onto his thigh. Livie's heart rate increased at the feel of the powerful muscles beneath the buckskin.

"I am going home to Hemsworth Place. I will be gone most of the time you are away."

"You're leaving London?" she asked rather loudly.

"I will return before you. Darling, I have to prepare my household staff for the future …" His words trailed off and she found herself feeling hopeful once again for a lifetime with him.

Her heart stopped beating. Her mouth dropped open. There was no mistaking what future he spoke of.

The carriage came to a stop. The marquess and Julia exited first. She turned back to them. "Livie, are you two coming?"

"Yes, of course." Remington stepped out of the carriage. He reached out his hand for Livie, who took it.

"Wait for me in the parlor," he whispered in her ear.

Chapter Sixteen

Lady O is not ruined! However, there is some new tantalizing information regarding Lady E. The question is, who is the father?

A FTER HE TOOK THE NOW-FAMILIAR PATH TO THE EARL'S office, Remington found himself once again sitting in front of Hempstead.

"How was the Egyptian Hall? Anything happen?" Hempstead asked, tapping his hand against his wooden desk.

"Heads did turn, but that is to be expected." Remington turned, watching the other man carefully. "I'm leaving tomorrow for my estate."

"And will you return?" The earl intertwined his hands together, sitting his chin on top of them.

"Yes. When I return, I will have my mother's ring. I will ask Lady Olivia to be my wife if you have no objections." Remington locked eyes with the older man, not willing to show any sign of weakness.

The earl smiled slowly; the shape of his eyes so like his daughter's. "Of course. I shall hold your secret until you ask her yourself." He stood and rushed over to Remington, offering him his hand.

"Good, if you tell your wife, I believe she will inform my mother." Remington rose to his feet, taking his offered hand. "I was worried you would object."

"I acted very hastily after the opera. I can see you care for Livie and her you." Hempstead gave him a healthy pat on the back before releasing him.

"I would like to say goodbye to Lady Olivia without a chaperone if you would not mind." Remington surveyed the earl's reaction.

"Of course. I suppose I can allow it, since you will be my son-in-law soon." Hempstead led Remington out of his office.

Remington felt overjoyed at the thought of marrying Livie, and could not stop the wide grin on his face.

Once they reached the parlor, they found Lady Hempstead and Livie chatting happily over the chessboard.

Livie looked up at her father. "Checkmate, Father." She gave him a wide smile.

"Impossible!" The earl rushed to the chessboard, staring down at her move, Remington behind him.

"Your Grace, I did not see you." Livie stood.

"You were too busy celebrating your win to notice me," he teased her, taking in the color of her cheeks and the smile at the corner of her soft lips.

"I protected my king!" Hempstead proclaimed, glancing from Livie to the board.

"It would seem not well enough. She appears to beat you often," Remington said, catching the earl's attention.

The earl looked up at him with a scowl on his face, before he went back to examining the chessboard.

Remington cleared his throat. "Wasn't there something you wanted to speak with Lady Hempstead about?"

Hempstead straightened. "Yes, I did. Lady Hempstead, if you would come with me." He offered a bewildered looking Lady Hempstead his arm.

"Yes, of course. Shall I call for Abigail?" she asked.

Remington knew that she very much liked to abide by the rules of propriety, and so did Hempstead, especially after the opera debacle. But was allowing him to say goodbye before they were separated for a fortnight.

"That will not be necessary. They will only be but a moment. Karrington is leaving tomorrow for his estate, so he will not be here when you all are off to Essex," the earl explained.

"Oh, I see. Please return safely, Your Grace. Lady Diana has sent me a missive everyday regaling me with all the things we will do at Talbert Abbey," she said, her smile wide like a child.

"Please enjoy every comfort as if it was your own home, my lady." Remington bowed gracefully.

The earl escorted his wife out of the room, closing the door slightly behind them. Once they were gone, Remington pulled Livie to him for a brief kiss.

"Mmm, I miss kissing you," she whispered against his lips.

Remington smiled, enjoying how much more comfortable she was in his arms. "Then I shall kiss you every day for the rest of our lives." He bent down and placed another much longer kiss on her lips.

Her arms wrapped around him, her head tilted back to open up more to him as one of his hands gripped the nape of her neck. A silky strand of hair tickled his finger as he plundered her mouth with his tongue.

He backed her against the wall, one arm caging her in, while he massaged her neck with the other. A deep wanton moan escaped her, sending a heat of electricity straight to his manhood.

Livie sucked softly on his tongue, causing a growl to emanate from his chest. He trailed desperate kisses down her long neck to the valley between her breasts. Remington licked and nipped at the exposed flesh, the hand that was against the wall now traveled up her spine, and around to her heaving bosom.

He looked up at her, watching for any signs of discomfort as he slowly pulled the front of her day dress down, revealing her large orbs to his greedy eyes. "My god, you are exquisite, my Livie," he groaned out before wrapping his lips around a dusky pink nipple.

"Remington," she cried out in pleasure, gripping his hair tightly in her hand.

He lavished her nipple with attention, kissing, sucking, and biting, until she was limp in his arms. He moved to her other breast, licking a slow trail from one to another. His hand played with her free nipple, pinching and rubbing it between his fingers.

Livie laid her head against the wall, shaking in complete, unadulterated pleasure. He held her in his arms, wanting nothing more than to say to hell with propriety and claim her right there in her parents' parlor, but he knew she deserved more. So much more than a quick fling with a house full of people.

Remington released her nipple, stood, and righted her dress. He kissed her lips sweetly as her eyes opened questioningly. "We must stop before I forget myself."

Livie clutched her chest, the motion drawing his gaze. "Goodness."

"Are you well, darling?" Taking her hand, he escorted her over to the settee, where he sat beside her.

"I am quite well. I have never experienced anything like this in all my life. I am a little out of sorts."

He lifted her from the settee and onto his lap. "In that case, I am glad it was I who made you feel such a way." He looked deep into her eyes before he pressed a tender kiss to her swollen lips.

When the kiss ended, he pressed his head against hers. "I must go if I am to leave first thing in the morning."

Livie stared sadly at him. "If you must. I shall miss you," she whispered, running her fingers through his hair.

"And I, you." He gave her one last kiss, before she rose from his lap.

Once they were at the parlor door, he pulled her to him, pressing a kiss to her forehead. "I'm leaving my heart and soul with you, look after them," he whispered before he released her and left the room.

As he walked towards his waiting carriage, he felt no truer words existed.

Livie, and Julia sat across from each other in the carriage as it stopped in front of Madam Beaumont's modiste in preparation for their trip to Essex. Julia had received a note from Madam Beaumont asking her to come for additional measurements. Livie accompanied her since both Helena, Julia's maid, and Abigail were busy packing.

She tried to focus on Julia's voice as she read from the gossips, but all she could think of was Remington leaving. It was the first time they had been apart since they began courting, and she found she missed him desperately. Him and his kisses.

"Should I ask Henry about it? The gossip says they believe she had a child! Can you believe that, Livie? A child, and she's been a widow for nearly three years!" Julia made a high pitch sound that made Livie focus on her.

"What?" she asked a perturbed looking Julia.

"Livie! I said Lady Evers has a child!" Julia yelled at her, crossing her arms over her small chest.

Livie took a much-needed breath, trying to calm herself down and resist the urge to throttle Julia. "We mustn't believe everything we read in the gossips, especially after what was said about me." Livie glared at her cousin, who seemingly ignored her, the paper practically touching her nose.

"I suppose you're right, but really, Livie, this could make my wedding a scandal!" Julia said in horror.

"It will not, and besides, she is to be your sister, too. You must show her kindness as if she were me," Livie insisted as the carriage came to a halt.

"Really, you would never do such a thing!" Julia shook her head as the footman opened the door.

Livie was quiet as they exited the carriage, thinking about the last time she saw Remington and all she allowed him to do to her. Perhaps, she was a ruined woman after all.

Julia pressed forward, always in a hurry. Livie followed her cousin at a more leisurely pace but stopped at the sound of a crying baby. She turned to see a maid rocking a beautiful little girl in front of a fine carriage. The baby had white-blonde hair and crisp green eyes. She was a stunning child that reminded Livie of someone.

"Come on, Livie. Auntie and Lady Diana want to leave first thing in the morning, and I have a hundred things to do." Julia urged her cousin forward and into the shop.

Madam Beaumont was in a heated discussion with none other than Lady Evers.

Livie couldn't contain the loud gasp that escaped her, at the likeness between Lady Evers and the small baby outside the shop. Her mind quickly went to the gossip sheet that Julia had read in the carriage.

It was true, she did have a child, and she was not married.

Madam Beaumont looked up, a forced smile on her thin face. "Lady Julia, please go to the back. My assistant will help you."

"Lovely! Lady Evers, how very nice to see you again," Julia said nervously.

"Lady Julia, Lady Olivia, what a pleasant surprise. I trust the wedding plans are going well?" Lady Evers had dark circles under her eyes indicating that she had gotten very little sleep.

"Very well, indeed. I trust you've received your invitation?" Julia shifted from foot to foot, a sure sign of her nerves.

"I did. Henry delivered it personally."

"Oh, he did not mention it, but I suppose we don't tell each other everything. He did forget to mention he had a half-sister." She rambled, not noticing Lady Evers slight glare.

Livie noticed the lady's reaction to her cousin and decided to intervene. "You should hurry."

"Oh, dear! You're right, Livie." Julia turned to Lady Evers. "We should have tea before the wedding, shouldn't we, Livie?" Julia gave her cousin a tight smile, tilting her head toward Lady Evers.

"Yes, of course. I shall send you a card upon our return from Essex," Livie replied before she walked around the small shop.

She knew Julia was judging Lady Evers for what was printed in the gossips, but Livie would not judge her harshly. How could she judge her when she did not know the lady's circumstances or the situation?

"Excellent," Julia said, causing Livie to turn around and watch their interaction. "It's all settled, Livie will plan everything." Julia left them alone as she rushed to the back in search of Madam Beaumont's assistant.

"Lady Olivia, if you would give me just a moment." The

modiste gave her a motherly smile before turning a hard glare back to Lady Evers.

Livie began perusing, taking note of material she may want to purchase in the future.

"As I informed you, my lady, I think it's best if you found another modiste. I cannot take the risk of losing customers and the rumors …" Madam Beaumont trailed off.

Livie tried desperately not to overhear their conversation, but she could not help it. Both women glared at each other, shoulders wire straight.

"I do not see how rumors have anything to do with my account. I am a paying customer, after all. I can assure you my coffers are in much better standing than most of your other clients." Lady Evers's voice was full of barely controlled anger.

"I understand that, of course. But please, Lady Evers, you must see the implications serving you will have on my establishment." Madam Beaumont wrung her hands together, becoming more agitated.

Livie felt it necessary to help both ladies. She walked toward them. "May I be of any assistance?"

"What could you possibly do?" Lady Evers turned to her with a look of annoyance on her too-pretty face. Her green eyes penetrated Livie's, holding her in place. She began second-guessing her decision to interfere.

"Lady Olivia, I'm sure the duke would not want you to concern yourself with such matters." Madame Beaumont shook her head emphatically.

Lady Evers rolled her eyes at the woman's comment. "No, of course, we wouldn't want to upset the duke's rules of propriety," she said in a sneering tone.

Livie reared back, aghast at her words and the sound of her

voice, not comprehending what she meant by that statement. "The duke has nothing to do with my offer of assistance, my lady. However, if you prefer I not interfere, then I will not." She met the other woman's stare, not willing to allow her attitude to affect her.

Lady Evers softened, her face instantly relaxing. "No, please excuse my behavior. I am just frustrated with society at the moment."

Livie let out an unladylike laugh. "That makes two of us. I was ruined one day and then the next I wasn't."

Lady Evers laughed, her head falling back. "Being nearly ruined is exceptionally better than being ruined since birth."

Shocked by her comment, Livie placed her hand on top of Lady Evers's hand. "You are not ruined; you're simply different."

Lady Evers blotted at her eyes, stopping the few tears that had fallen. "Thank you, Lady Olivia. You truly are good and kind. You will make the duke a wonderful wife."

Livie flushed, embarrassed at her comment. "We're not engaged, my lady." The words felt heavy against her tongue, but she did not dwell on it. Turning to Madam Beaumont, she gave her a wide smile. "Perhaps you can put the lady's purchases on my account, and no one would be the wiser?"

Beautiful fabric of pink, yellow, and white lace, along with different bright-colored ribbons, were stacked in the middle of the worktable. The items confirmed what Livie had perceived for herself, that the child was indeed Lady Evers.

"I could not allow you to do that. I have money … I can pay." She opened her reticule, pulling out some banknotes, but Livie shook her head.

"It's really not necessary. Besides, we will be family soon, will we not? My cousin is marrying your brother, after all." Livie placed her hands on top of the bundle and pushed it towards Lady Evers.

"I'm sure our paths won't cross in society for some time with the rumors about me—" Lady Evers began, but Livie cut her off.

"Nonsense. You will, of course, attend the wedding, and we are having tea when we return from Essex. Rumors do not concern me. After all, I'm courting the Bachelor Duke, and they said he will never marry." Livie laughed at the now silly title, remembering the words Remington spoke to her the last time they were together.

"I shall kiss you every day for the rest of our lives."

"Yes, they did say that, didn't they? It seems they may have been very wrong, indeed." Lady Evers took hold of the small bundle of fabric and ribbons in front of her. She clutched them to her chest, her eyes filled with tears. "Thank you again for your kindness."

Lady Evers left the shop, a sad smile on her face. Livie couldn't help but to dislike society for their treatment of Lady Evers, for any lady that does not behave as the ton expects.

"Lady Olivia, that was very kind, but truly, you should not concern yourself with such a woman." Madam Beaumont shook her head disapprovingly.

"Why ever not? We really shouldn't be unkind to someone based on gossips." Livie looked her in the eye, daring the modiste to contradict her.

"It's not just gossips. You saw the fabric with your own eyes, and I know you saw the babe outside as well."

"I did," Livie said simply. "But I still will not shun her for it, and neither should you."

"Perhaps you're right, but I can't afford to lose customers.

I'm sure loyal ones like yourself and your mother would not fault me for it, but there are others who are not so kind."

Madam Beaumont clapped her hands together. She walked behind a screen and pulled out an unfinished dress. The blue material was silky, shimmering in the light of the shop. "I still have much to do, but I believe it will be completed when you return. I think it is turning out fine, don't you?"

Livie stared at the dress hoping that both Mother Di and her mother's over eagerness was correct.

"It's perfect," Livie whispered, unable to find words to express how much she loved it, even unfinished.

She was ready to become his—forever.

Chapter Seventeen

While I'm sure we're all desperate to know what is going on with the Bachelor Duke and Lady O, the real question is who is the father of Lady E's daughter? The list, surprisingly isn't very long.

REMINGTON ARRIVED AT HEMSWORTH PLACE four days after he left London. He was greeted by his head housekeeper and butler, Mr. and Mrs. Taylor. The elderly couple had worked at the estate since they were in their youth.

The large, old house was hell on earth when his father was alive, but slowly he made it his own. It was now a place where he wasn't a scared little boy or the Bachelor Duke. Here, surrounded by decades of memories, he was just Remington.

"You've returned early, sir." Mr. Taylor took Remington's hat and gloves.

"We didn't expect you until the end of the season." Mrs. Taylor gave him a motherly smile.

Remington turned to face the two employees he'd known since he was a boy. "Yes, I have some news. I'll only stay for a day before I return to London. If you two could follow me to my study."

"Surely you would like to rest or wash the road off?" Mrs. Taylor reproached.

"I'm afraid it can't wait. There needs to be preparations. After all, you only have a short time to prepare." He walked past them, leaving the couple to stare at each other quizzically before they rushed to keep up with his long strides.

Passing century-old paintings of ancestors, antiques, gifts from kings, and family heirlooms, Remington imagined what the house would be like filled with the sounds of children. It would happen, his father be damned, society be damned. Livie was going to be his wife.

He hurried into his office to the large cabinet that stored his safe and used the key from inside his jacket to open the cabinet. He turned at the sound of the elderly couple coming into the room.

Remington turned back to the safe and entered the combination. It opened easily, his eyes searching the space for the small box. He found it in the back and pulled it out, his heart beating wildly in his chest, knowing this would be one of the most important decisions in his life.

"Your Grace, is everything alright?" Mr. Taylor asked, bewildered.

Remington faced them holding the box in the palm of his hand. Mrs. Taylor let out a loud heave, her hand covering her mouth and tears pooling in her eyes.

Remington lifted the box to reveal a delicate gold band intertwined with vines and five diamonds across the top. It was his mother's most beloved possession. She had worn it all her life in remembrance of her own mother.

His mind went to a long-buried memory of his mother on her death bed. He was just a young boy, and all he knew was that his mother was having a baby.

The room had been dark when he entered, his small hand

clutched in Mother Di's. With a sad smile, she pushed him to-ward the bed where his mother lay dying. Remington recalled the feel of her cool hand on his cheek. His mother removed the ring she wore from her hand and pressed it into his. He clutched it as if his very life depended on it as tears fell down his face.

"One day you will marry for love. Promise me that you will cherish her." He remembered how strong her voice was in that moment.

He wanted to give her any and everything, because she was his mother and he loved her. "I promise, Mama."

The diamonds caught the sun streaming through the win-dow, bringing him back to the present. He would do it. He would keep his promise to his mother and cherish Livie with every part of his being.

He wasn't a monster like his father or Bromswell, and he would prove it. Livie would never have to worry about a cruel, loveless marriage. He would make sure of it.

"Sir?" Taylor asked again.

"Everything is perfect. I'm getting married."

Talbert Abbey was a lovely home in the small village of Frinton-on-Sea in Essex. It sat three stories high and overlooked the North Sea. It was by far the most beautiful place Livie had ever been. She could imagine herself spending days there wrapped in Remington's arms, the fresh smell of the sea wafting through the window. Their children would play on the beach behind the home, and they would all be so happy.

It had a comfortable feel that she enjoyed immensely, each room full of warmth. Mother Di had said that it was Remington's mother's preferred home. Eliza had found the quaint place one day by chance when leaving the more popular sea town of Clacton-on-Sea. It was obvious by the way each room was cared for and decorated that Talbert Abbey held a special place in her heart.

According to Mother Di, Eliza Warren would spend months here without her husband—just her, Remington, and her friend. Livie sighed, understanding how she must have felt. Needing an escape, and Talbert Abbey being the perfect place for her.

Since they had arrived at the country home, Livie could finally breathe again. Society could no longer bother her with their whispers and constant stares. Daily walks on the estate seemed to lessen the ache she had in her chest for Remington. Not seeing him for almost an entire fortnight filled her with a loneliness she had never before felt. It was a good thing her mother and Mother Di kept them busy with different activities.

Livie walked through the bright and airy home. She was being treated like the duchess, and they weren't even married—not even engaged. Mother Di even insisted she took the duchess's chambers. The entire ordeal overwhelmed her.

Her mother and Mother Di sat in the breakfast room, conspiratorially whispering as if they were girls sharing a secret.

"Good morning, Mother, Mother Di," Livie greeted as she sat at the small, round table.

The room was cheery and bright with light green drapes and sixteenth-century French furniture.

"Good morning. Did you sleep well?" Mother Di had a huge smile on her face.

"Very well, although I really wish you hadn't insisted I take the duchess's chambers. It is your room, after all," Livie said.

"I've never slept in that room, it always belonged to Eliza, and now it belongs to you." Mother Di took a bite of her ham.

Livie shook her head, trying not to become cross with the older woman, but it was daunting how she acted as if Livie and Remington were already married. Although she had to admit, in their last meeting, it was abundantly clear that he would propose soon.

"May I remind you that we are not yet engaged—"

"That's just a matter of time. Besides, the other rooms weren't ready." Mother Di took a sip of her tea.

"I can't believe the day may soon come where my daughter will be a duchess." Her mother's voice was whimsical and full of awe.

Julia entered the breakfast parlor and sat, a despondent look on her face.

"Good morning. Is anything the matter?" Livie asked.

"I just miss Henry. I've never gone so long without seeing him. Don't you miss Remington?" Julia's shoulders hunched.

"Really, Julia, can you try to remember yourself," Lady Hempstead demanded as she looked up at her niece. "You're going to be a married marchioness soon."

"I don't know why I must follow propriety in front of Mother Di. Soon, we will be family," Julia huffed out, placing food on her plate, ignoring the look her aunt gave her.

Livie ignored Julia, seeing the signs of a temper tantrum. She was accustomed to her cousin's moods and hoped they would lesson once she was married.

Before Julia could continue on her rant, a footman came in carrying the mail on a silver tray and set it beside Mother Di. The tray was filled with letters and the gossips. Mother Di picked up the items, sorted through them, and passed Livie a letter then discarded the others to the side and picked up the gossip sheet.

"Di, you have the gossips delivered to Essex?" Lady Hempstead inquired.

Mother Di nodded. "I like to know what is being said in London. There is always news, even if it is not the best and it's late."

Livie turned the letter over to find the Karrington seal gleaming at her. Her heartbeat increased. It had been so long since she heard from Remington. Not wanting to delay a moment longer, she opened the letter and released it from its confines with shaky hands.

Her starving eyes roamed his neat penmanship greedily.

My Darling,
Love's not Time's fool, though rosy lips and cheeks
Within his bending sickle's compass come;
Love alters not with his brief hours and weeks,
But bears it out even to the edge of doom.
Thinking of you, my Livie. I will return to London immediately.
Yours, Always,
Remington.

"That must be some letter. You've hardly breathed since you opened it," Julia said.

"I'm breathing," Livie whispered, feeling the heat on her cheeks as she neatly folded the letter and put it away in her dress pocket.

They continued eating as Mother Di read over the gossips. Livie eyed the small breakfast room in awe, imagining it filled with children running around, while her and Remington enjoyed breakfast. A smile graced her lips as walks to the beach and nights playing chess filled her mind.

"Oh, dear!" Mother Di's loud voice caused every head to turn toward her.

"What is it? Surely it can't be about Livie and the duke? We've escaped London to avoid the gossips." Lady Hempstead leaned over, eagerly looking down at the paper.

"What does it say?" Livie sat up, anxious to know what was being said about her.

Her mother gazed up from the paper. "More gossip on Lady Evers and her supposed child. To even suggest such a thing is unheard of. I now know why we've never been to town before."

"It seems as if there is proof the child is hers. One of her maids has confirmed it." Mother Di's eyes were glued to the sheet. "Goodness." She dropped the paper as if it had burned her, her hand covering her mouth.

Lady Hempstead took the paper scanning it furiously until her own eyes widened.

"I believe the child is hers, but what concern is it of anyone's, really?" Livie asked, remembering the beautiful babe outside the dress shop and Lady Evers's confession to her.

"Livie, it's unheard of and scandalous. Can you imagine the spectacle it's going to cause at my wedding?" Julia's voice shook with outrage.

"I believe there is more at risk than that." Mother Di finally said, her face pale.

"Whatever do you mean?" Livie asked, concerned.

"My darling … Please know that it is just speculation, but the paper has listed a number of gentlemen that could be the father of Lady Evers's child. The duke is among the list." Her mother's voice was kind and unwavering.

All the breath in her lungs seemed to have left Livie. Surely a paper wouldn't be so cruel as to actually name men and ruin their lives. It couldn't be true. She stood urgently and took hold of the paper.

She scanned the names of the five gentlemen listed. At the very bottom, directly after the Earl of Windchester, Remington's title stood out among the others:

The Duke of Karrington

Her breakfast lodged in her throat. She had to leave before it threatened to return in front of everyone.

"Excuse me." She dropped the paper and rushed out of the breakfast room into the hall. When she turned the corner of the main hallway, she collided with something hard. Strong arms settled around her.

"Sweetheart? What is the matter?" Remington's deep voice was out of a dream. She must be hallucinating. There was no way he could be there, wrapping her in his arms, right when she needed him most.

She needed him to say the paper was a lie. Looking up into his crisp blue eyes brought an immediate calm over her. Remington really was there.

"What … What are you doing here? I thought you were still in Norwich." She tried to back away so that she could hide her tears, but he wasn't having any of that as his hands cupped her cheek.

He wiped at a tear she hadn't realized she shed. It was as if all of her fears were coming true.

"Are you going to tell me what's wrong?" he teased before kissing her lips.

She knew the kiss was supposed to be chaste. But from the moment their lips touched, a desperate need seemed to have taken over both of them. They clung to one another, making up for their time apart.

Suddenly, she didn't care about the atrocious article, and its insinuations, for she knew when they were like this, that Remington was hers and hers alone. Livie's fingers went to his nape, pulling him closer. His arms encircled her tighter. She wanted to forget about the paper.

"Livie?"

"Olivia?"

The muffled voices called in search of her. But coming through her kiss-ridden mind, she didn't care; she just wanted him.

Remington released her just as the footsteps grew closer.

Livie turned to her mother, heat and embarrassment spreading through her at the thought of being discovered in such an act.

Three shocked faces stared at her. Julia, her mother, and Mother Di all stood gaping.

"Your Grace ... w-what a surprise," her mother stuttered, making the situation infinitely more embarrassing as she tried to hide the gossip sheet.

Chapter Eighteen

How does Lady O feel about the Bachelor Duke possibly being the father of Lady E's child? It's bound to come out sooner or later, who the father really is.

REMINGTON CLEARED HIS THROAT, AWARE OF WHAT they must look like. He had been so desperate to see Livie that after he saw his solicitor and requested a special license for them to marry, he had immediately set off to Essex. He had to see her, had to ask her the question that had been building since the first day he saw her. She would be his wife, promptly, if he had anything to say about it.

Once at the house, he had practically sprinted in like a boy, not saying a word to his servants, just going in search of his Livie. Finding her distraught caused him pain. A kiss meant to soothe her seemed to have taken off on its own course, a fact that pleased him very much if it wasn't for their audience.

"Ladies, forgive my interruption. I thought I would come and escort you all back to London." He pulled his jacket down, trying to hide his discomfort.

"We were just having breakfast." Lady Hempstead huffed out a breath as she held the gossip paper in her hand.

Remington eyed her, his gaze locked on the sheet in her clutched grasp.

"I'm afraid the gossips have arrived." A worry crease formed between his mother's brows, one he hadn't seen since his father was alive.

Livie shifted uncomfortably at the mention of the gossips. She nervously chewed her bottom lip, her eyes red from her tears.

"What was said?" His voice was harsh, his eyes never leaving his intended.

"Perhaps you would like to freshen up first?" Mother Di gave him a sad smile.

"No, I would very much like to know what has upset Lady Olivia." He reached out his hand to Lady Hempstead, silently asking for the paper.

She handed it to him before she turned to Julia. "Come along. Let's prepare for our walk."

"I really must stay with Livie—"

"Julia!" Lady Hempstead's voice raised a fraction, causing her niece to jump before scurrying away.

"Lady Olivia, please find us when you are done with the duke." Her mother bowed her head before following Julia.

Mother Di looked at her son, who took Livie by the elbow and led her into the adjacent library. His touch caused Livie to visibly relax, the tension in her shoulders disappearing quickly.

"It's just gossip," Mother Di said simply, trying to excuse the papers as she followed them into the room.

Remington's eyes widened and his jaw tightened as he scanned the sheet. "Trash!" He threw the paper across the room, causing Livie to jump slightly. "How dare they ruin people's lives like this! To name possible fathers."

"Yes, it's abominable, but we know there is no truth to any of it." Mother Di eyed Livie, who remained quiet. "Don't we?"

Livie gave Mother Di a small smile, her eyes shifting nervously.

"Mother, may I speak with Lady Olivia alone?" Remington gave his mother a pleading look.

"Of course." Mother Di left the room, closing the door behind her.

Livie walked to the window; the drapes were opened to reveal the grounds that overlooked the sea. Remington watched her carefully before he joined her. His arms wrapped around her shoulders, enveloping her in his embrace.

She leaned her head back against his shoulder, letting out a shaky sigh. "I'm sorry I reacted in such away." Her voice broke a little.

He gently turned her around to face him. "You have nothing to be sorry about." He cupped her cheek. "I'm sorry that it upset you. But you must know, I have never had any personal relationship with Lady Evers, aside from being her brother's closest friend."

He wanted to tell her that him and the lady could hardly stand each other. They had a difference of opinion on gossips and propriety.

Livie let out a sigh of frustration. "I know, it's just when we saw Lady Evers at the ball, and I saw her at the dress shop before we came here, she seemed to be familiar with you."

Livie took a step away, creating space between them. Remington cleared his throat and gestured to the sofa. She walked over and took a seat but refused to look at him.

Kneeling down in front of her, he held her hands in his, bending to brush soft kisses against her knuckles. "Livie, I swear to you there is no truth in that article. I only have eyes for you," he whispered staring into her eyes.

"I just don't understand how they can print such a thing if there is no connection." Her voice was quiet as she stared over at the chessboard in the corner.

Remington stood taking the seat beside her, before he took her hands again. He intertwined his fingers with hers, trying to reassure her of his innocence. "Sweetheart, I don't want there to be any discord between us. I became familiar with Lady Evers last season. We were often thrown together as she and Heartford formed a relationship. There were jokes, and we did become familiar with each other's company, but nothing more." He took a breath, his eyes locking with hers. "The lady and I often did not agree on her lifestyle. As you know, I deplore gossip, and she seemed to shine in it, especially with the freedom she has as a widow. Other than that, there is no connection between us, especially one where I would father her child—"

Livie leaned into him, squeezing his hand. "I never thought such a thing. I was just unsure of how familiar she was with you."

"Rest assured, no one is as familiar with me as you, Livie." He pulled her to him so that she was on his lap.

"Good," she whispered before her lips captured his in a searing kiss.

His fingers gripped the nape of her neck, deepening their connection, while his other arm wrapped tightly around her waist. "My God, I've missed you," he whispered urgently against the base of her neck.

"Yes," she called out as he lavished the sensitive area with his tongue. "I've missed you too," she mewled as his teeth nipped at her skin.

Her fingers found a home in his hair, pulling him closer to her. He massaged and kneaded one full breast, while trailing kisses down the column of her throat. She arched her neck giving him greater access to her delicate skin.

Remington growled out in frustration as he lifted her

up and then laid her down on the sofa. Livie stared at him in round-eyed surprise as she watched him remove his waistcoat.

Taking her by the hand, he kissed a slow trail starting at her fingertips, "You are ..." he began before continuing up the long span of her arm, "... the only woman ..." He stopped at the crook of her elbow, eliciting a giggle. Her gray eyes were warm and welcoming. "... that I want ..." He moved up her body, spreading his larger frame on top of her, propping up on his elbows so that he wouldn't crush her. Wrapping his hand around the back of her neck, he pulled her toward him, his lips hovering over hers, their eyes locked in a heated gaze. "... now and always."

His lips ravished hers hungrily; his tongue plundered her mouth like a greedy pirate searching for treasure. Remington pulled down the bust of her dress, freeing her bosom. He released her mouth, trailing heated kisses down her magnificent flesh.

He had dreamed of her body every day they were apart, and now, he couldn't contain himself any longer.

"Remington," she moaned out in pleasure, her head pressed into the embroidered cushion.

He took the pebbled pink flesh into his mouth, swirling his tongue around one perfect nipple. Reaching down with one hand, he began lifting the edges of her skirts. Livie gripped the muscles of his arms as his fingers trailed up the bare skin of her leg to the opening of her pantalettes.

She quivered beneath him when he touched her sensitive flesh. Her response emboldened him to part the folds of her sex, dipping in and out, tracing a slow delicious trail to the sensitive ball of nerves.

God, he wanted her more than he had ever wanted anyone in his life. His lips slowly traced from her jaw to the shell of her ear. "You're mine, Livie," his voice sounded husky to his ears as his fingers circled and dipped. Her walls closed around his fingers.

"Oh, yes! Yours." Livie moaned.

He continued to ravish her swollen breast, licking and sucking, while his two fingers filled her over and over. "Let go, Livie," he begged. She tightened and then exploded around him.

Remington covered her lips with his, so in awe of her beauty while in the throes of pleasure. His mouth slanted over hers, wanting nothing more than to take her right there in the library, everyone be damned. "And I am yours." His voice was soft as he removed his fingers from her sex.

His eyes searched hers, and he saw trust, absolute devotion, and—

"You're mine," she whispered, reaching up again and kissing him softly.

His heart soared in his chest because he knew that soon, they would belong to each other—forever.

The duchess's rooms at Talbert Abbey were large and beautiful, made for royalty. The entire room was covered in light furnishings and drapes that reminded her of the color of a light peach.

She glanced around, trying to avoid the insistent questions and stares from Abigail and Julia. Livie was preparing to go on a walk with Remington. However, what she really wanted was more of what occurred in the library. She had never in her entire life experienced anything like that, and she did not know what to think of it.

A knock on the door on the far side of the wall shocked

CECILIA RENE

all three ladies. Abigail quickly went over to answer, finding a shocked duke standing on the other side.

"Your Grace," she said, dipping a curtsy.

"Ladies, I was in search of Lady Olivia, and I heard voices." He looked at Livie, causing heat to blossom in her cheeks as she remembered the delicious ways he had tortured her body. "Are you staying in here?" he asked.

"Yes, Mother Di insisted. I'm sure she did not expect you to join us. Perhaps we can have another room prepared for me?" she asked nervously, not sure how he would react to her being in his mother's room.

"No, that will not be necessary. It's fitting." The last part was whispered as he walked over to her and offered her his arm. "Shall we go for our walk?"

"Y-yes," she stuttered, feeling butterflies dance in her belly after being so intimate in the library.

"Did you see Henry while you were in town?" Julia prattled on behind them as she and Abigail followed them out of the room.

"I'm afraid I did not. Once I arrived, I had urgent business to attend, and then I had the urge to see Lady Olivia." Remington looked down at Livie, his eyes twinkling in mischief.

"Oh, that is just the sweetest. I wish Henry had the same urge," Julia practically whined as they walked down the stairs where Lady Hempstead and Mother Di were waiting.

"Abigail, you do not have to walk with Lady Olivia and His Grace today." Her mother smiled, sharing a look with Mother Di.

Abigail gave her a nod before going back up the stairs.

Once outside, Livie and Remington parted from the others, her arm around his, ignoring the whispers and giggles behind them.

"What do you suppose they are up to?" she asked Remington, who was leading her down a trail toward the back of the property. The women seemed to have been conspiring all morning after catching her in his arms.

"Who knows?" He intertwined his fingers with hers. "Are you enjoying Talbert Abbey?"

"It's so beautiful, Remington, and the view from my room is breathtaking. Waking up to the sea has been divine. I love it here." The visit had only been made better by his arrival.

The path led to a clearing that overlooked the sea and the sandy beaches below. He wrapped his arms around her, bringing her to him. "I'm glad you love it here. It was my mother's favorite place. I wanted you to see it."

A cool breeze from the sea swept past them, and Livie nuzzled closer, basking in his presence. "I'm glad you suggested to Father that we escape the city. It's now my second favorite place in the world." She kissed the underside of his jaw, enjoying their closeness.

A deep chuckle sounded from his chest, "What is your first?"

She squeezed her arms around his hard middle. "In your arms," she whispered, closing her eyes.

Silence followed for a few moments before he released her, forcing her to open her eyes to look up at him. Wordlessly, he took a step back, taking her hand in his.

Remington bent down to one knee, never taking his gaze off her. Happiness threatened to burst inside of her as she gazed down at this glorious man.

"Livie ... From the moment I first laid eyes on you, I was completely and irrevocably yours. You captured me—body, and soul—and I never want to be freed from you. Please do me the great honor of becoming my wife and my duchess." His voice was rich and filled with emotion, his eyes watering.

He took her hands and pressed his lips against her fingers, waiting for her answer.

Livie opened and closed her mouth several times unable to speak. She nodded emphatically, letting the tears fall freely, her reply was a small whisper. "Y…yes." She swallowed excitement coursing through her belly. "Yes!" she repeated louder.

Remington rose to his feet, sweeping her up in his arms and sealed their fate with the sweetest kiss known to man.

Chapter Nineteen

*The Bachelor Duke was in town for one day. I'm sure all of
the available young ladies would like to know what he was
preparing for at his solicitor's office.
Should we pull out the handkerchiefs yet?*

R EMINGTON WAS HAPPY. HE COULDN'T RECALL EVER
being as happy as he was in that moment. There had
been small moments in his life, of course, when he'd
felt happiness. When he finished school. Annually, when he
celebrated his birth. His mother and him picnicking in the
very spot he asked Livie to be his wife. His life was filled with
small bits of happiness, but this feeling of being blissfully and
completely joyous was new to him.

"Did you plan this all along?" Livie broke their kiss briefly.

They had retired to the house when a light rain descended
upon them, finding shelter in the parlor with a pot of tea in front
of them. Their lips only parted for seconds at a time, so incredi-
bly content were they. She found a home on his lap, and he was
happy to accommodate her there. Remington would do anything, be anything she needed.

"Yes," he said at the base of her neck, halting his kisses
momentarily.

"Father knew?" she asked in wonderment.

"Mmhmmm," he hummed against her neck, lavishing it once again with attention.

Kissing a trail back up to her lips, he captured the bottom one in his mouth, seductively teasing it with his tongue. He felt her body melt in his embrace, as his hands roamed her body. He absolutely loved the feel of her in his arms and could not wait to feel her completely.

Breaking their kiss, Livie tried to rise off his lap, but he refused to release her. "Neither one of us can think like this, and I want to know everything." She pouted at him, her lips swollen from his kisses.

Remington leaned in, pecking her lips, happiness seeping out of him. "I can think perfectly well like this." He settled back on the sofa, giving her a challenging look, as one of his hands trailed up her back to massage gently at the base of her neck.

"Good. Now, as I was saying, Your Grace, who was aware that you were proposing?" Her eyes closed, the more he touched her.

"Your father knew, of course. I informed him before I left for my estate—"

"What? You knew you were going to propose before you left for Norwich?" she asked, bewildered.

"Yes, I had to get my grandmother's wedding band. My mother wanted my wife to have it." He lifted her hand, peppering her wrist with kisses, unable to contain himself. She was going to be his wife, and he would spend his life worshipping every part of her.

"Your grandmother's ring?" Tears pricked her storm-gray eyes.

Remington slowly pulled her closer, his lips trailing up her bare arms, her bosom, then the long curve of her neck, until he reached her lips, offering her a slow sensual kiss. "I wanted you to have my grandmother's ring, not some gold band purchased on Bond Street." His hand cupped her face, stroking the silky skin with the pads of his thumbs. "I need you to become my wife as soon as possible."

The nail of one of his fingers trailed down her cheek, causing her to bite her bottom lip with desire.

Livie sat up straighter, her eyes wide. "When would we be married? I don't want a large wedding; all I really need is you and our family." She leaned in, pressing a kiss to his lips.

Adoration soared within him for this beautiful woman in his arms. "I have requested a special license. We can be married in a fortnight. Will that be enough time to prepare?" Remington continued to caress her cheek with his lips.

Footsteps and happy chatter in the hall alerted them to the end of their time alone. They stood and straightened themselves.

"I also mentioned to the mothers that I had something important to ask you." He gave her a teasing smile.

The door burst open to reveal their mothers and Julia, all with expectant looks upon their faces.

"Well?" Mother Di rushed over to Livie, who was turning a bright red color.

Lady Hempstead went to her daughter's other side, taking hold of her free hand. Both she and Mother Di anxiously looked from Remington to Livie while Julia vibrated where she stood.

"Well, what?" Remington tilted his head, trying to hide his amusement at the appalled look on all their faces.

"Don't tease them." Livie's voice was a playful warning, her eyes sparkling with joy, and he wanted nothing more than to ravish her once again.

Remington gave a hearty chuckle, so happy at this moment

that she was going to be his. "Lady Olivia has agreed to be my wife."

"How wonderful!" His mother wrapped her arms around Livie, tears springing from her eyes.

"Livie, we're getting married!" Julia rushed to her cousin, squeezing in between the other ladies, all thought of decorum out the window.

"I can't believe my daughter is going to be a duchess!" Lady Hempstead cried into Livie's neck.

Remington watched the entire scene with amusement as Livie cried her tears of joy.

"Have you set a date yet?" Julia pulled Livie to the chaise to have a seat.

Mother Di walked over to Remington, her hand cupping his face in a motherly fashion. He fought away his own tears at the sight of her in front of him.

"I wish your mother were here," she whispered before pressing a kiss to his cheek.

He cleared his throat several times, unable to speak from the longing he suddenly felt. His mother had been gone for so many years, Remington was used to not having her around, and rarely felt her absence because of Mother Di's constant love. But in that moment, Remington wished she was there to share in his happiness and meet his future duchess, because he knew she would love her just as—

He blinked several times, his heart pounding and sweat forming at the back of his neck.

"We are getting married in a fortnight." Livie's cheery voice interrupted his train of thought, halting him from spiraling out of control.

"That will be sooner than Henry and I." Julia looked wide-eyed at her cousin.

"Yes, not by much. You two will marry a sennight after us. I saw no reason to delay and requested a special license." Remington spoke casually as he took a seat in an armchair.

Mother Di rang the bell that was on the table. The butler came in immediately, giving her a bow. "Yes, Lady Diana?"

"Horace, please have champagne sent in. We are celebrating His Grace's and Lady Olivia's engagement."

"Right away." Horace turned to Remington, his eyes brimming with affection. "Congratulations, Sir."

"Thank you, Horace. I am truly a happy man." He looked over at Livie, who was now patting her mother's hand, and for once in his life, he truly felt it.

Livie couldn't breathe. She knew what she wanted to do but didn't have the courage to open the door that stood between her and the man she loved. She loved him; it had come to her like a summer breeze, fleeting, and reassuring.

Taking another deep breath, Livie tried to calm herself. She only wanted a kiss goodnight. One kiss, and then she could sleep. Surely, that wouldn't be too scandalous between an engaged couple. They hadn't been alone since earlier that day, and after that, there was a flurry of activity to celebrate their pending nuptials. They discussed the wedding and the breakfast, and finalized their return to town. When they finally all retired for the night, she and Remington were forced to say goodbye at the doors of her room because of their audience.

Livie smiled to herself, thinking that they would be married in a fortnight. Tomorrow they would return to London and start making the arrangements for their wedding.

She took one last stuttering breath, squeezing the doorknob tight. Before she could open it, there was a brief knock and then the door swung open, causing Livie to yell out in surprise.

"Goodness!" She clutched her chest, startled by Remington standing in front of her, wearing nothing but a shirt and breeches.

The top buttons of his shirt were unbuttoned, showing off his cravat-free neck and chest. Thin, curly hairs peeked through the opening, begging for her to run her fingers through them.

"Darling, are you well?" He entered the room, closing the door behind him.

"Yes, I wasn't expecting you." She giggled nervously, looking down at his bare feet.

He reached out and combed his fingers through her loose silky hair, his eyes glistening in want. "I wanted to say goodnight properly." One of his hands slipped around her waist, pulling her closer to him.

"So did I." She stood on her tiptoes, wrapping her arms around his neck. He made her feel so bold, wanted, and adored.

"Great minds think alike," he whispered against her lips before taking them in a slow sensual dance.

Livie moaned in pleasure while his tongue caressed hers and his hands gripped her behind. Lifting her off her feet, she dangled slightly off the ground as he walked them over to the waiting bed.

Placing her down on her feet, they kissed passionately, his hands roaming her body in slow, deliberate movements. She gripped the nape of his neck, wanting to feel more of him against her.

Never in her life had she experienced such a feeling; it was like a thousand nerves had awakened inside of her. She needed to know what it felt like for him to touch every single one.

Their kiss slowed as his lips slid deliciously against hers. He released her, causing her to open her eyes to look up at him in question.

"Do you wish for me to go?" His voice was husky, the desire to stay evident in his intense blue gaze.

Her hands slipping from around his neck, Livie felt bold and empowered by his presence. Turning around, she crawled onto the large bed. She settled in the center and looked up to find Remington staring at her hungrily.

"Stay." Her voice was strong as they locked eyes.

Completely mesmerized, she watched as he slowly moved to the bed with a predatory look on his face. Biting the corner of her bottom lip, she suppressed a wanton moan, desire dancing in her belly. The bed shifted beneath his weight as he put one knee then the other and crawled toward her.

A strong hand gripped her neck, pulling her to him in a searing kiss. The weight of his body on top of hers made her feel secured and cherished. Guided by his expert hands, she moaned in desperation as he trailed fire-inducing kisses down her neck to the opening of her nightdress.

"Remington," Livie sighed out, her voice needy and breathy.

His lips on her aching bosom felt like heaven. When he took her nipple into his warm mouth, she cried out in pleasure. Remington's free hand found the triangle of curls underneath her dressing gown and let out a deep throaty moan. She was wet and eager for him, and in that moment, she did not care about propriety.

"May I remove your gown?" Remington asked, before kissing her lips. "I assure you, darling, I will not take you until you are my duchess. I wish only to explore you tonight."

A small smile graced her lips when he called her *"his duchess,"* and the only thing she could do was nod her head in consent. Livie wanted to allow him the liberties due to him as her future husband; she wanted to be with him, more than anything.

Removing her gown over her head, he placed it to the side and sat up to gaze down at her. Her gaze shifted around the room, nervous she would see disappointment in his eyes.

Her middle was not as firm as other ladies, her breasts were too large, hips too wide and curvy.

Firm hands guided her gaze back to his. "You are exquisite, Livie."

Remington kissed her, putting every ounce of what he felt for her in that one kiss. Her back arched off the bed. His hands roamed and caressed every part of bare skin that was revealed to him. Soon his lips followed the same path, stopping to nip playfully at her sides.

Every piece of her that was touched, kissed, and sucked by him was scorched and forever changed.

Tender touches in her most sensitive area, caused her heart to stop, she watched wide-eyed as Remington buried his face in her curls, slowly licking up her center. A wanton sound escaped the back of her throat, as he repeated the movement continuously until he found a particularly pleasant spot that led her legs to open wider of their own accord.

Remington let out an animalistic groan and pulled her roughly to him as he devoured her.

Livie pressed her head further into her pillow, her body quivering in need as he inserted two fingers inside, while his tongue swirled her sensitive nub. His free hand massaged her heavy breasts, and she rejoiced in ecstasy, unable to control herself as emotion and feelings crashed through her body.

She took hold of a free pillow and placed it over her face as a wave of the sweetest feelings took over. Her body stiffened, her toes curled, and her back arched practically off the bed.

"Oh God, Remington!" she called out, trying to muffle her sounds in the pillow.

Kissing up her body, he stopped to ravish her breast before lying beside her and removing the pillow. His hands continued to move about her body as if he needed to touch her.

Livie opened her eyes to find a smiling Remington staring at her. "Am I no longer a maiden?" she asked, for surely such an act would rob her of her virtue.

He chuckled, before bending down to kiss her. "You are still a maiden. There is a little more involved in the act." His eyes twinkled, yet desire darkened the blue depths.

"More?" she asked, her eyes widening at the thought.

He picked up her discarded dressing gown, helping her into it before he stood and lifted the duvet. Livie crawled under the cover as he slid in beside her. His arms enveloped her, and she felt so at peace, so at home within his arms.

"I'm sure your mother will explain everything, but now you have an advantage. When I truly take you as my wife, you will know it, and you will be mine forever," Remington whispered, his lips caressing her forehead.

"I'm already yours forever." She nuzzled his chest, taking in his scent. Sleep was quickly taking over her. Her lids lowered, and her limbs were numb.

"Sleep, my duchess." His voice was thick and sensual.

Livie drifted off, but before she fully succumbed to sleep, she swore she heard him whisper, "Sleep, my love."

Chapter Twenty

Prepare the smelling salts! Take out your handkerchiefs! Put away
your best gowns! The Bachelor Duke is engaged!

THE DAYS LEADING UP TO HER NUPTIALS WERE A whirlwind. While Remington secured the church, Livie sent out the invitations.

Madame Beaumont's assistant buttoned up the back of Livie's dress. She guided her fingers down the silky blue fabric, loving the feel of it. She couldn't wait to see the look on Remington's face when he caught sight of her. The fabric hugged her curves and the blue matched his eyes.

"You're all set, my lady." Agnes, Madame Beaumont's assistant, took a step back and smiled.

Livie returned the smile before she walked out into the now-closed shop where her mother stood along with Mother Di, Madame Beaumont, and Julia. They were all happily chatting about the upcoming weddings of both St. John ladies and turned at the sound of her approach.

"Gorgeous!" Her mother was the first to speak, tears pooling in her gray eyes.

"You look stunning, my darling." Mother Di clapped her hands together and brought them to her lips.

"You look ravishing, Livie." Julia gave her a playful wink.

Madame Beaumont led her over to the floor-length mirror. Livie had no words at the sight of herself in her wedding gown. Her mind traveled to her wedding night, and she could not wait to be with him intimately. If what happened in Essex was any indication of what was to come, then she could not wait

The thought of his lips against her most sensitive flesh kept her awake every night days after they returned to London. Now every time they were in each other's presence, she wished they had more time together, but soon they would have forever.

Madame Beaumont tugged on different parts of the gown. "It is a perfect fit, but maybe I can make some adjustments in the bosom."

"I was thinking that as well." Lady Hempstead came to stand beside her daughter and pushed on the fabric at one of Livie's breasts, causing her to blush profusely. "Unfortunately, everything she consumes goes straight to her bosom and rear."

"Mother!" Livie shouted, turning to glare at her mother.

"What? You know it's true. As a married lady, try to control your consumption of biscuits and pudding." Her mother patted her shoulders, giving her a loving smile.

"As a married lady, I shall eat whatever I like." Livie gave her mother a matter-of-fact nod.

"I wouldn't worry about what you eat. The duke looks at you as if you were something to devour. I don't think he would mind one bit." Julia teased from behind her.

"Lady Julia St. John, you will control your tongue." Lady Hempstead's voice was firm and authoritative.

"Very well." Julia folded her arms and stomped her foot in defiance.

Madame Beaumont cleared her throat. "I shall make the last of the adjustments tonight, adding a little more room at the top. It will be ready for pickup tomorrow, late morning."

"Wonderful!" Livie still could not believe that she would be a married woman in five days' time.

Livie returned to the small dressing room, changing quickly into her day dress. Once she was out, she returned the gown to Madame Beaumont with promises that either she or Abigail would pick it up tomorrow.

The ladies exited the store, excitedly chatting with each other. The sun was setting on the busy London street, shops closing for the day. Livie walked behind her companions, her thoughts on her upcoming wedding.

It was really happening.

Someone bumped into her, officially taking her mind off of her pending nuptials. Before she could stumble, a pair of strong arms secured her. Her mind quickly registered danger, her skin crawling from the touch of the unknown person. She looked up and into the cold eyes of Baron Bromswell.

"E-excuse me," she stammered, pressing her hands against his chest and pushing him away.

"Lady Olivia, what a surprise running into you." The baron's voice was devoid of any emotion.

"Yes, you as well. Goodbye—"

Before she could leave, he took her by the arm and pulled her forcefully toward him. Her mind immediately went back to the Ratchford's ball. It was the last time she had been this close to him.

"Congratulations on your engagement. How does it feel being a pawn in his game?"

Livie snatched her arm away from him. "What are you talking about? I'm not a pawn in anyone's game." She raised her head high, refusing to be intimidated by the man.

"Oh but you are, and soon everyone will know. You should've

chosen me when you had the chance." His voice was cruel and condescending, causing a feeling of trepidation to run through her.

Livie ignored his comment. "I was never going to choose you." She turned to catch up with the others.

"Is everything all right here?" Mother Di asked, walking toward Bromswell.

Livie nodded her head, trying to plaster a reassuring smile on her face. "Everything is fine. The baron was just offering his congratulations."

"Indeed, I was just telling Lady Olivia how happy I am for her and Karrington." The baron bowed his head before he gave Livie one last sinister look and walked away.

She watched him leave, so relieved the vile man was no longer near her. His words made her uneasy, but she did not want to give him any power over her and Remington.

"Are you sure you're all right?" Mother Di asked again, rubbing Livie's arm in a motherly fashion.

"Yes, it was nothing." Livie forced a smile as they returned to the carriage.

Remington sat in the corner of O'Brien's surrounded by a few select gentlemen who he'd called friends over the years. Although he wasn't as inebriated as his companions, he did find himself leaning slightly. He was sure other men would have at least ten to fifteen close acquaintances but looking around at their very intoxicated faces gave him a sense of pride. He trusted each and every one of them, and was glad they were celebrating with him.

He took a sip of O'Brien's finest Irish whiskey, which the older man had opened especially for this occasion. Remington replayed the night at Talbert Abbey in his head, the taste of Livie's sweet nectar on his tongue, the sounds she made as he pleasured her. He ran his hands over his face trying to hide that he now had a growing problem beneath the wooden table. At this rate, he didn't think he would ever let Livie out of their bed once she was his wife.

"What are you thinking about so hard?" Hempstead asked him loudly, causing Remington to cough.

He could feel heat spread over his face as it did when he was a boy and Mother Di discovered he had done something wrong. He tried to hide the fact that he was having impure thoughts about the man's only daughter.

"Thinking about the travel arrangements for the wedding trip. So much to do." Remington cleared his throat several times, avoiding eye contact with Hempstead.

No doubt, a father did not wish to think about his daughter's honeymoon, even if he was friendly with the groom.

"Aye! Where are you going for this trip?" O'Brien yelled out drunkenly, his green eyes clouded.

"To our country house in Essex, Talbert Abbey." A slight smile played on the edges of Remington's lips at the word *our*.

He would forever be part of an *our*, or a *we*. The thought pleased him, giving him that damn happy, blissful feeling again, the one that had been building since he first saw her across the ballroom.

"Fine idea to get away from the city. A newly married couple needs time to explore each other." O'Brien moved his brows up and down suggestively, causing Hempstead to look as if he was going to be sick.

"O'Brien, try to remember that's my daughter you're speaking of." The earl's voice was strained as he took a sip of his whiskey.

"Aye, that's why you should only have boys." O'Brien laughed loudly before sobering slightly. "But I have two girls myself, so I know the feeling."

"I'm glad she's going to be happy. I couldn't have picked out a better gentleman out myself!" Hempstead raised his glass, and the other men followed suit.

"I personally never thought the day would come!" Windchester slapped Remington on the back.

Heartford stood, raising his glass, making a grand show of it. "I'd like to toast farewell to the Bachelor Duke!" He flourished his hand in Remington's direction, ignoring the scowl on his friend's face. "May we never see the likes of you again!"

"Hear! Hear!" A drunken Prescott banged on the table, causing the other occupants to look at the rowdy group of men.

Remington shook his head, smiling happily. "Thank you. I can assure you, I will never again be the Bachelor Duke. Livie is it for me."

"And that, my friends, is a man in love!" O'Brien shouted cheerfully.

Remington blinked several times as his companions continued to chat around him. The revelation had been slowly building inside of him since Essex. He remembered thinking that his mother would love Livie as much as he did. It came to him as easily as breathing—he loved Livie.

The thought hit him like a ton of bricks falling from a building. He was in love with Livie. He loved her most passionately, heart, body, and soul. Dear God, he loved her more than he loved anyone or anything in the world.

He wanted to shout it from the rooftop, tell everyone he loved her and that she was going to be his wife.

But first, he needed to declare his love to her.

Before he could make a decision about rushing to her and declaring his love, a footman rushed over to Heartford, whispering furiously in his ear. Remington watched as his friend turned an odd greenish color before he stood abruptly, swaying slightly from inebriation.

"I must go, Amelia needs me!" he shouted and then turned to Remington. "Karrington, would you mind accompanying me? I feel we may need your assistance."

"I'm coming too!" Windchester shocked them both by standing.

Remington bid the other gentlemen a good evening, barely standing on his own two feet, and followed his friends out into the darkening night. His carriage was readily available, so the three men hurried inside once Heartford informed the driver of their destination.

"What is happening?" Remington pressed his hand to his head to stop it from spinning.

"The current Viscount Evers is throwing Amelia and her child out of her townhouse." Heartford's voice shook with rage.

"In the middle of the night?" Remington asked, horrified that Lady Evers was being treated as such.

"Can he do that?" Windchester vibrated from his seat, his anger barely controlled.

Remington looked at his friend's balled-up fist and rigid demeanor. He found it strange that Windchester was so upset over Lady Evers's situation.

"I'm afraid he can. The townhome is entailed to the estate." Heartford looked out the small window as the carriage slowed to a stop. "Bloody hell!" he called out before practically jumping out of the moving carriage.

Once the carriage was fully stopped, Remington

disembarked to find an enraged Lady Evers arguing with Viscount Evers. Her maid held a tiny bundle in her arms, as gowns and baby clothing were being thrown from the house.

In his opinion, it was outrageous to treat a lady in such a way, especially in the middle of the night. A small crowd was assembling, watching the spectacle.

"What the hell do you think you're doing?" Heartford grabbed Evers by his lapels.

Viscount Evers was the heir and only son to Amelia's late husband and his first wife. Evers had been a grown man of thirty years when Amelia had married his father. "I'm putting that whore and her bastard out! She will no longer be associated with my family!" His cold eyes glared at Heartford, who was much thinner compared to his bulkier frame.

Windchester, who had exited the carriage behind Remington, rushed the two men, grabbing Evers by the shoulders and turning him around. "How dare you!" he yelled before he punched the man in the jaw.

Sensing that the situation was indeed getting out of hand, Remington took hold of Windchester, pulling him off the other man. "Control yourself!" He turned to Evers. "There must be something that can be done without you making such a spectacle. Surely, as your father's widow, she deserves some respect."

Viscount Evers wiped his mouth with the back of his hand. "There isn't. For years I have turned a blind eye to the whispers surrounding her, but now they are affecting my own life." He faced Lady Evers. "Get out. And effective immediately, your accounts are frozen."

"You bastard! You can't do that! There is a marriage contract! I earned every penny of that money, after being married to your father." Amelia tried to rush after him, intent on harming him, but Heartford took hold of her. "I will appeal in the court of Chancery."

"Well, until then, they are frozen!" Viscount Evers' voice was shrill, and spittle spewed out of his mouth.

The crowd was growing larger. "Heartford, please get Lady Evers and the baby in the carriage while Windchester and I grab her things. I'm assuming she can't go to your home because of your mother?" Heartford nodded in agreement. "Go to my townhome, we will follow behind you in a hackney."

"Aren't you quite the savior, Karrington? Perhaps the bastard is yours after all," Viscount Evers sneered.

Remington walked over to the man, not saying a word. The viscount took a step back in fear. "Unlike you, I know how to treat a lady, which does not include throwing her out on the street like trash."

"She can come in the morning and get the rest of her things." Viscount Evers quickly walked away from Remington, rushing into the townhome and slamming the door behind him. Remington and Windchester stayed and gathered the remainder of Lady Evers's belongings from the street.

Once everything was piled inside a hackney, Remington eyed his friend closely, noticing how upset the man was over this situation. "Are you going to tell me why you are so concerned for Lady Evers?"

Windchester bowed his head, avoiding his friend's gaze. "I do not wish to burden you. You are to be married; we should be celebrating."

Remington sighed. "Are you the child's father?"

"Yes … But I had no idea Emily even existed until Amelia returned from France. She refused to let me see her. Every time I tried to visit, she refused me. We didn't part well last Season." Windchester pulled at his hair, grimacing in pain.

"When you married Lady Windchester?" Remington sat forward, peering at his friend's tormented face.

"I would've married Amelia, but she refused me over and over, saying I was only marrying her for her fortune, which would have ceased once she was remarried." He bowed his head. "I couldn't do that to her. I had nothing to offer."

"Yes, but that did not stop you from getting her with child. My God, man! Do you ever use your brain?" Remington asked as the carriage stopped. "You will tell Heartford today." He pointed to Windchester, knowing that their friend will be upset.

"I will tell him, and I will tell my wife. I love Amelia and Emily, and I want to be with them." Windchester hung his head.

Once they were out of the hackney, Remington's servants helped bring Lady Evers' things into his house. Remington walked in to find a flustered Dayton.

"Sir, this is most improper, especially since the new duchess will arrive in a matter of days," the butler whispered hurriedly.

"I'm aware. However, it is getting darker by the second, and you wouldn't have me put the lady and her child out on the street, would you?" Remington challenged.

"Of course not, sir, but please think of what a rumor of this magnitude can do to your reputation, and that of your future wife," Dayton said seriously, looking at his employer.

Remington nodded in agreement. "Please make sure none of the servants say a thing." He began walking away and then turned. "Send in tea, and coffee for me. I need to sober up."

He entered the parlor, watching as Heartford paced back and forth. Lady Evers' maid sat in the corner crying with the child in her arms. The baby was now awake, sitting up alert and focused.

Lady Evers stood, smoothing out her skirts. "Karrington,

thank you, but I can't bother you with my problems. I will find us lodgings for tonight and get out of your way."

"Amelia, you and Emily have no place to go. Please stay here until I can figure something out," Windchester said, rushing over to her.

Heartford stopped his pacing, turning to watch his friend and his sister. "What are you talking about?" Windchester took hold of Lady Evers's hand. Realization dawned on Heartford's face. "Are you saying you're the child's father? And you kept it from me?" Heartford walked over and shoved his friend, anger taking over his countenance.

"Yes, I am Emily's father, and I love your sister." Windchester stood his ground.

Lady Evers lifted her arms, her fists balled in anger. "Ha! Love? What do you know about love, William? You don't love anyone or anything but money. You proved that last Season when you married that harlot of a wife." She crossed her arms over her heaving chest, glaring at Windchester.

"I know I failed you, but it doesn't change that I love you and our child. Let me spend my life making it up to you." Windchester tried to walk over to her, but Heartford pushed him away.

"You lied to me an entire year, and now you think you can just say you love her and forget about your wife?" Heartford pushed him forcibly, causing the larger man to stumble.

"What we need to figure out right now is where Lady Evers and little Emily are going to stay tonight. There's no point in fighting amongst ourselves." Remington stood in between his friends, looking back and forth at them.

"My mother is at my townhome, but to hell with her." Heartford's hair was a mess, his eyes filled with fire.

"No, I won't stay with that woman. She's hated me since I was born. I'm sure I can find us lodging for the night." Lady Evers walked over and took the baby from the maid's arms.

"You will stay here tonight. In the morning, the three of us will find you and little Emily suitable accommodations." Remington's voice was final.

"I can't ask you to do that. Lady Olivia was kind to me ... kinder than anyone has been in a long time. I don't want to cause her pain, and staying here will only cause tongues to wag." Lady Evers took a seat, rocking the child back and forth. Her voice was full of sadness.

"I will explain everything to Livie, and she will understand. For now, I must insist you stay here." Remington walked to the door calling in his butler. "Please have the guest rooms prepared for Lady Evers and her maid."

Dayton's eyes widened. "Yes, sir."

Remington turned to face Heartford. "I think it's best if you stay tonight as well."

"Yes, I think so. That way, if there are any questions of propriety at least it could be mentioned that I was present." Heartford turned to Windchester. "I think you should leave. You've done enough."

"I'm not leaving until I speak with Amelia, and there is nothing you can do about it, Heartford. I love your sister; I made an egregious error, but I'm still your friend, and I want to make up the time I missed with my daughter." Windchester walked over to Amelia, kneeling at her feet.

"I'm right here, so you two can stop speaking of me as if I'm not in the room." Her green eyes turned to Windchester, cold and unfeeling. "If any of that is true, you know what you have to do. I will not play second to your wife any longer and neither will my daughter." Amelia kissed the top of Emily's head.

"I will." Windchester stood and bent to kiss Emily's downy head, while Lady Evers ignored him.

Once Windchester had left, Heartford turned his cold gaze to Remington; he didn't look like himself at all. There were no signs of the jovial man Remington knew his entire life. "Did you know?"

"No, but I surmised it on our way here. He seemed very much affected by the wrongdoings of Viscount Evers, even more so than you." Remington walked to the sideboard to pour himself a drink.

"Karrington, do you mind if we retire for the evening? I'm afraid we have had a little too much excitement for one day." Lady Evers smiled down at her daughter, running her fingers through her hair.

"Of course. Dayton will show you to your rooms." Remington walked out to call for the butler, who readily showed himself. "Please make yourself at home. In the morning, Heartford and I will go and find you suitable accommodations."

"Thank you, and please inform Lady Olivia that I'm sorry to be a burden." Lady Evers gave him a small smile before she and her maid followed the butler out of the parlor.

Taking a gulp of his brandy, Remington turned to face Heartford. "I'm afraid to tell Livie about Lady Evers." She hadn't reacted well when the gossips named him as a possible father to Emily.

Heartford joined him at the sideboard, pouring his own drink. "I do not see why. She's levelheaded, more so than her cousin, in fact. Just inform her that you are doing me a great favor, which is true, as well as for that blaggard, Windchester. He is the real father, after all, and your cousin."

"Windchester is one of your oldest friends. Sometimes a

man is blinded by love." Remington's voice was low as he swirled the brandy in his glass.

Love. He still needed to tell Livie how much he loved her, that she was the only person in the entire world for him.

"I'm glad you love her. I was worried it was all a cruel jest at first." Heartford turned fully to his friend.

Shaking his head, adamantly, "Never a jest. Maybe at first it was not my true intentions, but now…"

He loved her, but admitting it to his friend before he admitted it to Livie wasn't an option.

Heartford slapped Remington on the back. "Good. Perhaps start with that when you tell her you have a famous widow and her illegitimate child staying at your home."

They glared at each other before laughing at the situation they now found themselves in.

Chapter Twenty-One

The Bachelor Duke's secrets revealed!

L IVIE ROSE LATE IN THE MORNING WITH A SMALL headache from indulging in too much claret with the ladies. The previous night, Mother Di and Lady Hempstead had decided it was time to have the marital talk with her and Julia. It was a very informative night, filled with drawings and demonstrations. Although their night at Talbert Abbey had given Livie a slight advantage, she still was shocked at some of the information the matrons shared.

"You're all ready, my lady." Helena put the final pin in Livie's hair and took a step back. Julia had been too happy to loan Livie her maid while Abigail went to collect Livie's wedding gown.

Julia entered, looking as if she were wrung out with the laundry. "Aunt and Uncle want us to come down to breakfast right away. Something about spending our last days together as a family."

Livie gave Helena a small smile. "Thank you for helping me; I know you have other things to do."

The ladies walked out of the room, arm in arm. "What are we going to do when we live apart?" Livie had been so excited about her time with Remington, she had given little thought to leaving her closest friend behind.

"We will make Henry or Remington bring us to the other as often as we would like." Julia laid her head on Livie's shoulders. "I can't believe you'll be married soon, and then I'll be here alone."

"It will only be for a matter of days, and then you will be with Lord Heartford in your new home." Livie reminded her as they descended the stairs.

"With his mother and his uncle. I wish they were like Mother Di and lived separately. Perhaps she will marry again one day." Julia's voice was hopeful as they walked through the house.

"That reminds me, we must have tea with Lady Evers." Livie's voice wavered slightly, as she tried not to hold what the gossips printed about her and Remington against the lady. "We could do it tomorrow or after my wedding, but perhaps days before yours?"

"Tomorrow. After your wedding will be the week of my wedding, and I'm going to be too busy to entertain. I'm shocked you want to have tea with her at all. After everything they are printing in the gossips, her reputation is bound to affect yours," Julia huffed out as they walked into the breakfast room.

Livie's parents sat together. Her mother was holding on to her head, while her father gazed at his wife lovingly. Livie's thoughts went back to the previous night, and the teachings of Mother Di. The knowledge that her parents were more than likely engaged in marital acts the night before made her queasy.

The maid entered with the mail and the gossips. Livie stiffened, not wanting to hear more rumors about Lady Evers and the potential father of her child.

Livie was glad she hadn't been participating in any balls or functions as of late, since she was so busy planning her wedding.

It would be painful to see Bromswell again, especially after the incident outside of the modiste. She knew he was a foul man, but she could not help but to wonder what he meant.

"Karrington mentioned going away for a wedding trip. You didn't mention that to me?" her father questioned, looking up at her.

"Really? I had no idea" Excitement began to replace the doubts she had about Remington's intentions. He had planned a trip for the two of them, a sure sign of his commitment.

"My lord! I hope you haven't ruined a surprise." Her mother shook her head at her husband.

"Uncle, you must try to hold your tongue." Julia reached for a roll.

"I had no idea it was a secret. He mentioned it while we were all at O'Brien's before he left with Heartford to assist his sister." Lord Hempstead took a sip of his coffee.

"The duke left to assist Lady Evers?" Livie tried to control the negative thoughts that threatened to take over her mind.

"Yes. She was being evicted from her husband's townhome by his son. A footman told O'Brien all the sordid details. Heartford insisted the duke go with him." Lord Hempstead retold the story with little interest at all, but Livie caught every word.

Her mother picked up the gossips, but then sat them down, looking around the table at her family. "I can't believe this is one of our last meals together as a family under one roof." She dabbed at unshed tears. "Both my girls wed their first Season. I saw Lady Jameson yesterday, and she couldn't help but praise me on what wonderful matches my girls had made."

The family continued to eat breakfast, until Thomas entered the room. "Sir, Baron Bromswell is here to see you. He said it's urgent."

Livie stopped chewing, apprehension taking over her at the mention of Baron Bromswell.

"Whatever could he possibly want so early in the day?" Her mother picked up the gossip sheet and looked down. "Oh God."

Her face went ashen. Her father's brows drew together in a frown as he read over her shoulder. Livie knew immediately it was about Remington.

"I'll call him out!" her father shouted before turning to Thomas. "Bring Bromswell in here."

Livie sat in her chair, refusing to move as Julia and her parents all read from the paper. She didn't want to know what it said. It was no concern of hers. Whatever it was, they would get through it together.

Julia came and wrapped her arms around Livie. "Oh Livie, it says Remington caused the death of a girl!"

Gently but firmly, Livie pushed her cousin away, stood, and walked to her parents. She held her hand out in silent request for the paper.

"Oh my darling, I'm so sorry." Her mother passed it to her, tears in her eyes.

Livie scanned the paper.

"It would appear that our Bachelor Duke has a dark secret. A reliable source has informed us that the Duke of K was involved in the mysterious death of an unknown light skirt. Stay tuned as the saga unfolds, but our source says the duke is not what he appears to be."

"Baron Bromswell, Sir," Thomas announced then exited swiftly.

Livie looked up from the horrible article with tears in her eyes as Baron Bromswell entered the room looking smug.

"What are you doing here?" Livie spit out unable to hold her disdain for the man any longer. How dare he come to her home?

Baron Bromswell walked into the room. "I thought it was time your father knew the truth about Karrington, Lady Olivia."

She grounded her teeth together at the sound of his voice and how he said her name.

Her father walked beside her, pointing to the paper. "Does it have anything to do with this trash!"

"Yes, it's all true. Karrington murdered a girl ten years ago." Bromswell placed his hands on his hips, as if he wasn't ruining Livie's hopes and dreams.

Murdered?

She couldn't believe that Remington was capable of such a thing, it was like she knew nothing about the man that she was marrying in four days.

She shook her head, not willing to believe the baron. The room was spinning, her stomach felt sick. "How do you know?" Her voice quivered.

She hated how weak she sounded, but she was unable to be stronger.

"I think you, Julia, and your mother should go." Her father tried to reason with her, but she shook her head side to side.

"No." Everything was becoming increasingly difficult for her, speaking, breathing, everything.

Her mother stood quickly. "Come along Julia, Livie, let your father handle this—"

"I'm staying, Mother." Livie held her head high when all she wanted to do was run far away from everything.

Her father turned to object, but Livie glared at him, her head held high, shoulders firm. It was how Remington always presented himself in society, and she noticed it always commanded respect. She refused to be dismissed. This concerned her life, and she would not allow her father to make a decision without her.

She felt as if her world was crashing in around her. The pain threatened to consume her entire being, but she wouldn't let it, not in front of Baron Bromswell.

Her mother and Julia left the breakfast room, and she waited for the baron to speak.

Livie crossed her arms over her chest and glared at the man. Her father began nervously pacing back and forth, and she wished that she could go back to minutes ago when they were all happy as a family eating breakfast.

"It may surprise you all to know that Karrington and I were at Eton together. When we left, we spent a great amount of time together, doing what young, rich gentlemen do." The baron cleared his throat, his icy gaze on Livie.

"One day, when we were out enjoying the company of some ladies at a place of ill repute—"

"Livie, perhaps you should leave." her father interrupted, looking at her.

"I will not leave." Her voice was firm, but inside she was crumbling into a million tiny pieces.

Remington had never informed her of the connection between him and Baron Bromswell, but Livie knew there was mutual disdain.

"As I was saying, there was an incident that happened between Karrington and a young woman. I'm afraid she did not survive—"

"What?" Clearly, she had misheard. She could not comprehend the Remington she knew ever harming anyone, especially not a helpless woman.

Her father glared at Baron Bromswell. "You do not mean he harmed her?"

Livie shook her head repeatedly not believing that

Remington would do such a thing. How had he harmed the woman, was it an accident?

She didn't think he was capable of violence, but perhaps she was fooled by his charm and handsome face.

"I was not in the room. I only know that I heard the screams and came to investigate, only to arrive too late. The girl was undressed and dead." The baron shook his head in horror.

"Dear God!" Her father sat abruptly.

Livie clutched the table next to her for support. The tears that she tried so hard to contain fell without her permission. It couldn't be true, she knew Remington, didn't she? He would never harm anyone.

"That cannot be true. I know Karrington." Her father's words mirrored her thoughts.

Livie balled her hands into fists, trying to stop them from shaking uncontrollably. Her tears continued to fall.

"Forgive me, but it is true." Baron Bromswell had a slight smug smirk on his face. "Forgive me, I know this must come as a shock to you all, especially with the wedding only days away." He walked over to her father, placing his hand on the older man's shoulder. "There is only one way to stop Lady Olivia from being ruined, and that is for her to marry, but I worry about her safety if she were to marry Karrington."

Livie couldn't find her voice. So, that was his intention, to come here and gain her hand after no one else would have her.

She closed her eyes, not wanting to hear any more. If she did, surely she would collapse from the pain. "Leave, you vile despicable man," she yelled, having heard enough.

"Olivia! I know you are upset, but you must control yourself. It is not Bromswell's fault that we have been so deceived," her father insisted, but she ignored him.

Baron Bromswell looked taken back by Livie's anger, but she saw a flash of amusement in his cold gaze. "There is no need for apologies. I do understand that Lady Olivia is shocked to hear such news about Karrington. I just hope that she will see that marrying me is the best course of action."

"I won't marry you," Livie gritted out through clenched teeth.

Her father walked over and took her arm in a tight grip. "You will do whatever needs to be done to save your reputation and this family. I won't live forever. You need to think about your future!"

Livie stood up, facing off with her father. "I'd rather die a penniless spinster than be his wife. I won't do it, and you can't make me." She glared at him, causing him to take a step back.

"You will see that marrying me is your only option." Baron Bromswell gave her a sneer that turned her stomach, nearly causing her to recall her breakfast.

"Over my dead body."

Remington glanced from Hempstead to Bromswell and then finally to Livie.

She looked broken, and it was all his fault. The very thing he didn't want to do was happening, and he couldn't reach her in time to tell her the truth.

"What lies have you told them?" His body vibrated with anger.

"I told them the truth. The pretense is over. I've informed Hempstead about your part in that girl's terrible death all those years ago. The papers tell the entire story," Baron Bromswell announced triumphantly.

"You have some nerve coming here. My daughter is ruined! I trusted you Karrington!" Hempstead came to stand in front of Remington.

He turned to Livie, her tears like swords to his heart. "I swear to you none of it is true, Livie." His voice broke under the weight of her gaze.

"We both know that all of it is true. You killed that girl ten years ago—" Bromswell began but stopped abruptly upon seeing Remington's glare.

"That girl? Her name was Lillian, you heartless bastard, and you killed her!"

Bromswell took a step back, his gaze shifting around. Remington felt a small victory at the look on his face. He knew that Bromswell was not aware of his continued relationship with Lillian's family.

"Karrington! Control yourself." Hempstead placed a hand to Remington's chest to stop his pursuit of the baron.

"Is it true? Did you kill Lillian?" Livie asked, her voice small to his ears.

Rushing to her, he took her by the hand, shaking his head. "No, Livie. Please you must believe me."

She wrenched her hand free of his. "Believe you! How can I believe you when you've confided nothing to me?"

Remington turned back to Bromswell. "You accused me of killing Lillian Cooper? Have you really stooped so low?"

"It's the truth," Bromswell sneered.

"We both know that is not the truth. You killed Lillian all those years ago." Remington stalked the other man, intent on unleashing the fury of the Warren legacy on the vile creature.

"It's your word against mine." Bromswell looked victorious. "You're done, and now everyone knows that you're not the saint you pretend to be. How does it feel to be low like the rest of us?" he asked, giving Remington a sinister smirk.

His body vibrated with the urge to hit Bromswell again.

"I think you should leave, Karrington." The earl's eyes were cold and void of emotion, a look that Remington had seen from his own father. It was strange coming from who he thought was a friend.

"Hempstead, you can't be serious. Bromswell is lying, and I will prove my innocence to you and Olivia."

"Stop this façade, Karrington, there is no proof. Hempstead, if you want to save your daughter's reputation from this mess that Karrington has made, you will give your consent to our marriage." Bromswell's triumphant stance made Remington want to kill the bastard.

"I won't marry you," Livie said slowly, each word said with a fierceness that Remington had never seen before, and it filled him with pride. Until the stormy eyes he worshipped turned to him. "You lied to me." Tears pooled in her eyes, causing his heart to break in a million pieces.

He shook his head. "I didn't lie. I was ashamed for my part in Lillian's death. You must believe me, Livie. I did not kill her."

Livie straightened her shoulders, looking so much like a warrior to him. "You didn't confide in me, your future wife. I had to learn everything from Baron Bromswell and the gossips! Do you have any idea how absolutely humiliating that is!" she yelled, taking a step back. "The wedding is off." She walked past him and toward the door of the breakfast parlor. He rushed over to her taking her by the arm.

"Livie please!" His voice broke, and he could feel tears in his own eyes.

She stopped and faced him, the stormy gray eyes he loved so much, now dull and lifeless. "Goodbye, Your Grace."

She left the room, and Remington wanted to go after her and grovel at her feet. He loved her, and she wanted nothing to do with him.

Anger took over him and he turned toward Bromswell and punched him in the jaw. "Damn you! Damn you and your lies." He grabbed the other man by the lapels, slamming him against the wall.

"Karrington!" Hempstead shouted, rushing over to them.

"I buried Lillian Cooper three days after you brutally abused her and her friend Mary. So, don't you ever accuse me of killing her. That was you, you're the fucking monster, not me!" Remington shoved him against the wall before he released him.

"You have no proof," Bromswell sneered, wiping the blood from his lip.

"I have proof, and they will vouch for me." Remington swallowed, hoping that Livie would listen and know that he would never do such a thing.

He would clear his name and then he would prove to her that she was all that mattered in this world.

Hempstead's features were hard, no sign of the jovial gentleman Remington became friends with. "Is that true Bromswell, did you kill the girl and now accuse Karrington? Why would you do that? Why would you come into my home and lie?" Hempstead looked between the two enemies.

"The girl is dead, Hempstead. There is no proof, and now everyone knows that the great Duke of Karrington is a murderer. Your daughter is ruined, regardless." Baron Bromswell's cold voice made Remington want to pound the man even more.

"Your lies won't get you Lady Olivia's dowry," Remington stressed, glaring at the detestable man in front of him.

The baron shrugged his shoulders. "Maybe not, but now I have received something much more satisfying."

220

"What's that?" Remington clenched his hands, ready to land another punch on the baron's smug face.

"I got to take away the one person you really love. There will be other heiresses for me, but seeing you crumble was worth it." Bromswell straightened his jacket before walking to leave the room.

"Get out of my house, Bromswell." Hempstead stared at the other man in total disgust.

Bromswell shrugged his shoulders before he walked out of the room. Remington released the breath he was holding, the fear that Hempstead would force Livie to marry Bromswell gone.

Silence hovered over them. His head was bowed and he looked as if he aged years in the minutes that Remington had been there.

"I'm sorry, Karrington, you should leave as well." Hempstead turned around, his eyes wary as he looked at Remington.

"Please. I beg you to come with me so that I can prove my innocence," Remington pleaded, feeling a stray tear fall.

He hadn't cried since his mother died, but the fact that he may have lost Livie forever sliced through him like a knife.

"Even if you do prove your innocence, I'm afraid that Olivia may not forgive you," Hempstead said gravely.

"If she won't forgive me once I have cleared my name, then I will live without her forever, but I must try. Hempstead, I must try … I love her." Remington's voice broke, and he bowed his head ashamed of his tears.

"Very well," the earl agreed. I will go with you, and once your name is cleared, the rest is up to my daughter."

Remington breathed a sigh of relief. He would prove his innocence and he would win Livie back. If it was the last thing he ever did.

Chapter Twenty-Two

The Bachelor Duke and Lady O are no more! It appears that the duke's deep dark secret was too much for her. Or was there something more? Is the Bachelor Duke really the father of Lady E's child?

REMINGTON RAPPED ON THE DOOR OF THE SMALL home that sat behind a grocer in Cheapside.

The door opened, revealing a shocked Benedict Cooper, Remington's valet. "Your Grace, we saw the papers. My family is outraged."

"Yes, there's been a mistake. May we speak to your parents about … Lillian." Remington whispered the last part, watching as the younger man's face filled with sadness.

"Of course. Please come in." Benedict opened the door wider and moved aside, allowing the two gentlemen to pass.

The hall was filled with old paintings with a discolored wooden table against the wall.

"Benedict, allow me to introduce the Earl of Hempstead." Remington introduced the two men, waving his hand between them. "Hempstead, this is my valet."

The earl nodded in greeting, before they followed the young man to a tiny room where his parents were sitting, enjoying tea.

Mr. and Mrs. Cooper both looked up when Remington and Hempstead entered the tidy space that was filled with well-worn furnishings. A painting of Lillian Cooper sat above the mantle in a place of honor, fresh flowers on either side. She had been a lovely girl. The combination of her long red hair and hazel eyes made her look as if she was painted from a dream.

Her face had haunted him for years, her hazel eyes lifeless as he held her hand in his.

Mrs. Cooper, a robust, serious-looking woman with graying, brown hair, stood hurriedly when she saw the two gentlemen enter her parlor. "Yer Grace! We saw the lies in the gossip!"

"Mr. and Mrs. Cooper, forgive us for intruding. This is my acquaintance, the Earl of Hempstead—"

"Yes, Lady Olivia's father! We're sorry that all this is coming up now with yer wedding so close," Mrs. Cooper interrupted, her head shaking from side to side.

"Please make yerselves comfortable." Mr. Cooper nodded toward the sofa.

"Thank you." Remington looked from husband to wife as they sat down. "If you both are up to it, I would ask that we speak of Lillian's death. Baron Bromswell has wrongly accused me and I need to clear my name."

"That's a lie! It was Baron Bromswell who killed our Lilly and got away with it. No one cares about a girl from da slums. They didn't lay a finger on him, just let him walk free after he killed her. The nerve of that man accusing you, Your Grace." Her body shook with grief and anger, tears ran down her round face. "Lilly ran off fer a better life when she was only fifteen. Mr. Cooper was in da army, sending his commission home, but it wasn't enough ta feed us and keep a roof over our heads."

"After I lost me leg in da war, we could barely live. Both Lilly and Ben went to work, sending money home." Mr. Cooper shook his head, his hands gripping the armchair as if he was struggling to tell the story.

Mrs. Cooper nodded her head in agreement, continuing the story. "One day da constable came to where we were staying and informed us that our girl was murdered by a gentleman. They wouldn't tell us his name, but her friend Mary was with her. We went to visit her in da hospital, and that's where she told us everything.

"Mary was in da room as well, seems as if the gentleman was having a bit of fun with both of them. But Mary said he liked our Lilly best fer pain, yew see." Mrs. Cooper dabbed at her eyes, trying to catch the tears that fell freely.

Mr. Cooper pulled himself up, adjusting what was left of his leg. "We met the duke in the hospital, he was making arrangements for Lilly's body. Mary had told us everything, how da duke came into da room and stopped da bloody baron. He took both the girls to the hospital and stayed with them. Lilly died holding his hand and asking him to tell us that she loved us. Mary says that if it wasn't for the duke, she would've perished along with Lilly."

"No," Remington said, his voice full of pain and regret. "If it wasn't for me, Lillian would still be alive, and Mary wouldn't have suffered so greatly."

"What do you mean?" the earl asked, the shape of his round eyes reminding Remington of Livie.

"The night we went to the brothel, we were drinking to excess, gambling." Remington's shoulders slumped at the memories of his foolishness. "I was inebriated, hardly able to stand on my own. I was in another room with a girl when I heard the screams … I thought they were in my head at first, but they grew louder and louder. They were horrible, and I felt as if my heart were quet

being gripped within my body. In a place like that, no one would dare interrupt a lord to protect a working girl, but I couldn't stand by and allow it to continue."

He stopped to take a much-needed breath, his hands shook in his lap. After years of watching his father abuse his mother as a child, he knew the sounds of a woman being abused.

"I had to hold on to the wall to stand upright, but I followed the screams to where I knew Bromswell was with two girls. I burst in and was shocked at the scene in front of me." He stopped abruptly, taking a moment to compose himself. He could see it as if he was in that room once again. "Rage filled me, and I attacked Bromswell. I could not believe I had befriended such an animal."

What Remington did not reveal to the earl and the Coopers was that the entire scene reminded him of his childhood. Finding his father standing over his beaten mother when he was just a boy of five years old, Remington ran to him, hitting him with his small fist to no avail.

When he found Baron Bromswell standing over Lillian and Mary with his bloody walking stick, he had to save them. It was as if he was a little boy all over again, unable to protect his mother from his father. And yet he still could not save Lillian, a regret he would always carry.

"What you have done for our family is a far greater deed than we could ask for." Benedict gave his employer a small smile.

"Lilly chose her own path. It wasn't your fault." Mr. Cooper sat back in his chair, tears glistening in his eyes.

"If I were not so inebriated that night, Lillian would still be alive, and for that, I am very sorry." Remington placed his hand to his chest.

"Benedict has a good job, we have da store and a home. Mary is now a respectable woman living in Ireland with her

225

husband. Yew did not have ta do any of those things fer us. But yew did, Your Grace." Mrs. Cooper turned to the earl. "He's a kind man, nothing like Baron Bromswell."

"Thank you for saying that and for reliving the ordeal for the earl." Remington stood and turned to Hempstead, who sat shocked at the story. "We should be going; we've taken up enough of your time. I may need you all to confirm my innocence to the gossips as well."

"Whatever yew need, we will be happy to do it." Mr. Cooper gave him a firm stare, and Remington was relieved that he could depend on the Coopers.

"Thank yew fer coming, Your Grace. Yew know you're always welcome, and I expect yew ta bring Lady Olivia for dinner when she's da next Duchess of Karrington." She walked over to the duke, patting his shoulder as if he was a boy.

He nodded his head, unable to voice out loud that Livie would not be his duchess. To admit it would bring attention to the pain he felt in his chest. "Hempstead, are you ready?" Remington looked over to the earl, wondering if he had sealed his fate by revealing his deepest, darkest secret.

The earl shook his head, standing abruptly. "Yes, thank you both for telling me the truth."

Silence followed them out of the small home and into the waiting carriage. Hempstead stared out into the crowded streets of London.

"Hempstead …" Remington said, waiting on the man to acknowledge him. When their eyes met, Remington cleared his throat. He knew what he wanted, more than anything in this world. "If Livie will forgive me for keeping the truth about Lillian from her, I am going to marry her. Do you have any objections?"

Hempstead shook his head vehemently. "No, I have none. What about the rumors about you and Lady Evers?"

Remington pinched the bridge of his nose, tired of the damned gossips and their assumptions. "They are false. I assisted Heartford with Lady Evers yesterday evening, and they both stayed at my townhome because the lady and her child were put out on the street like trash. Heartford took her to look for a new place this morning. Once I saw the gossips, I came straight to speak with Livie." He felt exhausted from the day he had and wanted nothing but to lay himself at Livie's mercy.

He was nothing without her, and he had to win her back. He loved her, more than his own life. Now he just had to prove it.

Chapter Twenty-Three

Does the Bachelor Duke have a child?
It seems our duke may be the father of Lady E's child! Witnesses saw him
come to their aid, and now she and the babe are staying at his townhome.
No word on how Lady O is taking the news.

NATHAN, THE BARON OF BROMSWELL, stormed into his meager home in a rage. Damn Karrington and damn Lady Olivia for refusing to marry him. He had hoped that the information he gave the gossips and Hempstead would've made the spineless man make his daughter marry him.

Walking into the small empty parlor, Nathan found Josephine, Lady Windchester, sitting on his threadbare sofa drinking the last of his wine. Curse her, she knew his funds were low, and simple things like wine were becoming further and further out of his reach.

"What are you doing here? Isn't your mother or husband wondering where you are?" He removed his hat and threw it on an armchair.

"My mother is having tea with Lady Wilcox and Lady Jameson. As for my husband, if I have to see his fucking happy face another second, I'm sure I'll kill him." She took a sip of wine. "Especially after the news he delivered to me this morning."

He sat down beside her, eyeing her suspiciously. "What has the oaf done now? You really could've married better."

She sat back in a huff shaking her head. "He's gone and ruined every damn thing. He is the father of that harlot Lady Evers' child, and he wants to be with them."

"I'm sure your mama will delight in cutting you both off. That was her one rule, was it not, no bastards from either of you?" Nathan raised an eyebrow in challenge, crossing his long legs.

"Yes. That's precisely why I must handle the brat and the whore who had her." Josephine took a gulp of wine, grimacing slightly. "The nerve of Windchester, thinking I would allow him to leave me for her."

"That entire group has always been a pain, especially Karrington. I needed that fucking dowry!" His voice was cold, his fist balled tight. "I was looking forward to breaking Lady Olivia, too, but she had to go and insist that she wouldn't marry me."

"So, your plan for Karrington and Lady Olivia didn't work? Did she forgive him?" she asked with interest.

"No, she ended their engagement, and I swear he was going to cry like a babe. I think he loves the chit."

He couldn't believe that the cold Karrington he hated all these years was in love. Karrington's suffering brought Nathan immense pleasure. If only he could cause him pain permanently.

"Well, that's disappointing, but I knew he had terrible taste when he refused me last Season. Perhaps I can get him into bed now with Lady Olivia gone." Josephine stood a little perkier at the thought.

"Don't get too excited, I'm sure she will forgive him. Karrington always wins." He propped his feet up on the table thinking of how to make the duke pay.

Nathan watched as she deflated before she turned to face him. "I need your help getting rid of the whore and bastard."

He sat up suddenly; an idea had come to him. "I'm in, only if we add Lady Olivia to our plans."

Lady Windchester barked out a sinister laugh. "You want to kill Lady Olivia? Why?"

"Because I want him to know what it's like to have nothing." Nathan rose, feeling much better now that he had vengeance on his mind.

Josephine walked over to him, seductively running her hand up his chest. "I'm listening."

Karrington and that cow would pay for ruining his plans. He was tired of having nothing, of being nothing, while men like Karrington had everything. Nathan had used the duke's hatred of his father to help him squander the dukedom's coffers.

It was all going splendid until the night he took Karrington to one of his preferred brothels, where they never cared what Nathan did to the girls. It all went up in flames.

Damn Karrington for interrupting. It wasn't really Nathan's fault he killed her, he simply got carried away. It was the first time he had lost himself completely, but not the last.

After that incident, Karrington made his life a living hell for years, shutting doors that would usually be open to him. No, it was time he knew exactly what it felt like to be Nathan. The only way to make that happen was to take away the one person the duke had allowed himself to love.

Lady Olivia St. John.

After returning Hempstead to his townhome, a despondent Remington walked up the steps of his home. Livie had refused to see him.

He'd lost her.

"Your mother is in the parlor, along with Lady Evers and Lord Heartford," Dayton said.

Remington stopped walking and ran his hand through his hair. He didn't feel like being around anyone, especially his mother, and why the hell was Lady Evers still here?

"Please have the staff prepare for my departure tomorrow. When Benedict returns from his parents, have him pack my things." Remington instructed in a lifeless tone.

"Sir? What about the new duchess?" Dayton asked, his voice sounding as confused as Remington felt.

She would not be his duchess.

"There will not be a new duchess, Dayton." A part of him crumbled as the words came out of his mouth.

Remington wanted nothing more than to drown himself in a glass of brandy. Deciding it was best to face his mother now, he took a deep breath before he walked into the parlor.

His mother was bouncing Emily on her lap but looked up when she heard him enter. "All will be well," she said, and it unnerved him that she was always tried to be positive when he was upset.

When he was a boy, she had an uncanny ability of knowing just when he needed her, but even she would not be able to help him.

"It is not important. May I ask why all of you are in my home?" He saw Lady Evers bristle, and he felt bad for being so disagreeable, but he just wanted to be alone with his heartbreak.

"Lady Evers' new townhome will not be ready until

tomorrow. So we wanted to impose on your good nature one more day," Heartford said in his usual cheery voice.

"Of course, please stay as long as you need. I'm leaving for Hemsworth Place tomorrow, so the townhome will be empty—"

His mother passed the baby to Lady Evers before she stood. "What are you talking about? The wedding is in four days."

Remington swallowed and avoided eye contact with his mother. "Lady Olivia called the wedding off and is refusing to see me. I'm sure the St. Johns will inform everyone soon."

Silence filled the room, and Remington saw pity in everyone's eyes. He hated that look, and couldn't bear it at the moment. He didn't deserve or want their pity, he wanted Livie.

He wanted to grow old, have children, and make love to her for eternity, but she no longer wanted him.

"I'm sure it's just a misunderstanding. Surely she doesn't believe you killed that girl?" Mother Di asked, and he forced a sad smile.

"I believe it has more to do with the fact that I did not inform her of it. Since she is refusing to see me, I can't be sure." He walked past his mother, going to the sideboard to pour himself a much-needed drink.

"I'm sorry, Karrington. We can find some other place to stay tonight. I've written Evers and will get the remainder of my things in the morning," Lady Evers said from behind him.

"You and Emily are more than welcome to stay with me," Remington heard his mother say as he gulped down the brandy.

"Karrington, are you all right?" Heartford asked from beside him.

"I've lost her, Henry." He poured more brandy, trying not to cry—again. Drinking would numb the pain.

"May I speak to my son alone?" His mother's voice was soft but demanding.

Heartford squeezed his shoulder before he walked away. Remington heard the door close but refused to turn around and face his mother.

"Remington, you have to fight for her." He could feel her standing behind him.

It annoyed him how simple she made it sound. Throwing his head back, he let out a humorless chuckle. "She won't see me, Mother Di."

"Look at me!" she yelled at his back.

Remington turned around, his eyes were now blurry with unshed tears.

"You love her—"

"Yes, I love her, damn it! I love her so much that I can't breathe without her, but she doesn't want me, Mother!" he shouted, so angry at himself for believing that he could have any type of happiness.

"Fine then, give up. Run back to Hemsworth Place! Forget about Livie. It doesn't matter that you love her and she loves you." His mother stood glaring at him.

Remington blinked several times, not believing his mother's words.

His breath stuttered. "S-She loves me?"

"Yes, you fool of a man." She placed her gloved hand on his cheek wiping his tears like she did when he was a boy. "Now fight for her."

He nodded briefly, making up his mind to allow her some time. Tomorrow, he would go to her and fall at her feet. Livie loved him and nothing else mattered.

Chapter Twenty-Four

The Bachelor Duke cleared!
While Lady O is crying over her ended engagement. Mothers and daughters
all over England can rejoice that our duke is not a monster. Perhaps there is
hope for us all to wed him now that Lady O supposedly has snubbed him.

LIVIE AWOKE THE NEXT DAY, EYES RED AND PUFFY, feeling as if she had been run over by a carriage. She laid in her large brass bed surrounded by decorative pillows wishing that she could just go back to sleep. The grief from losing Remington and the lies he told her were heavy on her heart.

She knew he was innocent of Lillian's death, but she couldn't forget how he had lied to her. Before yesterday, all her hopes and dreams were coming to fruition, and now it was all gone in the course of a day.

The pain was too great and she wanted nothing more than to fall into a deep, dreamless abyss.

She did not want to face society. They were correct, she was plump, and he was the Bachelor Duke. Why would he want her?

He had never said he loved her. Every touch, or kiss implied something deeper, but perhaps it was just the heat of the moment.

She heard someone enter her room, and moments later the bed dipped. A firm hand began rubbing her back. She knew it was her mother. It reminded her of when she was small, a simple back rub from her mother would cure whatever it was that ailed her. It would not be that simple now that she was no longer a little girl.

The previous evening her father told her everything after he returned from the Coopers with Remington. She refused to see him, knowing there would just be more lies. He didn't trust her enough to tell her the truth, and that hurt more than anything.

Livie turned over and saw her mother's sad smile. Livie was thankful she had her family at this time. They were all she had.

"Abigail is bringing your breakfast up. Don't worry about getting out of bed today." Her mother kissed the top of her head.

"I'm sorry I called off the wedding," Livie whispered, wiping at the tears that were forming again.

"Oh darling, it's fine. If you can't forgive the duke, I understand. Whatever you decide, I will always support you."

"He doesn't love me, Mother. He didn't trust me enough to tell me his deepest secret. It was all a lie." She hugged her mother tightly and cried.

Her mother gently pushed her away and raised her chin, so that they were eye to eye. "Olivia, this is your choice, but I've watched you two together. I know love when I see it, and the duke does love you, my darling girl."

Tears fell down her face, and she felt her heart breaking all over again. Livie wished her mother was correct, but he never declared his love for her. If he loved her, she may have forgiven him, but the fact that he didn't trust her enough to tell her about Lillian, proves that he doesn't love her.

Her mother gave her a small smile, before she stood. "Stay in bed for the rest of the day. I will send out missives informing the guests the wedding has been canceled."

Livie nestled into her bed. She heard whispers until the door closed.

Her mind wandered to the proposal at Talbert Abbey, remembering his words, his kiss, no one would ever replace Remington in her heart. He ruined her for any other man.

The door opened and Abigail came in with a tray, her head bowed. "Oh Livie, I'm so sorry about the duke."

"Thank you," Livie whispered, watching her friend closely as she sat the tray down.

Abigail picked up a missive on the tray. "This came for you, it was delivered to the kitchens by a maid. I'm worried it will just upset you more."

Livie blinked, her hand shaking as she held it out. "What is it?"

She handed Livie the missive. "It's from Lady Evers. There have been more rumors about she and the duke," Abigail said in a quiet voice.

Livie threw her head back, letting out a frustrated groan. She wished she didn't care, wished her heart wasn't shattered into pieces, but it was, and she did care. She had to know the truth about the man she had planned to marry.

If he had lied to her about Lillian's death and his involvement, then he could've lied about his relationship with Lady Evers.

Livie looked down at the missive in her hand and ripped it open. Her eyes quickly scanned the words feeling another bout of tears threaten. Why would Lady Evers write such a thing if there was no relationship between them?

Looking down at the letter one last time, Livie set her shoulders, her resolve firm. "I'm going to see Lady Evers. If my parents ask about me, tell them I'm in bed, don't let Mother come check on me." She stood and walked around the room, grabbing a day dress that was laid out.

"Livie, no!" Abigail tried to reason with her.

Livie handed her the letter. "No. I want her to tell me. After all, she sent this for a reason, and it says for me to come alone!" Livie pointed to the note; her mind made up. "I'll return before anyone knows I'm missing."

Livie pulled the nightdress over her head, before she stepped into the simple day dress and went over to Abigail to lace it up.

"Livie, please don't do this. Why go if the engagement is off?"

Abigail finished tying the gown and Livie rushed to the armoire, pulling out a pelisse.

"I need to know if he lied about Lady Evers as well." Livie put on the pelisse, and gave Abigail one last look. She fled the room, down the servants' steps, through the kitchen, and out the door.

Livie took a deep breath as she stood in front of the three-story townhouse. She looked around noticing a carriage with the Oakhaven crest on it. She found that odd, not knowing of any connection between Lady Evers and the Earl of Windchester's wife. The driver and another man stood eyeing her, their cold eyes unnerved Livie, and she quickly turned back to the door.

She rapped the knocker twice then nervously ran her hands through the side of her hair for any loose strands.

The door opened, revealing the maid. "Yes?"

"Lady Olivia St. John to see Lady Evers." Livie gave a brief nod.

"Lady Olivia! Please come in. We weren't expecting you," the maid said, taking Livie by surprise.

Surely, Lady Evers was expecting her since she sent the missive. Livie followed the maid through the empty home that was void of any personal belongings.

Lady Evers was in the parlor, a small number of items in her hands when she turned to face them. She blinked several times looking at Livie.

"Lady Olivia, what a surprise. Are Karrington and Henry with you?" Lady Evers placed the objects down on the table.

Livie's brow crinkled as she concentrated. Was the woman playing a game with her? "No, you sent me a missive," Livie said in annoyance, waving her hand towards Lady Evers.

This was becoming very confusing to Livie, all she wanted to do was stay in her bed and cry. She was already in a foul mood with the cancellation of her wedding. Any time she thought about Remington, tears threatened to fall, and she couldn't cry if she was to face the woman the gossips said had his child.

"I assure you I did not send you a missive. I've been too occupied trying to secure a new home so that I can leave your home, before you are the next duchess." Lady Evers shook her head walking over to Livie.

Through her confusion, Livie thought of Remington and how she would never share his life. "That cannot be. I received a letter from you stating that you wished to speak to me about the duke's connection to you and your child."

Lady Evers tilted her head to the side as if she was trying to solve a difficult problem. She sat down on the sofa, her hands clasped on her lap. She looked at Livie and patted beside her. "Please sit down. I'm sorry you came all this way alone."

Livie sat down on the opposite end of the sofa. Her body

was tired, and she ached all over from the loss of Remington and the life they could have had.

"Lucy, if everything is loaded in the carriage, please take it to the new townhome." Lady Evers requested to her maid.

"Should I take Emily with me?" Lucy asked, from behind Livie.

"No, let her sleep. Send the carriage back for us once it is all unpacked, I'm sure Henry or William will accompany it."

"Very well." Livie heard Lucy respond.

Lady Evers took Livie by the hand. She looked up into clear green eyes and gave her a watery smile.

"Lady Olivia, you must know that there is no connection between Karrington and I. He was kind enough to let my daughter and I stay with him these two days, but that is it." She squeezed Livie's hand and gave her an encouraging smile. "I honestly have never seen the man in such a state. He looked as if he would cry when he informed us you wouldn't see him. He loves you dearly. The papers are wrong."

There it was again.

Love.

"I-I don't understand if you didn't send the missive who did, and why hint at a connection between the two of you?" Livie felt more and more confused.

"I'm not sure. Someone wants to come between you and Karrington. Do you have any idea who would do that?" Lady Evers relaxed back on the sofa.

"Baron Bromswell is slightly obsessed with my dowry, and I recently found out that he and Remington share a past. I just don't understand why insinuate that Remington is your child's father." Livie sighed in frustration, wondering why anyone would want her to believe that Lady Evers' child was Remington's.

"I don't like this. Once Lucy sends the carriage back, we will get you home. I'm not sure if Karrington has left by now—"

"Left? Left for where?" Livie asked in a panic.

For Hemsworth Place. Lady Olivia—"

Her heart felt as if it were breaking all over again.

"Livie. Please call me Livie, after all, it is I who is intruding on you." Livie gave her a small smile, wishing she could snap out of the melancholy she felt.

"Then I shall be Amelia." She gazed off toward the window, avoiding eye contact with Livie. "I feel that I may have some blame in you and Karrington's parting." Amelia clasped her hands together.

"I was upset with the constant rumors in the gossip. You also did seem very familiar with him. Then after the news of Lillian Cooper's death came out. I wondered if perhaps he lied to me about the relationship he had with you." Livie admitted, feeling as if she had been fooled by the gossips and society.

"The only relationship is that Karrington is Emily's cousin through her father, Lord Windchester." Amelia looked down and picked a piece of lint from her dress.

Livie's mouth fell open. The earl was married to Lady Windchester, although the couple seemed to have some sort of arrangement. "The Earl of Windchester is your daughter's father?"

"Yes." Amelia let out a weary sigh, exhaustion evident on her pretty face. "We began an affair last season. William was funny, kind, and unlike any other gentleman I'd ever met. We talked and laughed, and he actually cared for my opinion," she chuckled, a wistful look on her face. "His family estate was bankrupt, and he refused to borrow the money from Karrington. He needed to marry a lady with a fortune. I did not have one and I never wanted to marry again after my first husband died."

"Do you love him?" Livie inquired.

Amelia placed her fingers to her lips, pulling at the corner. "I did not think I was capable of loving anyone, after I was forced to marry a cruel older man." She closed her eyes shuddering. "I fell in love with William, but when he married Josephine, he broke my heart. I discovered I was with child three days after his marriage."

Livie squeezed her hand understanding the heartbreak that Amelia must have felt. "I'm sorry, Amelia. You must have felt so alone during that time."

"I did, but I had Lucy, my maid, who has been with me since I was a girl. I decided to go to France and have Emily. I stupidly returned thinking I could hide Emily while I settled my affairs."

"Perhaps you can still escape society, but I'm afraid their reach is long. If only I could go with you," Livie said with a sad smile. She knew no matter where she went, she would never escape her love for Remington.

Amelia stood, laughing. "Although, I would enjoy your company, I'm sure Karrington would search until the edges of the earth to get you back." She began walking toward the door, and Livie rose to follow her out. "If William displayed half of the emotions that Karrington showed for you yesterday, I would forgive him. Unfortunately, the only thing he has done is to inform his wife that he is Emily's father."

Following her up the stairs, Livie's mind was on Remington. When she returned home, she would send him a missive, insisting they talk.

They entered the second-floor nursery, careful not to make any noise. Livie glanced around the bare room while Amelia went to the baby's steel cot and peered down.

241

Walking over to the cot, Livie saw the beautiful baby sleeping peacefully.

Amelia looked up at Livie. "She's the only good thing that has ever happened to me, Livie. I will always want and love her no matter what. My mother nor my real father have shown me any love."

Livie squeezed Amelia's hand. "That is what a dutiful parent should do, what your parents should've done for you."

It was difficult for her to understand parents mistreating their children since her parents always loved and cherished her and Julia.

A noise from downstairs grabbed their attention. "That was rather quick of Lucy," Amelia said as she grabbed the last of the baby's things.

Livie took what Amelia could not carry and followed her back downstairs.

"Lucy, did you return with Henry?" Amelia asked as they walked into the parlor, their hands full.

Suddenly, Amelia came to an abrupt stop causing Livie to run into her back, dropping the baby's things she was carrying on the ground.

Before Livie could inquire what caught her attention, she was grabbed by force and pulled against a manly chest. She looked around the room frantically and saw a man holding Amelia by the throat.

"Hello, Lady Olivia."

Livie froze hearing the cold menacing voice of Baron Bromswell at her ear.

"There isn't much time. Let's tie them up quickly," Lady Windchester said from in front of the fireplace.

Livie began struggling in Baron Bromswell's arms, fear

consuming her. She kicked at his shins, tried to scratch his hands and face, but he did not release her.

"I do like a woman who fights," he whispered in her ear, causing revulsion to course through her.

"What are you doing here?" Amelia demanded, as the man holding her flung her in a chair nearly causing her to fall.

"I want you and the bastard gone ... for good, and Bromswell has a score to settle with Karrington." Lady Windchester informed her sweetly as if she was speaking about the weather and not the death of innocent people.

Panic seized Livie as she saw Amelia's wide tear-filled eyes. Livie fought the baron with every ounce of strength she possessed. She would not fall victim to this cruel man.

"Lady Olivia, I see you received my note." Lady Windchester gave Livie a cold smile that sent terror through her.

"No! Release us!" she yelled, not believing that two members of society would behave in such a way. Bromswell slapped a thin hand across her mouth, muffling her cries.

"We're going to give them what they want, and I promise you, we'll get out of here." Amelia's voice was calm, calmer than Livie felt.

"You're a fool if you think we'll let either of you go. Josephine here really needs you and your bastard gone." Bromswell released his grip on her mouth, taking hold of Livie's arm.

"No! Emily is just a babe, please!" Amelia screeched.

"You can't do this! I demand you release us!" Livie screamed at Baron Bromswell, as he dragged her to a chair.

He laughed at her. "You have no power here. You should've agreed to marry me. Now you will be duchess of the ashes."

"You're evil. You killed Lillian Cooper and tried to blame

Remington. What do you plan to do with us!" Livie shouted, looking from Bromswell to Lady Windchester.

Bromswell gripped Livie's arm tighter. "We're going to kill you."

All the air deflated from Livie, and she felt as if she could not move. Kill them? Her mind went to her family, and Remington. The thought of never seeing any of them again, shattered her heart and soul.

"With Lady Evers and the bastard gone, my allowance from my mother will continue." Lady Windchester began starting a fire with the tinderbox.

"Your death will ruin Karrington. It appears he loves you, and what better way to make him pay than to take you away." Baron Bromswell flung her in the chair and one of the henchmen began tying a rope around her body. "Forever."

"No! No! Please stop this, Josephine. Emily and I will go away. I'll do whatever you want, just let Emily go. She's just a baby!" Amelia cried, struggling against the rope restraining her.

The henchmen started throwing things around the room, and Livie watched horrified as they lit candles from the fireplace. They began setting them around the room and sheer panic seized Livie.

"You're both crazy! You can't do this to us!" Livie cried, looking around wildly.

"Leave the bastard upstairs. No one will get to her." Bromswell turned to Josephine. "We have to go," he shouted taking a candle from one of his accomplices.

"Stop! Help!" Amelia yelled furiously.

Lady Windchester picked up a small figurine from the small pile Amelia had on the table and violently struck her with it. "I look forward to you and your daughter's death."

Livie watched horrified as Amelia's head lolled to the side, blood spilling down her face.

Dread and defeat filled Livie. She did not know how they would ever escape the fire. Her mind went to the last time she saw Remington, the devastation in his eyes when she announced the engagement was off.

Tears ran freely down her face as it came to her, clear and bright as a summer day. Remington loved her.

Chapter Twenty-Five

Fire in Mayfair!

LIVIE COULDN'T BELIEVE THAT SHE WAS GOING TO DIE. She was going to die without telling Remington that she loved him. She looked over at Amelia, who was bleeding profusely. This entire ordeal didn't feel real to her.

Lady Windchester bent down in front of Livie. "I'll be sure to comfort Karrington in my bed. He'll be too distraught to refuse me."

"You're mad!" Livie screamed, horrified by the two evil creatures.

Fear rocked her body as she watched a henchman set the drapes on fire.

"Goodbye, Lady Olivia. I am sad I won't get your dowry." Bromswell bent down and gave her a hard kiss on the lips.

Anger fueled Livie, and she bit his bottom lip hard until she tasted the bitterness of his blood.

Baron Bromswell wrenched away from her. "You bitch!" He slapped her across the face. The strike was so hard, it caused her teeth to rattle. She blinked several times, her vision now blurry.

"Let's go before we burn with them!" Lady Windchester's voice was piercing and afraid as the fire began taking on its own mission, spreading quickly through the room.

"Amelia!" Livie screamed, worried when she did not get a response. "Amelia! Wake up!" She wiggled and moved, trying to free herself.

"I'm up … Emily. You have to save Emily." Amelia blinked several times as blood poured into her eye. "She's upstairs in the nursery … promise me." Her voice was desperate, her green eyes pleading.

"No." Livie coughed, trying to speak through the heavy cloud of smoke. "We will both get out of here and go get her to-gether." Livie's voice was soothing, so much calmer than she felt.

Inside she felt helpless and wanted nothing more than to give up and allow the fire to consume her. But Livie had to fight for herself, for little Emily upstairs, for Amelia, and Remington. She had to fight for all of them.

She had to get out of there, so that society could know what monsters Baron Bromswell and Lady Windchester were.

Livie wiggled from side to side, pulling her arms up as she did it. She was accustomed to trying to fit in a gown once she out-grew them, for no other reason than to prove her mother wrong about her addiction to sweets. She jerked her hand through, feel-ing the burn of the rope on her wrist. Livie pulled at the ropes with her free hand, trying to ignore the heat that seemed to grow by the second.

"Livie! Go save Emily!" Amelia pleaded.

Ignoring her, Livie went to pull on Amelia's ropes. Amelia shook her head, causing blood to fly onto Livie's pelisse. "No! Please! Go! … Please."

Livie stopped working on the ropes and rose to her feet. She glanced frantically around the room, taking in the fire. "I'll come back for you. I'll get Emily and come back for you."

Running out of the parlor, Livie was met by fire. It was

engulfing the entire front hall of the townhome and traveling up the stairs, officially blocking them.

"Oh my God," she cried, pulling at her hair.

Quickly, she ran toward the back of the home, pushing the door open to the servants' stairs that led down to the kitchen. Thankfully, they weren't burning—yet. She ran up the steps, trying to move quickly as she ran to the nursery.

She found Emily crying in her cot, the heat and smell of the smoke so thick she could barely breathe.

"Shh, it's going to be okay. We're going to go get your mama now." Livie took off her pelisse and looked around the room.

She found a basin of water and poured it on the pelisse, soaking it. She then tore a piece of her chemise, wetting it as well and wrapped it around her face, trying to block the smoke from suffocating her. She took Emily and covered her in a blanket, placing the pelisse over the baby's face.

The fire was everywhere, and she feared she wouldn't be able to get them out. Squaring her shoulders, she ran out into the burning hallway, determined to get to Amelia and save them all.

Remington took a deep breath as the carriage stopped in front of the Hempstead's townhome, and he quickly disembarked. He was going to fight for her. He loved Livie and would not give up on them.

The smell of smoke pierced his nose, and he looked up to the sky, noticing a fire beginning not far away.

"Looks like it's going to be a bad one if they don't get control over it." His driver voiced, looking in the far-off distance.

A prickling feeling crept up the back of Remington's neck as he made his way to the door. Thomas, the butler, opened it, and Remington handed him his hat and gloves.

When he followed the butler into the parlor, Hempstead, Lady Hempstead, Julia, and Abigail stood around wide-eyed. They all turned toward him when he entered.

"What is going on?" Remington asked, seeing everyone's distress.

"Your Grace, thank goodness you're here. Have you seen Livie?" Lady Hempstead's voice was frantic, her eyes filled with tears and utter fear.

"What do you mean? Where is she?" Remington's hands gripped at his sides, trying to control the panic that was now seizing him.

Gone. She was gone.

"We do not know. She was in her room resting but when Lady Hempstead went to check on her, she was nowhere to be found." Hempstead began pacing back and forth.

No, he couldn't lose her like this, he had to find her. Remington looked over at the maid who was avoiding eye contact with him, tears in her eyes. "Abigail do you know where Livie is?"

Abigail looked down at her feet, her hands in her pockets. "T-There was a note from Lady Evers, and she went to her to discuss the duke."

"To discuss what exactly?" Remington asked hurriedly.

Abigail cleared her throat several times, her face reddening. Her dark eyes avoided looking into his. She took a missive out of her dress pocket and passed it to him. "She wanted to know if you were the father of Lady Evers' child."

He tore open the letter.

Lady Olivia,
I would like to meet you in person, so that we can discuss the duke and my
connection more in-depth. This is a sensitive matter and needs discretion.
Please come to my townhome at 22 Mount Street alone.
Lady Evers

"This makes no sense! Lady Evers wouldn't write this. There is no connection between us." Remington was dumbfounded as he read the words over and over.

Lady Hempstead walked over to him as her husband reached out his hand for the note. Remington thrust the missive into Hempstead's waiting hand in frustration.

"Is there a possibility ... the child—" Hempstead began but was cut short by Remington's hard glare.

"No. The child is Windchester's!" Remington yelled in anger, livid over all the damn gossip.

"Karrington, perhaps I should look for her since the engagement was called—"

Remington turned around, glaring at Hempstead. "Try to stop me Hempstead and see what will happen."

He turned to leave, prepared to go to Lady Evers and demand she explain the absurd letter, but suddenly he knew it wasn't her.

Lady Hempstead's voice shook. "I don't understand why Lady Evers would send this then?"

"She didn't write this. When I spoke to her the night she was evicted from her townhome, her only concern was for Livie's reputation." He shook his head, absently. "She cared more about Livie than she did for herself and her child."

Heartford walked into the parlor and took in the mood of everyone, noticing how tense they were. "Is everything all right?"

Julia ran to him, wrapping her arms around him. "Oh, Henry, Livie's missing, and we think she went to your sister's."

"I'm going to Lady Evers' townhome to find out what the hell is going on," Remington said.

"The streets are blocked. There's a fire on Mount. I hoped Amelia was on her way to the new townhome by now. I left Windchester there since he refused to leave me be," Heartford rushed out, noticing the color had drained from everyone's faces.

"A fire? Olivia went to Mount!" Lady Hempstead yelled in horror. Remington rushed out of the room, outside, and into his carriage.

"Get me as close to Mount Street as you can!" he demanded of his driver as Heartford ran from the house and jumped into the carriage with him.

"What the hell is going on?" Heartford's voice was bewildered.

Remington shook his head. "I don't know. Someone sent Livie a letter pretending to be Lady Evers, insisting they discuss my involvement with her and her child."

"Who would do that? We all know you have no connections with Emily." Heartford's leg bounced up and down.

"I know. I just pray that fire is nowhere near them." Remington's voice was shaky as the carriage bounced over the uneven cobblestone.

The carriage came to a halt as crowds of people ran past it, causing it to jostle roughly. Remington opened the carriage door, standing to see ahead.

"It's blocked off, sir."

Panic started to run through him. Remington peered ahead on Mount Street, noticing the crowd going further down near Lady Evers' old townhome.

CECILIA RENE

"Heartford, let's go!" he screamed, jumping out of the carriage into a sea of bodies and running as fast as his long legs would take him.

"What is it!" Heartford yelled as he ran beside Remington.

"I think Amelia's townhome is on fire! Livie, is in there!" The words were wrenched from Remington's lips. He prayed to God that he was wrong, and that for once, his senses had failed him.

They reached the fire brigade, who was using a pump and a hose to try to stop the massive fire that had spread to four other homes.

"Good God!" Remington screamed, his heart lodged in the pit of his stomach.

"Amelia!" Heartford gasped as he looked up at the large fire swirling out of control.

Remington searched frantically for Livie in the crowd, but she was nowhere to be found. He grabbed one of the men holding the hose.

"Has anyone been taken out of twenty-two! My fiancée was there, along with Lady Evers and her child," Remington demanded, his voice on the verge of hysteria. The fear was like nothing he'd ever felt before.

Remington couldn't lose her. Dear God, he couldn't lose her like this. Once she was safe, if she never wanted to see him again, he would gladly stay away from her as long as she was alive. He couldn't lose his Livie. It would be like losing his own heart, and how could one live without a heart?

"No, sir, I'm sorry, but if anyone was there, they're gone. The front is blocked by fire." The man bowed his head.

Remington's felt cold all over. His mind went wild, and he took off running.

The servants' entrance! There had to be a way in, and he would find it no matter what! The corner of the stately, three-story terrace house had a servants' entrance not yet consumed by fire.

His mind was set on one thing as he ran ahead and past the crowd. "Sir! Stop! Stop!" He heard a man scream, but he kept moving, adrenaline pumping through his veins.

Heartford joined him as Remington kicked furiously at the servants' door, causing it to burst open, releasing a cloud of dark smoke.

Without further thought, Remington lunged into the burning townhome—thinking only of Livie.

Livie carefully edged her and Emily past a fallen beam on the second floor. The ceiling was caving in on her, and she still needed to make it down the servants' stairs and back to Lady Evers. Two flights of stairs, in a burning house. She had no idea if she could do it, but she had to try. She couldn't die here—wouldn't die here—and if she could help it, she wouldn't let Emily or her mother perish either.

Her hands squeezed Emily tightly to her chest, checking every now and again that she was well. She was afraid she would drop her, so she clung to her desperately. The baby constantly whimpered in her arms, a sound that thrilled Livie, because she knew Emily was alive and well.

Livie cleared the burning beam, relief fueling her momentarily at her accomplishment.

The smoke was so thick that a cough consumed her. Pulling the rag down that was covering her face she yelled, "Help! Help!"

Her voice was desperate as she struggled to breathe with the smoke growing around her.

Livie reached the servants' stairs, so happy that the first part of her task was over. She took off running toward the clear space, hope filling her that they all would survive.

Taking the stairs as fast as she could, she was careful not to trip while carrying the baby. When she was near the first floor, she felt relief build inside of her, knowing that she only had one more flight to go before she was in the kitchen. Livie stopped walking, barely able to see from all the smoke and ash in front of her.

Debris from the ceiling was falling all around, and she feared another beam would come crashing down on them. She could sense the heat from the first floor and feared it was covered in flames. She desperately needed to find a way to get to Amelia. Perhaps she could get Emily outside and come back for her mother.

"Livie! Livie!" The sound of Remington's deep voice could be heard through the fog of the smoke.

"Remington!" Livie yelled, so happy to hear him. Her heart soared at the thought of him risking his own life to save her.

Love for him took over her, and she wanted nothing but to fling herself into his arms and forget about everything.

"Livie! Thank God! Thank God!" he screamed, coming into view in front of her eyes.

He took a step forward until parts of the ceiling fell between them, making a large hole in the stairs and bursting the door of the first floor open. Fire came gushing out of it, causing Livie to scream and press herself and Emily against the wall.

"I'm trapped!" she cried, holding Emily to her bosom.

"No ... I'm coming," he assured her. "Trust me, love." He slowly eased onto the edge of the remaining stairs toward her.

The servants' stairs were barely wide enough for his body. He wobbled precariously on the small pieces of wood, shuffling slowly toward where Livie stood. It was a gap as wide as a carriage seat, but it seemed like it was as large as Hyde Park with his slow progression.

Heartford stood behind Remington, looking on wide-eyed. "Lady Olivia, where is Amelia?"

She looked at the open door, horrified at what she saw. "Baron Bromswell and Lady Windchester ... they tied us up and set the place on fire," she choked out, her eyes on Remington's careful steps toward her.

He slipped at her words and then clung to the wall catching himself. Parts of the stairs remained, but one misstep and he would fall to his doom.

"Remington! Please be careful," she cried, fear for all of them now swarming inside of her.

"I'm going to try the main staircase and see if I can get to Amelia," Heartford called out to them.

"It's completely consumed, Henry," Remington yelled.

"I have to try! She's my sister!" the marquess yelled with determination before he ran back down the stairs.

Remington gradually made his way to her. When he reached her, he took her into his arms, and placed a quick peck to her forehead.

"You came for me?" She was overcome with emotion and love for this brave man.

"Always. I'll always come for you ... I love you, Livie." He removed Emily from her arms and secured her against his chest.

"I love you and I'm—" She looked up at him with teary eyes as she felt the heat of the fire around them.

"Not here. We have to go." He said urgently. Leaning down, he gave her a stern look. "Let's get out of here. Take hold of my arm and don't let go." He instructed, leading her toward the edge and away from the massive hole in the narrow passage.

Livie wrapped her arm around his as if they were going to take a stroll in the park. Her grip was tight, and she was afraid to loosen it. "Remington …." Her voice cracked, not wanting to admit out loud the fear that was consuming her.

"I promise we will get out of here, and in three days, you will be my wife … my duchess." Remington's blue eyes bore into hers as he shifted the baby in his free arm.

Livie nodded her head. "Together."

"Always," he confirmed before he took a step toward the edge.

He shuffled side to side with Livie beside him, her breath ragged. It was becoming more and more difficult to breathe in the burning townhome. Pieces of the ceiling were falling, and at any moment, it threatened to cave in around them.

They slid, side by side together. Fire from the first floor blocked the entrance, and Livie feared it would burn them. Remington guided their way until finally, his foot reached a solid stair.

A cough wracked Livie as she tried to breathe. Her foot twisted painfully, causing her to slip and lose her footing. Her leg dangled, causing her to let out a gasp of fear. Remington flexed his arm tightly, yanking her forward with speed before she fell. She crashed against him and Emily, but he steadied the three of them, the size and power of his body saving them all.

"I have you, love," he whispered against her hairline, placing a swift kiss there.

Livie tried to put weight on her ankle but cringed painfully, as Remington led them down the stairs. He looked up at her in alarm. The townhome was close to being completely consumed by the flames.

"Take Emily!" he rushed, handing her the baby.

Once Livie had Emily safely in her arms, Remington picked her up and rushed down the stairs to the kitchen as fast as his legs could carry them.

It was becoming increasingly harder to see and breathe. The fires were just reaching the kitchen when they reached it.

Remington turned and looked behind them. "Heartford! We have to get out of here!" His voice was swallowed in the fire.

Livie looked down at Emily, who was now crying loudly—a sound she cherished in this terrible situation.

Heartford returned, looking defeated. His hands bloodied. "It's blocked! I need help lifting the debris! I can't get to her!" he yelled, the agony in his voice causing Livie to cry.

"I'll come back and help. Let me get Livie and the baby out!" Remington shouted before he ran out of the kitchen and into the fresh air.

Livie coughed, trying to catch her breath. Remington sat her and Emily down, kissing her forehead before he turned and rushed back into the fire.

"Remington, no!" she yelled in panic, afraid he wouldn't return to her. She clutched the crying baby in her arms.

Tears ran down her face from the failure she felt inside; the darkness of despair threatened to consume her. She had failed Lady Evers—Amelia. She had failed her. Livie was unable to make it back to her in time, and her heart broke in two for Amelia and the little girl in her arms.

"Livie!" her mother cried, breaking through the crowd and running toward her. Her hands pushed Livie's undone hair out of the way, and she kissed her dirty cheeks repeatedly. "I thought I lost you." She cried into her neck, her body rocking.

Her father was at her other side, helping her off the ground.

She winced as she tried to put pressure on her ankle. "Lady Evers is still inside!" she cried frantically to her parents.

"Amelia!" the Earl of Windchester yelled, rushing toward the burning inferno but was stopped by the fire brigade.

Whispers grew louder as the crowd realized that Lady Evers was in the house, along with Remington and Heartford.

Livie waited for any signs of them to come out, but time slowed. Her mind swirled with countless possibilities.

"Back away! It's going to collapse!" everyone around them yelled as the crowd ran away from the building where the roof was caving in.

"Remington! Remington!" Livie repeatedly yelled, her body shaking hysterically.

Her parents held on to her as she waited with bated breath for any sign of the man she loved. The man she was going to marry.

The building shook violently, and Livie crumbled to the ground, closing her eyes tightly. She prayed Amelia was alive and would be able to raise her daughter. She prayed that the marquess wouldn't be lost to Julia. And most of all, she prayed that Remington would return to her safely.

"Thank the Lord!" her mother cried out as the crowd gasped loudly. Remington came out of the building, dragging a wounded Heartford.

Windchester came and grabbed Heartford on the other side. Livie handed the babe to the countess and limped over to Remington. She wrapped her arms around him as relief flooded her. He clung to her, whispering his love and how sorry he was over and over in her ear.

Livie looked up into his blue eyes, so happy they were together again.

Chapter Twenty-Six

Lady Amelia Evers was a beautiful, poised, sophisticated lady. She was a pillar in our society, the Daughter of the late Duke and Duchess of St. Clara. Lady Evers will be greatly missed by all.

R EMINGTON HELD LIVIE THE ENTIRE CARRIAGE RIDE from the fire to her parents' townhome. She had Emily in her arms, checking her tiny little body for any injuries. Remington knew he should release Livie and that kissing her forehead, cheek, and occasionally her nose in front of her parents was against propriety. But he couldn't contain the relief he felt. It was as if fate had given him a second chance because his Livie was safe in his arms.

"I love you," he whispered softly in her ear for the millionth time, not caring they had an audience.

She turned to face him, giving him a soft smile in response. "Me too," Livie whispered back shyly, having a little more decorum than him.

Remington couldn't help himself; he'd thought she was lost to him. Propriety be damned, she was his, and she was breathing.

"Who will take care of Emily?" Lady Hempstead asked, tears forming in her eyes as she looked from Remington to Emily.

The carriage was heavy with the loss of Lady Evers and the memory of the fire. Both Remington and Livie were covered in dirt and soot, their clothes completely ruined. Only little Emily seemed to have escaped unscathed, except for the blankets covering her.

"I'm sure Windchester will take care of her. He is her father, after all. Lady Windchester will not be free much longer if I have anything to say about it," Remington barked, anger spiraling through him, threatening to explode at the thought of what the baron and Lady Windchester had done.

Hempstead took a deep breath in, his eyes void of emotion. "I will assist in any way I can. What they did was abominable!"

Livie sat up, looking down at Emily's green eyes and white-blonde hair like her mothers. "I-I'd like to take care of her, if he doesn't, or if he needs help. Would that be alright?" She turned to Remington, her gray eyes hopeful.

He blinked several times, knowing what she meant by asking him that one simple question. She was going to be his wife.

"Of course, darling. Whatever you would like to do. I think Lady Evers would've loved that. She seemed to think highly of you." He kissed her forehead.

Livie smiled softly. "Amelia gave me strength, and she wanted me to save Emily and come back for her. I'm just sorry I couldn't do both."

Her mother shook her head. "You were so brave. Going after Emily in a burning building. So very brave." Her mother covered her mouth with her hand and cried.

Hempstead looked at Remington, his eyes cold. "Bromswell and Lady Windchester must pay for what they did. I don't give a damn who they are. They tried to kill my daughter, Karrington!" the earl yelled as his arms wrapped around Lady Hempstead to comfort her.

"They will pay!" Remington nodded his agreement. Lady Windchester and Bromswell had intentionally killed Lady Evers.

Livie and Emily would've perished as well, if he hadn't ran into the fire.

The carriage came to a stop, and everyone disembarked at the Hempstead's townhome. Lady Hempstead took Emily in her arms while Remington lifted Livie out of the carriage, carrying her into the house.

The countess began ordering the servants' around. "Thomas, we will need a room prepared for Lord Heartford and assistance helping him out of the other carriage. Immediately call a physician for everyone, especially the baby."

"I assure you I am fine, my lady. Where is Livie's room?" Remington's voice was calm as he held Livie.

"Karrington." Livie's father's voice had a hint of a warning in it. "We have it from here. Why don't you go home and come back after you've rested?"

Remington glared at Hempstead. "I'm sorry, but either I stay with Livie here, or she comes home with me right now."

Sensing a confrontation, Lady Hempstead walked between the two men.

"Abigail, please show His Grace to Lady Olivia's room," Lady Hempstead instructed the maid, who stared wide-eyed at everyone.

Livie rested her head against Remington's chest as he carried her upstairs. His gaze traveled around the modestly sized bedroom, that was still in the process of being packed, and the reason for that gave him some confidence.

He placed her on the bed, knowing there was hope for them again after the ordeal in the fire.

"I'll go prepare water for your bath ..." Abigail stopped walking and turned to face her friend. "Livie, I was so worried." She cried, wiping at her tears hastily.

Livie reached out her hand, and Abigail came to her, hugging her fiercely. "I was as well, but I—I survived."

Abigail gave her friend another squeeze before she left her alone with Remington.

Livie patted the space on her bed, giving Remington a small smile. He sat down beside her, wrapping his arms around her.

"I'm sorry I didn't tell you about my connection to Bromswell and Lillian's death. I have lived with my guilt and shame for so many years—"

"Shh." She tilted her head up and gave him a soft peck on the lips. "It doesn't matter anymore. The only thing that matters is that we're alive … together."

They clung to each other in silence for several moments, both overcome with emotion. The memory of the fire still swirled in Remington's mind. "I can't be separated from you." His eyes watered, he had lost her once because of his own foolishness, and then he almost lost her forever. The fear of losing her forever haunted him and he would spend the rest of their lives showing her how precious she was to him.

Livie ran her fingers through his hair. "I'm right here because you saved me. You came for me." She kissed him lovingly, their lips molding together in a soft, gentle caress.

Emotion swirled inside of him like a raging storm. Tears filled his eyes; the words of the volunteer still fresh in his head.

"No, sir, I'm sorry, but if anyone was there, they're gone.

Remington could still feel the weight of those words and the impact it had on his heart. It led him into that burning building, and he would do it a thousand times over to have Livie alive and well.

Remington buried his head in her neck, so overcome with his emotions. His body shook from his tears, as he replayed the events from the fire over in his mind.

Livie clung to him, her own pain and fears swirling through her.

"Forgive me, Livie. I was so afraid that I would never see you again—"

Livie pressed her fingers to his lips. "There is nothing to forgive. I'm here, and you're here, that's all that matters." She kissed him gently, a sad smile on her face that was covered in dirt and soot. "I love you."

He kissed her once more, this time more passionate than the one before. All his love and devotion were tied to the kiss. Remington wanted to marry this woman today, to hell with everything. He loved her, and she was alive and his. "My God, Livie, I love you, too." He kissed her cheek, squeezing her to him.

"Marry me, Livie, in two days. Say you'll be my duchess," he begged, his hand cupping her face gently.

She smiled softly, her gray eyes filled with tears. "Yes."

It had been an excruciating five hours for Livie. The doctor had come and examined Remington, Lord Heartford, Livie, and baby Emily. Out of all of them, Remington was in the best of health. Heartford was the worst with burns to his entire right side, where the fire had raged through the servants' door as he was trying to get to Lady Evers.

Emily was having some difficulty breathing. The doctor instructed them to make sure she received plenty of rest and to prop her head up on a pillow in case she coughed while sleeping. He also advised that Emily have constant monitoring for any signs of difficulty breathing.

Livie also had trouble breathing; anytime she took a deep

breath, pain would form in her chest, causing her to cough. Her ankle was sprained from where she nearly fell off the stairs. The doctor informed her to rest and to reevaluate how she felt the day of her wedding. If her ankle was still bothering her, he suggested a walking stick. She hoped it wouldn't come to that, as she did not wish to stroll down the aisle with the assistance of a stick. The bruise on her cheek was a nasty, light purple color where Baron Bromswell struck her. But other than the mark, there was no lasting damage.

Remington had not seen the bruise due to how filthy she was from the fire. But after her bath, it was clear she had been struck by someone, and he demanded she tell him what happened. Once he discovered that Baron Bromswell laid hands on her, it took what felt like hours for him to calm. She purposely did not inform him about the forceful kiss, which still caused revulsion to run through her.

The constable had come to hear Livie's testimony before he took any action to arrest the baron and Lady Windchester. This act enraged Remington greatly. He paced back and forth in front of her, where she laid on the chaise lounge, trying to hold herself together as she retold the gory details of the fire.

She hated reliving it, especially the part where she abandoned Amelia. If only she had stayed just a second longer, perhaps she would have freed her, and Amelia would be with her daughter, alive and happy.

Constable Huckabee was a rail-thin man with a mustache and a small stutter that seemed to increase when he was nervous. He certainly looked extremely uncomfortable under the watchful gaze of both Livie's father, Lord Heartford, and her fiancé.

"I want both of them in custody, immediately!" Remington's voice was full of anger, his body shaking in rage as he stopped in front of the poor man. "The longer you wait, the more time they have to avoid arrest!"

"You are wasting time, man!" Heartford spoke up from his seat at the desk against the wall. He was wearing an open shirt and no jacket. Bandages covered his entire right side and his right hand, covering the burns he received from the fire. He insisted he must attend the questioning, even after Julia demanded he rests. Livie hated the look on her cousin's face when the usually calm and friendly Heartford yelled at her to *leave him be.*

"Y-yes. I understand, but we must verify Lady Olivia's testimony—" the constable said.

Lord Heartford slammed his good hand down on the desk. "My sister is dead! What else is there to verify? Lady Olivia has told you everything! They tied them up, struck my sister with a statue, and struck Lady Olivia! They also left my niece to perish. What more do you need! If you do not apprehend them immediately, I will spend every cent I have ruining your life, and theirs as well!"

A red-eyed Julia stood by his side, trying to calm him down. Heartford then rose suddenly and left the room, walking with a slight limp.

Julia followed behind, trying to hide her tears. Livie wanted to go to her cousin but was unable to move. Her ankle was wrapped and elevated with a cold compress on it.

Remington walked to the other side of the chaise and took Livie by the hand, his glare never leaving the constable. "As you see, both Heartford and I feel very strongly about this. We will use everything in our power to make sure they pay for what they did! I want them both apprehended instantly!" Remington yelled, causing the poor man to jump in his seat.

"Y-yes, of course, Your Grace," the constable agreed before

his dark eyes turned to Livie. "Did Baron Bromswell or Lady Windchester mention why they were doing this to you and Lady Evers?"

"Lady Windchester indicated she was doing it because Lady Evers had a child by her husband, which meant her mother would stop supporting her. Baron Bromswell acknowledged I was there because he wanted the duke to know what it was like to lose someone he loved." Livie nodded her head, her voice trembling.

Remington squeezed her hand, causing her to gaze up at him. His jaw was set so tight he could break his teeth. Livie stroked her thumb across his hand, reminding him she was here and alive. "Lady Oakhaven's fortune supports Lady Windchester's lavish lifestyle as well as her husbands. I believe most of the dowry that my cousin received after his marriage was used to restore my grandfather's estate."

"Is there a connection between Baron Bromswell and yourself, Your Grace?" Constable Huckabee tried to hold Remington's hard glare.

"Yes. We were acquainted when we were younger. There was an incident where a young woman died. Bromswell was accused, but at the time, his father had friends in high places. The entire ordeal was forgotten, but never by me," Remington explained briefly.

Taking in his demeanor and tone, Constable Huckabee stood, holding his hat in his hands. "I will keep you all updated."

Remington shook his head. "Keep Lord Hempstead, Heartford, and Windchester all abreast of the situation. I'm getting married in two days, and we're going to go on a wedding trip."

"Of course, You're Grace. Congratulations to you both on

your upcoming marriage." Constable Huckabee bowed, and her father escorted him out.

"Shall I continue with the cancellation of the wedding?" her mother inquired, gently.

"No. We would like to marry on our original wedding day." He turned to gaze at Livie as if he was unsure. He had a vulnerability in his crisp blue eyes that she'd never seen before. It made her love him even more.

To postpone after they had been reunited, would mean Lady Windchester and Baron Bromswell won. Livie could not allow them the satisfaction.

"We will marry in two days." She sat up taller on the chaise. "I won't give the Baron and Lady Windchester power over us. They already cost Amelia her life, and Emily, her mother."

Her father re-entered the parlor. "Lord Heartford has gone. Perhaps you should go check on Julia? Thomas said they did not part on the best of terms." His voice was tired, and he looked as if he had aged years in one day.

"I should go to her. He was being very distant, which is understandable since he lost his sister." Livie tried to rise but was detained by a strong hand on her shoulder.

"You're not going anywhere on that ankle. I'll carry you to Lady Julia's room." Remington's voice was firm as he walked around the chaise to her side.

"You're being a very bothersome nursemaid. Father nearly had to drag you out of the room for my bath," she reminded him, and her father began coughing.

Remington knelt in front of her. "I'm finding it very difficult to be parted from you." He kissed her knuckles gently, causing heat to rise in her cheeks as they were in front of her parents.

"Soon, you will tire of me." She gave him a teasing smile.

"Never. I'll never tire of you, love." They stared at each other intently as his free hand stroked her cheek.

"Please remember yourselves. I'd hate to have Lord Hempstead have a fainting spell," her mother warned them. "I will go see after Julia." She stood and left the room.

Livie turned to find her father turning a strange shade of green she had never seen on him before. She knew that seeing her and Remington so affectionate toward each other made him uncomfortable. She was thankful when Thomas entered the room, followed by a flustered Mother Di and Mr. Prescott. Mother Di rushed past the butler and straight to Livie on the chaise.

Remington took a step back, allowing his mother space with his fiancée.

"We came as soon as we received Len's note. The streets were absolute chaos with the fire and news of Lady Evers' death." Mother Di choked up. "How are you?"

Livie squeezed Mother Di's hand, giving her a small smile. "I'm fine, just some scrapes and bruises ... but I'm alive, thanks to Remington."

Mother Di's eyes widened, her gaze moving from her son to Livie. "What happened? Len only said there was a fire, and you all were injured. Then the maids beguiled us with gossip. Is it true, about Lady Evers?"

"I'm afraid so." Remington bowed his head.

"I wouldn't be here if it wasn't for Lady Evers ... Amelia." Livie whispered her name, remembering her strength in that dark time.

"Prescott, make yourself comfortable. We are all family, after all. Besides, both Karrington and my daughter have thrown propriety out of the window today." Her father gave them both a side glance.

"It is no bother at all, and we must forgive them after the ordeal they have been through." Mr. Prescott walked over to Remington and put his hand on his shoulder. "How are Heartford and Windchester taking Lady Evers' death?"

"I'm not sure about Windchester. He stayed behind to recover the body, but that was hours ago." Remington's shoulders dropped, and he blinked several times. "Heartford is in a really bad place. He was here, but he blames himself. If I wouldn't have dragged him out of the burning townhome, I fear he would've perished trying to save her."

Mother Di and Mr. Prescott both gasped as they listened to Remington retell the calamity of the fire.

Livie laid on the chaise, trying not to relive the entire nightmare over in her mind, but she could not help remembering every detail. It was as if she was still trapped in the house, surrounded by the flames with the ceiling falling around her. Panic rose in her chest as she remembered how helpless she felt that she could not reach Amelia.

Livie's heart was heavy. At that moment, she vowed never to abandon Emily. She would always do whatever the child needed—be whoever she needed. Livie would never forget what Emily's mother sacrificed to save them both.

Chapter Twenty-Seven

The Bachelor Duke is no more!
After his courageous rescue of Lady O and baby E from the fire,
Lady O forgave the duke. It's official ladies, our bachelor duke is
gone. Take out the handkerchiefs and wish him well.

ON HER WEDDING DAY, LIVIE ALLOWED THE STRESS OF the past few days to fade to memories. She wanted to focus on the simple fact that she was marrying Remington, the man she loved and who loved her. Nothing else mattered beyond that.

She barely recognized the woman staring back at her in the mirror. She was very much the soon-to-be duchess, and not the girl who came to London at the start of the Season. Every inch of her body was scrubbed to the point of redness, and she was primped to perfection by Abigail and a despondent looking Julia.

When the countess and Mother Di walked into the room, they were both overcome with tears of joy. The countess held a small jewelry box in her hands as she walked to Livie. She lifted the top to reveal a pair of gold, flower-shaped earrings.

"No crying, you two," Livie warned, pointing a stern finger at them.

"How can we not cry? Our children are getting married." Mother Di pressed the corner of her eyes with her knuckles. "I just wish Eliza was here."

"She is here, through your memories." Her mother gave Mother Di a soft reassuring smile. She turned to Livie, holding up the small box. "I believe these will match the necklace your grandmother gifted you." She removed the jewelry and placed each one on Livie's ears.

"You know, my mother was a very cold woman. I had vowed never to treat my children the way she treated me. She gave me these earrings on my wedding day, but never the necklace. Maybe she had hoped she would have another daughter." She chuckled to herself. "I was glad when she gave you the necklace. They belonged to her mother, and now they belong to you. One day you will give them to your daughter."

Trying to control her tears, Livie hugged her mother. "Thank you, Mother."

Mother Di approached Livie holding two boxes with a note on top. "Remington wanted me to give you these." She handed Livie the letter first.

Livie scanned the letter, tears threatening to fall as she read Remington's and Shakespeare's words.

My Darling,
Love comforteth like sunshine after rain,
Love's gentle spring doth always fresh remain,
Love surfeits not,
Love is all truth
The hair comb belonged to my mother, and I want you to have it and wear it
today, our wedding day. The bracelet is my first gift to you as my duchess.
I love you with all my heart and soul.
Your soon to be husband,
Remington

Livie handed the note to her mother then took the objects out of Mother Di's hands. The first box had a large hair comb that greatly favored a tiara. Its intricate design and the rows of diamonds were simply breathtaking.

"It's beautiful," she whispered in shock.

"Eliza would wear this to every ball and event. She always said it made her feel like royalty." Mother Di's voice was full of love for her friend.

"Abigail, can you assist me?" Livie asked her friend, handing her the hair comb.

Once it was placed on her head with her veil in place, everyone looked on with happy tears and joy.

"One more, and then we must be going. We don't want you late for your wedding," Mother Di reminded her, nodding down to the small box.

"Yes, we can't have that," her mother agreed before turning to a quiet Julia. "Julia, will you go and make sure Emily and her maid are ready for the wedding?

"Yes, of course. I'll meet you all in the carriage," she said, before leaving the room.

Livie smiled after her cousin before she opened the small box to reveal a diamond bracelet. She gasped at its brilliance and handed it to Mother Di to help place it on her wrist.

"Now, let's get you married, Your Grace," her mother teased, happily bouncing in place like a little girl.

Livie laughed at her mother, ready to begin the new chapter in her life. They made their way down the stairs; all the servants had stopped working to send their young mistress off to her wedding.

As she descended, they all clapped and cried. Livie smiled at each and every one of them. They had all been a part of her life since childhood.

"This isn't goodbye; I will visit often. Not even marriage could keep me from Cook's biscuits." She laughed, looking over at the crying cook that had known her since birth.

"I'll be sure to give the recipe to your new cook," she said, crying into a handkerchief.

Lord Hempstead walked over to Livie, holding out his arm. "We must be going now." He cleared his throat, blinking several times to control his own emotions.

"Yes, Father." Livie took her father's arm, so eager and happy to become Remington's wife. She walked out of the townhome and to her new future.

The wedding of the Duke of Karrington and Lady Olivia St. John was supposed to be a small affair, but most of society came out to view the nuptials.

It mattered not to Remington, as he only had eyes for his bride as she walked down the aisle toward him. Livie was radiant in a blue gown, wearing his mother's hair comb. His bride's gray eyes danced as she stared at him. He held back the need to run and carry her, hoping she wouldn't reinjure herself. But she walked slow and steady beside her father, who had watery eyes.

The ceremony lasted for what felt like forever to Remington, but finally, the bishop pronounced them husband and wife, and his world was finally set right. After years of being afraid to allow anyone in, to love anyone in fear that he would become a monster, Livie freed him from himself. She was everything to him, and he would spend his life proving that he was worthy of her.

After their wedding, they went to her parents' house for the wedding breakfast. The guest list was only their family and close friends. Both Heartford and Windchester had sent a note asking for forgiveness. Their grief was too great for them to attend a happy affair.

Conversation at the wedding breakfast turned to Lady Evers' death since every newspaper in London mentioned her. News of the fire and her death was spreading due to the involvement of two prominent members in society. The Gazette praised her life, her fashion, and her beauty; in fact, every newspaper only listed all her good qualities, and none of the petty gossip that seemed to follow her throughout her short life.

The gossip sheets surprisingly praised her character and qualities, conveniently forgetting they had indeed printed vicious and personal things about her life.

Remington was happy when the talk of Lady Evers' death came to an end as he was afraid the conversation would bring up the emotional events of the fire to the forefront of Livie's mind. But one look at his bride's happy face, and he knew that all was well with her.

Little Emily was the belle of the wedding breakfast, every woman wanting to hold her, except Lady Heartford. She and her brother-in-law, Mr. Livingstone, attended to represent Lord Heartford.

Standing from the table, Remington looked to Livie. "We should get home since we will be leaving at first light for Essex."

She smiled at the word "home" and took his hand. "We should."

"Oh, will I not see you before you leave?" Lady Hempstead asked, looking distressed.

"Mother, we will return the day before Julia and Lord Heartford's wedding."

"Now, Len, I thought you were being strong?" Mother Di reminded her.

"Yes, I was, but then the fire happened, and now I find I'm more emotional than expected."

Hempstead took his wife by the hand and squeezed it. "Soon, we will be all alone." His voice was wistful as he smiled at Livie then Julia.

"We will always come back," Julia reminded them, her mood lighter since the wedding.

Remington led Livie out of the dining room, followed by the good wishes of their guests. They walked to the carriage with clasped hands and matching smiles on their faces.

Once they were alone, Remington kissed his wife passionately as he lifted her to sit on his lap. Her hands draped around his neck, pulling herself closer to him.

Their kiss was long and languid as the carriage bounced through the unsteady streets of London. His lips traveled down his wife's long neck, kissing and savoring the taste of her skin. "I love you," he whispered, causing her to shiver. He never would tire of saying it or feeling her reaction to his words.

"I love you," she moaned, her back arching wanting more of him.

Looking into her gray eyes, he could see her love and passion. He kissed her lips. "And I love hearing you say it, my duchess."

Her fingers ran through his hair as she pulled him to her, deepening the kiss. His hand traveled up her leg, massaging her calf, as their tongues slowly danced.

The carriage came to a stop, and a soft knock alerted them that they had arrived at their townhome.

"Are you ready to see your new home, my duchess?" he asked.

"Yes, Your Grace." Her voice was deep and sultry, her lips already swollen from his kisses.

Waiting a moment to allow his wife to adjust her dress, Remington opened the door and assisted her down from the carriage.

The door to their townhome opened to reveal Dayton and all the servants' lined up in the vestibule waiting on their new duchess.

"Dayton! Allow me to introduce my wife, the Duchess of Karrington." Remington's voice was filled with pride as he looked down at his wife.

"Your Grace, welcome home. It will be an honor to serve you." Dayton bowed gracefully.

"Thank you, Dayton." Livie gave the older butler a warm smile.

Remington watched as one by one each servant was introduced to his wife. He couldn't help the wide, permanent smile that refused to leave his face.

She was finally his duchess.

Remington walked into his bedroom, wearing nothing but his nightshirt. Livie was still in the adjoining duchess's rooms, preparing. He felt rather nervous for a man grown and familiar with the company of ladies. However, this was his wife—his Livie.

He walked over to the bed, noting the champagne and glasses on the night table. He poured two glasses, wanting to calm her nerves for their first night as man and wife. Although they were intimate in Essex, a night he constantly played in his mind, tonight would be different.

The sound of the adjourning door opening caught Remington's attention. He looked up to find Livie standing nervously across the room; her flaxen hair draped down her back in beautiful ringlets. Some of the tresses hung over her shoulder to the swell of her breast.

His gaze traveled the length of her body in the darkened room. The sheer chemise she wore revealed flawless skin, and he wanted nothing more than to kiss every inch of her.

He walked to her and handed her a glass. "I had champagne brought up. I thought we could toast our marriage, and it will help if you are nervous."

"Thank you. I'm not nervous about you, perhaps just anxious to be yours."

He slid his free arm around her waist, and his hand settled on the swell of her behind. "I'm anxious too, darling. Anxious to start our life together." His heart was full of so much love for his Livie … his wife.

Heat spread across her cheeks, and she bit her bottom lip. The movement was seductive to him, and he leaned down to trail his tongue across the abused flesh.

"Don't injure my wife's lips, I need them," he teased.

"What are you going to do with your wife's lips?" Her breathing hitched.

"I'm going to kiss them for the rest of our lives," he whispered, staring into her eyes.

Remington captured her mouth with his. Her hand moved to the opening of his shirt, her fingers curling in the light smattering of chest hair.

Livie broke their connection, panting. "We're going to spill the champagne. Perhaps we should toast first?"

"Yes, forgive me. I lose myself whenever we are alone." He released her, holding up his glass of champagne.

She held up her own, smiling at him.

"To a long and happy marriage with you, my duchess. You are my very heart and soul. I love you, Livie."

"To a long and happy life, Your Grace. I love you, too." They clinked their glasses together before they both took a sip.

Remington took her by the hand and led her over to the bed. He placed their glasses on the night table.

When he turned back to Livie, she reached out her hand for him. He took it, bringing her flush against his body. His mouth plunged the depth of hers, exploring and needy. She was soft where he was hard, and his hands freely roamed, ending up at her lush bottom.

He lifted her chemise, slowly pulling it up her body, revealing inch by inch of creamy skin. Breaking their kiss, he lifted it over her head. He took a step back to gaze at the perfection that was now his wife.

A rosy blush formed on her cheeks, and she shyly ducked her head.

"Don't hide from me. Never doubt my love for your body." His voice was deep and husky as he lifted her chin.

Livie's hands slowly traveled over him, her eyes wide and exploring. Soon her hands took hold of his nightshirt, lifting it. He raised his arms, giving her a devilish smirk. Livie stood on her tiptoes, trying to get the garment over his head. He pulled it the rest of the way, and they both laughed.

He flung his nightshirt across the room, not caring where it landed, only wanting to be with his wife.

"I remember how much you enjoyed my body in Essex," Livie whispered. Her hands traced slowly down his stomach, stopping at his navel.

His breath caught, his heart pounding in his chest. He

couldn't think or form words with Livie touching him so intimately. His cock was hard and ready for her warmth.

Livie's fingertips traced down to his hardness, taking it gently in her hand. Her grip was timid as she stroked him. The movement nearly brought him to his knees.

"I didn't know your member would be so large," she said wide-eyed.

Remington plundered her mouth hungrily.

As he lifted her, she wrapped her legs around his bare waist. "You're going to be the death of me," he growled against her lips as he laid her on the bed.

He explored her, familiarizing himself with every curve and dip of her delicious body. Remington slowly trailed kisses from her jaw to her ear. "Did you enjoy what I did to you in Essex, my duchess?"

Her back arched as his finger and thumb massaged a pert nipple as he peppered sensual kisses down her neck.

"Y-yes," she said with a breathy sigh, her head tilting to the side as he replaced his fingers with his warm mouth.

He lavished her full bosom with attention, nipping on the sensitive flesh, before soothing it with his tongue. His mouth trailed fire-hot kisses to her other breast, lavishing and praising it with attention.

Nimble fingers trailed down her tummy to the triangle of blonde curls at her sex. Her body shook with desire when he placed two fingers inside her.

"You're so wet and ready for me, my duchess," he whispered against her skin, his lips trailing a path down to her sex.

"Oh!" she cried out, when he reached her sex.

His mouth was slow and steady, licking a path to her

bundle of nerves. He teased it continuously as he savored the taste of his wife's sweet nectar. Livie's fingers intertwined in his hair, guiding him where she wanted him.

He loved how sure and passionate she was. Livie knew what she wanted, and he wanted to give it to her—always.

"Remington, please ..." she begged, her body practically bowing in half.

He continued to lavish the sensitive nub, a primitive growl escaping him as he lifted her bottom. He devoured her as if she was his last meal, the sounds of her pleasure spurred him on. He desperately wanted to bring his wife to completion.

"Yes, yes, yes!" she cried, coming nearly off the bed, pulling his hair.

Kissing her thighs, he crawled up her body. Their lips battled, hungry and needy, as he lined himself up to her wet heat.

Remington wrapped his arms around her, entering her slowly. Livie gripped his shoulders tightly, her eyes closed as her head pressed against his. Her body was tense at first. Slowly, she relaxed as Remington worshipped her with his hands and languid kisses. He took her mouth in a slow, steady dance, trying to allow her body time to adjust to him.

She was tight and warm, nearly causing him to come undone at the feel of her surrounding him.

It was simply heaven.

Remington guided her slowly, one hand on her waist, the other lovingly caressing her body. She opened to him, finally relaxing to the intrusion as he began moving slowly.

He trailed his fingers through her hair, his hand molding her scalp. She lifted her hips, causing him to groan in ecstasy. "That's it, darling, feel me."

She arched her back, tilting her head back. Long silky tresses were flowed out over the white pillows. Remington sat up, frantic for more, but not wanting to hurt her. Her breasts were on display, and he massaged the heavy flesh with one of his hands.

His hand traveled from her breast to her stomach, down to the triangle of curls at her sex.

Below him, Livie swirled and rocked against him, finding a rhythm that threatened to send him over the edge.

"Ahh!" she cried out, reaching for him.

Remington bent down, taking her mouth hungrily. "Wrap your arms and legs around me, Livie," he whispered against her lips.

Remington lifted her off the bed, taking her by surprise.

"Oh!" Livie called out as he held her weight in his arms. He moved her on top of him.

Remington looked up at her, giving her a smirk. "I won't allow you to fall." He pulled her bottom lip into his mouth, sucking slowly.

He began guiding her movements, his grip on her backside firm. Unable to hold back anymore, Remington moved her faster against him.

"Livie …" he groaned, feeling the precipice of ecstasy approaching.

"Oh, God!" Her body stiffened, just as Remington squeezed her to him, pumping up into her with a furious need.

Their world shattered together as they clung to each other, gasping for air. They kissed hungrily while Remington laid her gently on the bed, his lips worshipping every inch of her.

He laid down pulling her body nearly on top of his. "Is it always like this?" she inquired before kissing his chest.

His hands slid down her back, taking hold of her behind. He squeezed, causing her to moan. "It will be, if I can help it."

She gave him a lazy smile, her eyes drooping closed. "Am I yours now?"

He kissed the tip of her nose. "Yes … always."

Epilogue

Another Season!
Will Lady J finally find a match after her canceled wedding to the
Marquess of H? Or will this season be just as disappointing as the
others. The Duke and Duchess of K have a new addition to their
family, at this rate they will populate all of London.

Talbert Abbey
Three years later

EVERY YEAR, LIVIE AND REMINGTON SPENT TIME AT
Talbert Abbey enjoying the sea breeze. Their three
children, Emily, Theodore, and Frederick loved the small
home as much as the large estate in Norwich.

Livie had discovered she was with child not long after they
settled at Hemsworth Place. Their eldest son, Theodore, was
born the following year. Their second son, Frederick, was born
nearly two months ago, which was a shock since Theodore was
barely on the earth a year when she discovered she was with child
again. Emily lived with them most of the year much to their
delight.

Livie walked into the breakfast parlor to find her husband,
cousin, and the children at the table. She insisted Remington enjoy breakfast, as she had to feed a hungry Frederick.

"Good morning, Lady Julia," Livie said cheerily to her cousin.

"I don't find anything particularly good about it, Livie. I'm in for another season of whispers and ridicule. I don't see why I can't stay here or even Hemsworth Place or Hill Manor alone. I hate the Season. I don't want to get married," she said in one angry breath.

"Aunt Livie!" three-year-old Emily yelled, never knowing when to use her inside voice. Her light blonde hair was long and flowing on top of her tiny head.

Both Theodore and Emily ran to Livie, and she smiled at the two of them.

"Up, Mama!" Theodore called out in a loud voice, trying to get his mother's attention.

"Theodore, we do not yell at Mama," Remington warned his son patiently.

The toddler was thoroughly chastised and turned watery gray eyes to his father.

Remington picked him up, running his hand through his blond hair. "It's okay. You must use your manners. Try, *Up, please, Mama*," he instructed his son calmly.

"I have manners, Teddy," Emily said cheerily, taking a seat beside Julia.

"Up, please, Mama," Teddy said, reaching for Livie, who took him from her husband, kissing his curly head.

"Very good, my darling," she instructed, smiling proudly at him.

Remington took her hand, giving it a gentle squeeze. He was such a kind and wonderful father like she knew he would be.

The butler entered, carrying the mail. He set the tray down between Remington and Livie. Remington picked up the mail.

Opening a letter, he read intently, unable to hide the shock on his face. "What is it?" Livie asked, noticing the change in her husband's demeanor.

He cleared his throat several times, looking over at Julia uncomfortably.

"I know it's from him. You do not have to pretend he doesn't write to you. At least he cares enough for you to give you some sort of explanation." Julia took a sip of her tea.

"Very well." Remington began looking from his wife to Julia. "Heartford is returning to England. Apparently, he feels that he is missing the children's lives and wants to spend more time with Emily as well as Teddy and Frederick."

"Goodness, did he say when he was returning?" Livie eyed her cousin for any signs of discomfort.

"He should be in London in a matter of weeks." Remington cleared his throat setting the letter down on the table.

The words hung in the air. Emily and Theodore continued their happy chatter oblivious to the adults.

"That's simply wonderful. I'm sure the gossips will just love that." Julia's shoulders were stiff as she avoided eye contact with Livie and Remington. "Thank you for telling me, but Lord Heartford means nothing to me." She continued eating, the subject closed.

Once breakfast was done, Lucy, the children's nurse, took them all out for some fresh air, while Livie and Remington found their way to the library. Playing chess had become one of their favorite things to share.

Livie sat down on the opposite side of her husband. Remington had a smug grin on his face as if he'd finally beaten her. She had been defeating him since they first played together on their wedding trip. In the three years that they'd been married, he hadn't beaten her once.

"Are you feeling victorious today?" She raised an eyebrow at him.

The sound of the children squealing in delight caught Livie's attention, and she looked out the window to find Teddy and Emily running circles around each other as Lucy held Frederick in her arms.

"I believe I've finally won one," Remington said, taking her out of her thoughts. She turned to look at her husband. There was a smug look on his handsome face, his dark hair falling over his eyes. Teddy looked so much like him, but with his mother's blonde hair. "Check."

She inspected the chessboard, noticing where her husband had moved his bishop, putting it officially in check to capture her white king. Livie let out a contemplative sigh, her gaze never leaving the board. She could feel his eyes on her, waiting excitedly for her move.

Livie moved her king, officially getting it out of check, and causing her husband to utter an animalistic sound.

She had discovered over the years that he was a terrible loser.

Remington ran his hands through his hair as Livie waited patiently. She stood, went over to him and sat on his lap. He wrapped his arms absentmindedly around her waist, never taking his eyes off the board.

"Do you need a moment, Your Grace," she teased him, trying to control her laughter.

He squeezed her side, making her laugh as she pressed her head against his. "Don't be cute, you minx." He kissed her lips, a smile on his face. "I will beat you, one day, Livie."

She gave his lips a gentle peck. "Perhaps you will one day. After all, society said you would never marry and look at you now." She gazed into his blue eyes that had captured her from the beginning.

"Yes. Look at me now. Happily married, getting beaten by my wife at chess." His hand traveled up her back, taking hold of her neck.

"The point is, never say never. If the Bachelor Duke can marry, surely you can best me at chess."

His lips ghosted over hers, his eyes twinkling. "Perhaps one day, I will."

The End.

Acknowledgements

This book was a long journey, and I could not have finished without my incredible support team. First and foremost, my Lord and Savior, Jesus Christ for never leaving or forsaking me.

To my husband and son, mother, brother, and family thank you for supporting my dream and always loving me even when my head is far far and away.

To my friends, and my fandom,

thank you all for your unwavering confidence, love, for always grounding and cheering me on.

I appreciate each and every one of you in my life that has had some impact on me, no matter great or small.

To Fran, thanks for staying with me on this journey with our favorite bachelor.

This book would not be complete without the help of some very amazing ladies.

Pamela Stephenson

Fran Walsh

Cheryl Edmonds

Debbie Hannon

Faye Byrd

And my sister V.

About the Author

Cecilia Rene is a creative, happy, and outgoing Detroit native who majored in Broadcast Communication at Grambling State University. Immediately following her graduation, she started her new life in New York City. As a self-proclaimed New Yorker, her stimulating and diverse career in advertising sparked a drive for hard work and dedication. Her love and passion for writing followed her from childhood through adulthood, where she wrote short stories, poems, and screenplays. Always an avid reader, she stumbled across a book that ignited a deeper need for more and joined a fandom of like-minded individuals. Cecilia and her family made a huge move five years ago to the great state of Texas, where she currently lives with her loving husband, wonderful son, and spoiled fur baby, Sadie. Cecilia Rene loves romance, humor, and all things spicy. For this reason, she will always give you a Happily Ever After.

Made in the USA
Monee, IL
24 May 2021

69369573R00173